Methuselah's Revenge

George T. Hahn

—————

The Library Ship Saga

Tau Ceti: A Ship from Earth

Tau Ceti: The New Colonists

Tau Ceti: The Immortality Conspiracy

Voyage of the Capek

The Methuselah Conspirators

Methuselah's Revenge

The Ambassador: The Lost Colony

The Ambassador: Path to Contact

The Ambassador: Mission to Earth

The Timeline:

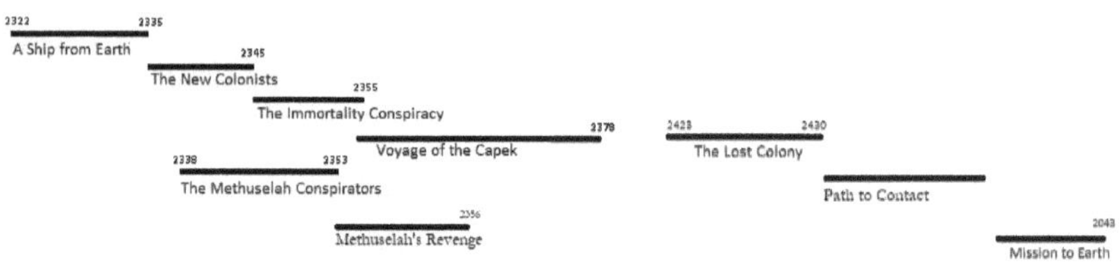

Contents

T HEY KNEW IT WOULD happen eventually but had hoped it wouldn't be so soon. Eddie and Joelle Bascomb stared at the image on the network screen where Western Alliance President Ana Sanchez-Smythe stood next to her husband, laughing at something he said to her. She had given a speech at a gathering of military leaders, urging them to maintain the strength that kept the Eastern Bloc at bay. General Salvador Juarez, leader of Project Methuselah, stood behind the executive couple in the cluster of ranking officials, a grim smile on his lips.

The Methuselah team had gotten back from *Lang* only a month before, after months on the library ship. Taken there against their will, Juarez had forced them to develop a device that could upload a human memory to the *Lang* computer, but they had outmaneuvered Juarez. Instead of a Juarez clone that would give the General complete access to the Western Alliance computer network, they created a sentient computer with a mind of its own.

With the computer, now calling itself Fritz Lang, helping, they left Juarez, Colonel Pizarro, and ex-President Castillo behind. Juarez should have taken months to get another starship to bring him to Earth from the Alpha Centauri library ship.

"Fritz will make sure he behaves," Eddie told his wife. "He can't touch us anymore."

Joelle nodded, but she pushed in closer to Eddie. At least Emile, their six-year-old, was asleep. Emile would have recognized Juarez, and that might have been traumatic.

M OST DAYS, EDDIE AND Joelle worked from home. They had made enough money when JEM Electronics went public that they didn't have to work at all. Their fortune grew during the fifteen months on *Lang*, but they stayed with JEM out of loyalty to its CEO, Max Estevez. Max had developed the original proposal for JEM and, along with Joelle and Eddie, founded the company.

After seeing Juarez, Eddie wanted to talk to Max. An aircar dropped him off on the JEM headquarters roof, and he was in his office twenty minutes after leaving his residence. Max was a busy man, and even Eddie had to schedule an appointment, but his phone negotiated one for 10 a.m. Eddie was lead on one of JEM's new projects, and he used the waiting time to visit the other two people working on the project. They traded status and ideas until a little before Eddie's appointment.

"Didn't you come into the office last week?" Max asked as Eddie took a seat on a chair in a corner of the spacious office. Max got up from his desk and joined Eddie.

"Just wanted to see your smiling face. I'm still catching up after not seeing it for so long."

"Uh, huh. So, what's up?"

"Juarez is back. I saw him on the network last night, standing next to the president."

Max nodded and frowned. "Well, you knew he'd be back eventually."

"I told Joelle that Fritz would keep him in line. I wish I believed it more. He could be looking for some payback."

Max scratched his head. "You told me Fritz can access all the computers in the Western Alliance, right?"

"If the computer is accessible via a Link connection. That would be anything of any importance, I suppose."

"That should give Fritz enough information to destroy Juarez if he continues Methuselah. Probably Sanchez-Smythe too."

"I know. That's the theory, at least. I worry, though, and I try to keep it from Joelle and Emile."

"How is Emile?"

Eddie smiled. "He seems fine. He doesn't remember much before *Lang*, so everything is new to him. We get a kick out of watching him sometimes."

"He's adjusting to school all right?"

"There doesn't seem to be a problem. He went to school on *Lang* with the children of the scientists stationed on *Lang*, so that wasn't a big change."

"Good. Oh, you might like to know that Alyssa Cleveland started here this week. I think she's the last of the Methuselah team to find a position."

"She's a good programmer. I guess no one else believed she was doing anything for the last year."

"It left a bit of a hole in the team's resumes. Emile has the lecturing position, but Lucinda is staying at home, at least until the baby is born."

"That should be any day now."

"Another month, give or take a week."

"We'll have to get everybody together to celebrate afterward."

"Everybody but Juarez and Castillo, anyway." Max grinned.

"Including Colonel Pizarro?" Michael Pizarro had worked for Juarez, but had helped them more than once in their conflict with Juarez. *I'm not sure how I would feel about seeing Michael again.*

"I don't know where he is. Would that be a problem?"

"I don't know. I hated him for a long time, but in the end, he helped us get away." *I tried to kill him, along with Juarez and Castillo. Thank God Fritz prevented that.*

"It's over now, Eddie. You all have to get on with your lives."

Eddie nodded, but the image of Juarez standing next to President Sanchez-Smythe wouldn't go away.

Tomás Xavier Hernandez was born on May 30, 2355. Eddie and Joelle visited Lucinda in the hospital. Emile wasn't there, scheduled to give a lecture he couldn't easily reschedule. It wasn't until Tomás's baptism a month later that most of the Methuselah team got together.

Tomás was baptized at Parroquia Medalla Milagrosa in Colón, a church familiar to Eddie and Joelle from their son's baptism seven years before. Emile and Lucinda had come to that ceremony, although Emile had been more limited then, with no vision and limited motion.

Emile Hernandez was much better now. An accident fifteen years before had damaged his brain and given him locked-in syndrome. At the time, Lucinda led a team working on improvements to the neuro-interrogator, a device that could read words from the brain and transmit them to a listener. An early prototype of the device allowed him to communicate, and JEM devices later gave him limited ability to move. More recently, Eddie and Joelle had helped design nanites that repaired the damage to Emile's brain, but his brain was still adjusting to normal activities three years later. Those ventures had brought them to the attention of General Juarez and Project Methuselah.

"My throat muscles are working well enough for me to drink from a straw," Emile told Eddie and Joelle after the brief ceremony. "My doctor says it could be a year or more before I can eat more or less normally, though."

"He's getting a lot better," Lucinda Hernandez said. She had Tomás in her arms, but he had fallen asleep.

Eddie nodded. The bed he designed so many years before no longer followed Emile everywhere he went. Once, the platform had been Emile's means of locomotion, but many of its functions were no longer necessary, and it had been stripped down to a gurney-sized box with only the intravenous feeding connections remaining. Emile could walk without even a cane now, and he had regained his hearing and speech, so the neurotrainer and neuro-interrogator connections were gone.

Eddie and Joelle's son had drifted off, but he joined them then.

"Little Emile!" Emile Hernandez said, beaming. "How are you doing?"

"He doesn't like to be called 'Little Emile' anymore," Joelle said.

"Except by Doctor Hernandez," the boy said, smiling up at the scientist. "He can call me that."

"Wonderful. Then you can call me 'Big Emile.' We've been through too much together to be so formal." He bent down and hugged Little Emile, not a simple action. Lucinda also hugged the boy.

Bill Bensonhurst, another neuroscientist from Project Methuselah, joined them. "So what do I call you?" he asked Little Emile.

Little Emile's face scrunched up, and he hesitated. "I guess you should all call me Little Emile if Big Emile is here, too."

Other people swirled around them, wanting to congratulate Emile and Lucinda. Eddie, Joelle, and Bill drifted away, leaving Little Emile with the Hernandez's. They were near the door and wandered out onto the steps in front of the church.

Eddie glanced around, noting that no one else was within hearing range. "Juarez is back on Earth."

"Is he?" Bill shrugged. "Not much we can do about that."

"I'm more worried about what he might do," Eddie answered. "We're counting on Fritz to protect us."

"We beat him," Joelle said. "Why would he do anything?"

"With someone like Juarez, if he thinks he can get away with it, . . ." Eddie's voice trailed off, and he looked around the street.

Bill, one of the few people who knew Eddie had tried to kill General Juarez, looked worried. He was a little older than Eddie and Joelle and acted like Eddie's big brother. Eddie wasn't sure he and Joelle would have ever gotten together if Bill hadn't pushed him into overcoming his shyness.

"Are you suggesting we do something?" Bill said.

Eddie shook his head. "No, I guess not. I just get discouraged. The Western Alliance government is supposed to be there for the people, but sometimes it doesn't seem that way. People like Juarez, Castillo, and Sanchez-Smythe think the government is there to give them power over people. It's not even a party thing. Castillo was a Liberal; Sanchez-Smythe is a Conservative."

"Too many politicians think that way," Bill said. "Castillo and Sanchez-Smythe are just bolder about using the system, and people like Juarez take advantage of them."

"One thing about our time on *Lang*. At least we didn't have to listen to the politicians."

Bill grinned. "Right. Just Juarez. We handled him once. With Fritz's help, we can do it again."

"I hope so," Eddie said.

"I hope we won't have to," Joelle corrected.

For two years, it seemed that might be true.

EDDIE SAT, GAZING OUT at Gatun Lake below. Joelle was reading inside the house they had purchased three months before, after finding the patio unseasonably cool. Emile played nearby, dressed somewhat more warmly than Eddie. Eddie wasn't sure whether that was Emile's preference or Joelle's, but Emile wasn't complaining.

It had been two years since General Juarez failed to take control of *Lang* and, in so doing, the Western Alliance, and almost that long since Eddie saw Juarez next to President Sanchez-Smythe. He rarely thought about Juarez, telling himself that either the general had given up on his plot or the library ships were keeping him in check.

The device they built on *Lang* could copy memories from people to a library ship's main computer. It could play back recorded memories to people too, but they destroyed the device, and Fritz Lang erased any trace of the work they did from its data storage. At least the Methuselah team had developed the improvements to the neuro-interrogator that made advances like Emile Hernandez's prosthetics possible.

Those thoughts were in the back of his mind when he tried to concentrate on his current JEM project, but he was too easily distracted. A powerboat passed on the lake, pulling a skier. *I guess they don't think it's that cold.* He was too far away even to determine the gender of the skier, but Eddie watched the boat until it passed out of sight. Emile didn't even look up, concentrating on whatever imaginary scenario he was playing out.

Eddie thought he dozed off because he didn't hear Joelle's approach. The urgency in her voice captured his attention instantly, though. "You left the phone inside, so I answered it when it signaled."

He looked up at her, and the almost frightened expression matched the tone of her words. She pushed the phone at him as if it were something repugnant. "It's Ambassador Shuford."

Why would the Pitcairn Ambassador be calling me? JEM did some business with Pitcairn, but Alan would talk to Max about that. Eddie understood Joelle's reaction; it was hard to think of a pleasant reason an official of another planet would call someone he had never met. He took the phone from his wife. "Hello, Ambassador."

"We need to talk," Alan Shuford said, and his voice seemed tense.

Emile had noticed his mother come out and give Eddie the phone. He looked over at them curiously, and Eddie waved his hands to indicate Joelle should take him inside. Joelle smoothly maneuvered Emile into the house but was back only seconds later.

"What's happened?" Eddie asked.

"Fritz failed. General Juarez is attacking Karel."

Alan told the story gradually, slowed by the limitations of library ship communication. "Some time ago, a group of colonists from Trist took over *Capek*. They planned to move more colonists to *Capek*, people who wanted to leave Trist, and move *Capek* to Pitcairn."

"Karel went along with that?" Eddie asked. Karel Capek was the name taken by the library ship's conscious computer.

"Apparently, General Juarez has kept Project Methuselah alive and is now looking at Karel to try again with a new team. Without the original team, they had to start again and tried to get the scientists on *Lang* to investigate Karel's consciousness with Alyssa Cleveland's software."

That program could kill Karel! No wonder it's cooperating. "You said tried."

"Yes, the scientists hesitated to install the software, and the colonists took over the ship earlier than they had planned to protect Karel. Now, Juarez is sending a ship, *Benjamin Sepulveda*, to take over *Capek*. Karel and the colonists are unarmed and cannot stop them. The colonists are hoping to leave Trist before *Benjamin Sepulveda* arrives, but they are cutting it close."

"How did Juarez do all this without Fritz knowing?"

"Juarez has been cautious about keeping everything off Western Alliance computers. Fritz can't monitor conversations, written communications, or computers not on the Western Alliance network."

"What can I do?" Eddie asked.

"I don't think you can do anything. Pitcairn Administrator Malley is working with Isaac to advise Karel. I wanted you to know that Methuselah is still active. If Juarez is successful, he may come after you and the team."

"Sanchez-Smythe supports him?"

"Apparently. Some evidence suggests that Juarez has not reported everything that happened on *Lang*. He would certainly not want his plan to double-cross the president to become known. The man is more capable than we gave him credit for, managing to run the project without being noticed."

"But there's nothing we can do?"

"Other than warning the rest of the team, I don't think so. We hope *Capek* gets away. If so, Juarez won't have any other library ships to attack."

"Unless he can get authorization to go after Pitcairn and *Asimov*. How long before *Benjamin Sepulveda* gets there?"

"Tomorrow. Trist has one more shuttle load to take up to *Capek*, and then they will leave. As I said, it is very close."

"Keep me informed." Eddie closed the connection and looked at Joelle. She had heard everything, and it showed on her face. "It will be all right."

Joelle nodded and walked toward where Emile had gone. Plainly, she wasn't convinced, and her first instinct was to go to her son. Eddie trusted she wouldn't do anything to pass their stress to Emile.

In theory, the Western Alliance was a liberal democracy, and mostly that was true. However, the theory failed when powerful people could subvert the government's institutions to further their own goals. That was what Juarez and ex-president Castillo had done in creating Project Methuselah.

The three library ships connected their planets to Earth through the Links. Juarez and Castillo, and later the new President Ana Sanchez-Smythe, had wanted to upload their consciousness to the library ship *Lang*, realizing that, from its position inside the Western Alliance's network of computers, *Lang* would have complete access to information that Western Alliance laws hid from them.

Emile and Lucinda Hernandez had foiled their plans by uploading Juarez's episodic memories but Emile Hernandez's semantic memories. The result was a conscious computer, Fritz, who knew all about General Juarez's ambitions and what he did to achieve them, but viewed those memories through the attitudes and morality of Emile Hernandez.

Eddie turned to his phone again. Shuford was right; the rest of the Methuselah team should know that Juarez was still active.

A LAN SHUFORD CALLED THE following day. Eddie sat on a couch with Joelle, the phone on a coffee table in front of them, listening while Shuford relayed the information he was getting from the library ships.

"*Benjamin Sepulveda* is in orbit near *Capek*. Karel sees a shuttle mounted on its hull, probably for an armed party to force its way into *Capek*. The former Trist Administrator, Ron Rigney, has docked with *Capek* on the last shuttle, and the ship is preparing to leave. He is hoping to avoid a confrontation."

"Once they are underway, the shuttle won't be able to catch them," Eddie said as Alan paused. He took Joelle's hand, and she gripped it tightly.

"Pitcairn Administrator Malley has convinced Isaac that it must intervene. It told Karel to use a gravity tractor missile to force a delay in the shuttle launch."

"The library ships have gravity tractor missiles to deflect dangerous asteroids," Eddie explained.

"I know," Joelle answered. "Earth has them, too. I don't think we've ever used one, though."

"Once, I think," Eddie said. "An asteroid that would have come too close fifty years from now."

"The missile is approaching the shuttle," Alan said. "It should come close enough to deflect the shuttle if it detaches from *Benjamin Sepulveda*. Yes, the missile will come within fifty feet. They won't launch into the shifting gravitational field, and that should delay the launch long enough." A brief pause. "Wait! The shuttle is separating. Don't they understand?"

"They may think it's a missed shot," Eddie said.

"The shuttle is wavering as it comes away from *Benjamin Sepulveda*. The pilot is trying to correct, but he's not handling the gravity changes." Alan's voice grew more agitated. "The shuttle has collided with a cooling fin on *Benjamin Sepulveda*. The fin has pierced the shuttle and broken off." Pause. "Karel sees atmosphere leaking out of the shuttle." Another long pause. "Karel has delayed its departure to help, but it is unlikely that the crew of the shuttle has survived."

T HEY LEARNED THE REST of the story over the course of the day. Alan's first impression was accurate; the ten people in the shuttle were dead. The shuttle rotated end over end near *Benjamin Sepulveda*, itself without the ability to move.

Karel had a dilemma. It controlled the Link, and if it left before a rescue mission could arrive, the crew of the *Benjamin Sepulveda* would have to wait for rescue. A ship would have to be sent at sublight speed from Pitcairn, a six year trip, and that was too long.

Ron Rigney, the colonist leader, decided to leave and convinced Karel that it was necessary. The *Benjamin Sepulveda* crew had little choice. When Karel left, it would take its passenger shuttle with it, leaving the crew no way to get to the planet's surface. Most of the crew reluctantly joined the colonists on *Capek*. Karel let the captain have a cargo shuttle, capable of carrying two people, to take down to the Trist colony, where he would await rescue. It would be a long wait, seven years for a ship to get there from Pitcairn, but the Trist colony was still viable, with half its colonists staying behind. *Capek* would get to Pitcairn at about the same time as a rescue vessel could get to Trist.

"Isaac and Karel are very upset," Alan said. "They are blaming themselves for the deaths on the shuttle. And the lives of the *Benjamin Sepulveda* crew. They've lost everything."

Eddie could barely speak, but somehow, he managed a few words. "It wasn't Karel's fault. This blood is on Juarez's hands."

J OELLE HAD SEEN THAT look on Eddie's face only twice before: the first time in Houston when Eddie realized Juarez was taking them from Earth; and again on their way to their captivity on *Lang* when General Juarez's aide, Colonel Michael Pizarro, frustrated an attempt to gain their freedom. His dark mood then came from the feeling that he had failed his wife and son. Joelle had calmed him the first time, and Bill Bensonhurst had calmed him the second by convincing him that his family needed Eddie more than Eddie needed to vent his anger.

She placed a hand on Eddie's shoulder but couldn't find words to say. She was shocked by what had happened, but her thoughts were on the people who died or would disappear, never to see their families again.

Eddie didn't seem to notice her hand. At first, he didn't even acknowledge her presence. He stared at a wall, eyes narrowed and hard, his lips compressed into a thin line. His fists clenched, whitening his knuckles.

Joelle had to say something. "Juarez will be punished for this." It sounded lame.

Eddie stared at her. "No. The government will cover it up just like they covered up what Juarez did to us. Only the library ships know what happened."

"Pitcairn knows. The captain of the *Benjamin Sepulveda* knows, and the colonists on Trist will know if they don't already. Questions will be raised about the missing people."

"Nobody on Trist counts. It will be years before any word gets to Earth now that the Link isn't operating. Pitcairn could do something if they're willing to irritate the Western Alliance that supplies them." He paused and turned away. "We know."

"Eddie, don't."

"Don't what?"

"You're angry now. Don't do anything foolish. Just calm down and let other people handle it."

"I have to call Emile and the rest of the team. They should know about this."

"Why? What could they do? You'll just get them angry, too. They'll probably hear about it from PNS, anyway."

"If the Pitcairn News Service dares cover the story." Eddie shook his head. "All right, I need to think about this, and I'll do it better if I wait. We'll see what PNS does about this first." He still looked angry, and Joelle put an arm around him.

T HERE WAS NO PITCAIRN News Service coverage of what happened at Trist. A story reported that Pitcairn Administrator Patrick Malley had resigned, and Eddie could only assume that had something to do with his involvement. Someone named Mary Norwood would take over Malley's position.

"The library ships asked Pitcairn not to talk about it," Alan told him. "The incident could further endanger Isaac and Fritz. People would think they are dangerous."

Eddie had cooled by then, but he was still concerned. "If Juarez is still bent on uploading his consciousness to a library ship, they could be in danger."

"This may have been his last chance. Without the work you did on *Lang*, he could only have been trying to take control, hoping to duplicate Methuselah. Since *Lang's* access to Western Alliance computers hasn't been cut off, we think Juarez has divulged little of what happened. We can't determine what he has told President Sanchez-Smythe, but given his success in hiding the attack on *Capek*, we think it's been as little as possible. He certainly would not want her to know he had planned to betray her."

"Are Fritz and Isaac willing to take that risk?"

"They are considering what actions they might take." Alan hesitated. "They could use human input from you and me."

"Juarez might threaten my family and the other team members, too. I'll help in any way I can."

E DDIE BEGAN CALLING EVERYONE, starting with Emile and Lucinda Hernandez. His phone connected immediately, and a hologram of Emile and Lucinda appeared. They were sitting on a couch, and Lucinda was feeding Tomás. It took ten minutes for Eddie to tell them about the attack on Capek.

"I can't believe Sanchez-Smythe would still support Juarez," Emile said when Eddie finished. "Fritz and Isaac must be . . .." He shook his head. "Hell, I don't know what they must be. How do sentient computers process this kind of thing?"

"Alan Shuford says they are agitated and would like human help in understanding it," Eddie said.

"This must be the end of Methuselah, though. Juarez can't keep the project alive after this."

"Maybe. I'm not so sure, and I don't think Alan and the library ships are, either."

Even as a hologram, it was clear Emile was disturbed. "This Capek situation suggests new dangers, Eddie. Any further work on Methuselah could be disastrous."

Eddie nodded. "Yes, it would be terrible if Juarez got access to the Western Alliance network. We knew that."

"We did, but there are other possibilities that might be worse. Isaac and Fritz have lulled us into assuming that a sentient computer would be friendly toward humans. There's no reason that should always be true."

"Karel was defending itself. It didn't mean to kill anyone."

"If Juarez is successful in creating a computer in his image, it would be bad. But if he is only partially successful and wakes a computer with his thirst for power but no human control, it could be much worse."

"Science fiction has used that scenario for years. It hasn't happened. What motivation could a computer have?"

Emile held up his hands. "I don't know, Eddie. I'm not a computer scientist. But I know the human brain and how it can be twisted."

Eddie frowned. Is Emile right?

E ASTERN BLOC PREMIER BON-HWA Boulos took the file folder from his Chief of Staff's hand. His predecessor had received the daily summary on his workstation, but Boulos preferred paper. He knew it was a hopelessly old-fashioned quirk, but, after all, he was in charge. People would have to live with his eccentricities.

The first item grabbed his attention. "Has this been confirmed?"

The Chief of Staff nodded. "It has. We don't know why, and there's been no official statement, but the Western Alliance has definitely lost contact with Epsilon Eridani."

"We need to know more. I want people working on this immediately."

The Chief of Staff bowed and left the office. Boulos knew he could rely on the man and settled back in his chair to think about what it might mean.

The Eastern Bloc should have been the dominant force on Earth. Compared to the Western Alliance, it had far more people, natural resources at least equal, and comparable technology. One glaring exception, however, made all the difference. For more than a century and a half, the west had lorded it over the east because they knew how to twist space itself to meet their profane desires. That technology gave them almost unlimited, inexpensive energy from their orbiting platforms, energy that they could dole out to the rest of the world in quantities that they decided on and at whatever price they deemed sufficient. The technology gave them the Stenhouse Drive, by which they claimed all of space as their own, flitting about the solar system at speeds approaching the speed of light while Eastern Bloc spaceships could barely achieve a tenth of that velocity. And, finally, it made the Links possible, allowing them to spread to the stars while the people of Allah languished on Earth.

But that technology had somehow failed the Western Alliance. They had lost contact with Trist, the world circling Epsilon Eridani twelve light-years away. Was there a way to exploit that? It was unlikely, but worth investigating. A chance to break the western stranglehold was worth any effort.

G ENERAL SALVADOR JUAREZ GRABBED the bottle of antacid tablets on his desk and wrenched the cap off. It came loose with a jerk, and pills shot out of the bottle and rolled around the floor. He swore and popped two still in the bottle into his mouth. *You would think they would have found a better way to package these damn things by now!*

President Sanchez-Smythe was not happy with him. She blamed him for the disaster at Trist and would have had him cashiered from the military if she hadn't feared he would go to the media. He suspected she was thinking about demoting him but leaving him in the army. Then, if he talked, she could have him court-martialed for leaking classified information. She had fewer options in dealing with civilians.

If she knew the whole truth, she would make him disappear. She had expected him to still work for her after he took over the *Lang* computer, but that had not been his plan. Why would he let a politician use the power when he could do much better? The government claimed to be protecting all its citizens, but its expensive programs were a barrier for the capable people that could give the Western Alliance victory over the Eastern Bloc.

It's the fault of that damn neuroscientist and his wife. I can't do anything about them without the computer noticing. It took all my skills to keep the Capek mission secret. That thought stopped him. Had he kept it secret? The Trist rebels were only waiting for the last shuttle from the surface before leaving Trist when *Benjamin Sepulveda* arrived. That couldn't have been a coincidence.

Who knew enough to warn the rebels? The crew of *Benjamin Sepulveda* and the ten soldiers who died on the shuttle. Maybe a couple of people involved in putting the mission together, but most of them didn't have enough information. The president and the cabinet? Juarez frowned. *I would bet money it was one of those damned politicians.* But which one?

A message would have to go to *Lang,* and it would have to go through the Earth Link. Juarez needed a list of the messages passed through during the relevant period, but privacy restrictions meant that a warrant would be required. The chances of him being able to convince a judge of the need without revealing why were nil, and the attempt would expand the list of people who knew something about the mission.

Sanchez-Smythe could probably get a warrant through the Executive Guard. She would have to come up with a sufficient reason, with backing documentation to convince a judge. That might have been easy, but privacy laws were in the way again; a computer selected judges for warrant requests at random to eliminate the chance of undue influence. He would have to hope that an amenable judge was chosen. It might work if Sanchez-Smythe still trusted him enough to do it for him.

All that was secondary, though, to the critical issue. How could he get Methuselah on track again? At least he knew it was possible to upload one's memories to a computer sufficiently powerful, but the device Emile Hernandez had used was destroyed, and its design documents, at least those from the time on *Lang,* were gone. Perhaps he should have sent updates to Earth as backups, but he hadn't wanted the data to get out of his control.

He would need Sanchez-Smythe to authorize a new team to rediscover the memory recorder technology. Now that he knew that uploaded memories could create a conscious computer, did he still need a library ship? Other computers in the Western Alliance were more powerful, but they might be missing something essential. The extensive sensory equipment on a library ship, for example, was likely a key element in bringing *Asimov* and *Capek* to consciousness. *Lang* hadn't become conscious on its own as the other two had, but it had the same sensors designed to investigate their star systems.

That, too, would need investigating. At least the original team's material on that issue was still available. Eventually, he would have to decide: could they build the required computer, or would they have to use *Asimov* or *Lang*? The former was under the control of Pitcairn, and the latter would be wary of any approach. Building a new computer had its advantages, but there could be problems, too, if the computer were in a facility on Earth. It would be too easy to take it offline once Sanchez-Smythe realized he had taken over.

Juarez pushed back from his desk and looked down when he heard a crunching sound. The wheels on his chair had rolled over one of the fallen antacid tablets, leaving a streak of white on the hardwood floor of his office. He swore again and called for his assistant.

"IF JUAREZ CAN KEEP Methuselah going, he will want to keep it secret," Eddie said.

Joelle nodded. "He would have to have government support still. I don't see how we can do anything about it if he does try again."

"You're right. Not by ourselves against the government. We need some high-level help."

"Who did you have in mind?"

"I see two possibilities. Japan and Pitcairn. And we can try both at once."

"You want to go to Tokyo? It's not likely Pitcairn or Japan could do anything."

"Emile should see more of the world. We can all go and make a vacation of it. I'll talk to the Japanese and visit the Pitcairn embassy. Maybe we can put a plan together."

Eddie could see that Joelle was skeptical, but it wouldn't hurt to talk to a few people, and they could make a pleasant trip out of it.

T HE WESTERN ALLIANCE AND the Eastern Bloc dominated the planet, but a few smaller countries such as Japan and Australia were not part of either. The Bascombs arrived at the Narita Space Annex five days later. JEM had an office in Tokyo, and a young man from JEM met them with a company aircar to whisk them to their downtown hotel.

"Ambassador Shuford sends his apologies," the man said. "He would have liked to give you lodging at the embassy, but it's a small embassy with limited facilities. He felt you would be more comfortable here."

"I understand," Eddie said. "When can I talk to the Ambassador?"

"He assumed you would want to rest and get used to the time change. He can be available whenever you're ready."

Eddie was tired and probably would be the next day, but he wanted to see Alan as soon as possible. "Late tomorrow morning, perhaps?"

"I will tell the Ambassador."

A bellhop met them on the roof with an automated luggage carrier. She escorted them to their suite on the top floor while the luggage carrier followed obediently behind. It took half an hour to settle in and then spend a few minutes enjoying the spectacular Tokyo view from their enclosed balcony.

"So, what are we going to do next?" Emile asked, his interest in the view exhausted.

"It's late," Joelle said. "We're going to go to bed and get some rest."

Emile looked at the time displayed on the network screen on one wall of the suite living room. "It's only eight o'clock in the morning!"

Eddie did a quick calculation. "It's late afternoon in Colón, and that's the clock your body is on. If you want something to eat, I'll have something sent up, but then we're all going to bed. It's been a long day."

Emile started to protest, but he looked as tired as Eddie felt. "No, we ate on the plane. We'll do something fun tomorrow?"

"You and I will," Joelle said. "Daddy has to talk to people."

With a display of reluctance that was probably fake, Emile allowed them to put him to bed in the smaller of the two bedrooms. They browsed the news for a few minutes and then checked on him. As expected, he was sound asleep.

"I DON'T HAVE MUCH new to tell you," Alan told Eddie. "Isaac has briefed Administrator Norwood and me. Fritz continues to monitor General Juarez's activities as much as possible, but apparently, the general is even more careful now about what he allows to be stored on Western Alliance computers."

"He can't hide everything." Eddie felt something approaching awe as he looked at Alan. The Pitcairn Ambassador was well over one hundred years old, and it showed in the wispy, white hair around the fringes of his scalp and the deep wrinkles in his face and hands. Yet there was a strength in the still-slim body, firm mouth, and sad brown eyes that told of a man who had seen more than his share of pain and had survived.

"No, not everything. Fritz is also watching the activities of scientists that Juarez might recruit. It thinks it has identified an obscure government project that might be the new Methuselah, but there are no recorded connections to Juarez. As far as Fritz can tell, the project is still staffing and not operating yet."

"I know I'm grasping at straws, but I'm trying to get help in stopping Juarez. I came here to talk to you as a representative of Pitcairn. While I'm here, I hope to talk to someone in the Japanese government as well."

"I'm not sure what we can do for you. Our influence with the Western Alliance is complicated, as I'm sure you know."

Eddie nodded. "Information from Fritz is useful. I guess I was hoping you might have some contacts within the Western Alliance government that might be helpful, too."

"Let me think about that. There aren't many right now who aren't allies of President Sanchez-Smythe, at least in public. Talking to any of them might reveal more than we would want them to learn about what we know."

"And possibly endanger Fritz's access. I understand. As you said, it's complicated."

"I think I can help you get in touch with someone in the Japanese government, though."

"That will help."

EDDIE STARED AT THE building from the window of the surface car that had brought him from the hotel. It was a busy area with crowds of people filling the sidewalks, but the address he had gotten from Alan didn't look busy at all. The blue roof and white walls were clean, giving the impression of a well-maintained structure, but it exuded anonymity. There was no sign of what the building was used for. People streamed past it, and no one gave it a glance. It hardly looked like a place where an important government official worked, and Eddie rechecked the address, but it was the correct building. He got out, and the automated car moved back into the traffic and away.

The front door opened to a featureless hallway about ten feet long, with another door at the other end. Eddie found a typical reception area beyond the second door and a man behind a counter watching as Eddie came in.

"Mr. Bascomb?" the man asked.

"Yes."

"Mr. Shijo will see you immediately." He came out from behind the counter and escorted Eddie through a door to the left of the counter. The room beyond was dimly lit, and it took a few seconds to see the man behind the desk to his right.

"Welcome, Mr. Bascomb," the man said. "I am Atsushi Shijo. My friend Alan has told me you wish to speak to someone in the Japanese government. Please, have a seat."

Eddie sat on the chair indicated. His eyes were adjusting to the light, but he could see that Shijo was a large man, overweight but not exceptionally so. His eyes bore into Eddie as if he could read Eddie's thoughts. Eddie glanced around the room and realized another man was sitting quietly in one corner.

"You are thinking that this doesn't look like a government office," Shijo said. "You are probably also thinking that I am some low-level bureaucrat and wonder why Alan sent you to me."

"Something like that," Eddie said.

"The Emperor himself could not help you more than I. Please, tell me how we can be of assistance."

Eddie hesitated and then shrugged. He was confident he could trust Alan, and Alan vouched for Shijo. "You are aware of Project Methuselah. I was on the project team."

Shijo nodded. "Alan briefed me on your involvement. He was vague about some details, however. Your concerns, he said, involve the reappearance of General Salvador Juarez two years ago and the loss of the Epsilon Eridani Link."

How much do the Japanese know about the library ships? "What is your position in the Japanese government, Mr. Shijo?"

Shijo's lips compressed into a thin line that might have been a smile. "I have certain duties in Japanese Security." He waved a hand toward the man sitting quietly in the corner. "Ikeda-san works for me and has had some experience with Project Methuselah."

Eddie looked over at Ikeda, and the man bowed his head slightly.

"We know that General Juarez took you to the Alpha Centauri library ship," Shijo said. "We don't know what you did there, but assume it had something to do with Project Methuselah. Ikeda-san and I are quite curious about that."

"I can't add anything beyond what Ambassador Shuford told you."

Shijo nodded. "Of course. Regardless, Ikeda-san will work with you to provide as much assistance as possible. I fear it will not be much, however."

7

K ENSHIN IKEDA MOVED INTO the seat Eddie had vacated as soon as the office door closed. Shijo looked at the dark network screen on one wall. "Show entrance hall."

The screen brightened and displayed the short room between the reception area and the outside door. In a few seconds, the inside door opened, and Eddie walked through. Shijo and Ikeda watched him until he disappeared onto the street.

"Your impressions?" Shijo asked.

"We know when Bascomb and the others went to *Lang*," Ikeda said. "It seems certain they were on the library ship for more than a year, but we're not sure when they came back. We have little information about what happened during that time."

"We can speculate, though. If we can believe the network reports from back then, Project Methuselah attempted to upload human consciousness to a computer. It is reasonable to suspect that the *Lang* computer was the target of the upload."

"I would also guess that they were successful," Ikeda said. "The Methuselah team returned to Earth and resumed their lives."

"And yet Ambassador Shuford and Mr. Bascomb say that Project Methuselah is still active and is a threat. How are we to reconcile those two circumstances?"

"Perhaps there was more to Methuselah than just uploading consciousness. Perhaps the task of the original team is complete, and the project continues toward additional goals."

Shijo nodded. "Perhaps. I would like you to return to the Western Alliance with the Bascombs and find out what you can. If appropriate, help Mr. Bascomb in preventing the project from succeeding. Its ultimate goal is unlikely to be favorable to Japan. Of course, if you should uncover something of use to our government, . . ."

Ikeda bowed. "Yes, sir. I understand."

KENSHIN IKEDA LOOKED AROUND the small Koenji apartment where he had lived for the last month. That shouldn't have been enough time to get attached to the place, but after the years in a Western Alliance prison, he knew he would miss it. His regret was worse because he wasn't sure he would be back.

His release from the Black Plains prison had been sudden and enigmatic. No one at the prison had told him why he was being released; they didn't seem to know. Outside the prison, an automated aircar met him and whisked him back to San Diego. A ticket for a suborbital flight to Narita was on the car's seat with his name on it. At the airport, the identification chip in his hand got him through security without trouble, and now he was back in Japan. Shijo had been as surprised as he when he had called his superior to announce his return.

It was impossible, but he couldn't help the feeling that the Western Alliance government, and General Juarez in particular, had not approved his release. Now he was going back.

That was not his only concern. Who was this Edward Bascomb? He had the basic information: electronics engineer and founder of JEM Electronics, making him a rich man; married with one child; and a former, supposedly unwilling, member of the Methuselah team. Back when Ikeda had been investigating Methuselah, he had concentrated mainly on Emile and Lucinda Hernandez, the neuroscientists who had led the project. Bascomb had not been a noteworthy subject.

He caught himself rubbing the spot on his hand where an agency doctor had implanted a new identity chip. The new chip was one of the illegal re-programmable devices developed in secret by a company in Hokkaido. A remote signal could change it to give him an entirely new name and background, but the chip had to be inserted surgically. The incision had been small and was completely healed, but some instinct or habit led him to rub it when his mind was elsewhere.

Shijo thought he could trust Bascomb, but that was because Shijo's friend, Alan Shuford, had vouched for him. How did the Pitcairn Ambassador know enough about the man to say that?

He could still resign and let Shijo send someone else. Shijo chose him because of his prior investigation, the reason for his imprisonment. He had considered resigning when he returned to Japan. But he hadn't done it then, and he wouldn't now. He had a duty to his country, and he wouldn't shirk it.

He met the Bascombs at a French restaurant in the Ginza shopping district. As it had been for centuries, the Ginza was filled with expensive shops, high-class entertainment, and fancy restaurants. It could be a dangerous place for the average tourist prone to impulse buying, but for Western Alliance moneyed families like the Bascombs, it was an expected stop in Tokyo. Ikeda's best suit was not quite up to the same standard, but it would do. Eddie Bascomb's attire was even less impressive, a sign of his humble origins or perhaps showing his indifference to the trappings of the rich. His wife, however, was dressed quite attractively in a dress that probably cost more than his clothes and her husband's combined. Eddie Bascomb didn't care about such things, but didn't mind spending money on his beautiful wife.

"I've been given diplomatic credentials with a new identity," he told Eddie and Joelle. Emile wasn't paying them much attention, his interest divided between his food and the unfamiliar surroundings. "My status with the Western Alliance government is delicate, and I don't wish it known that I am back in your country." Shijo had advised him to be honest with the Bascombs about his spying on Project Methuselah, and he spent the next half hour telling them about it.

Eddie accepted his narration of the events readily. "Your story explains something we had wondered about. The Captain of the *Hotaru* tried to stop us from disembarking at Alpha Centauri when General Juarez brought us there."

"Shijo-san did that based on what I had discovered," Ikeda said.

"We appreciated the effort," Joelle said. "We were desperate to get away from Juarez."

Ikeda noticed that Eddie Bascomb seemed troubled. Because he remembered their ordeal? Some instinct hinted that there was more to that in Bascomb's expression. Perhaps he would learn more when they returned to the Western Alliance. It was impossible to predict what information might be valuable to his government.

"Methuselah threatens the library ships," Eddie said a few minutes later. "We have to stop Juarez."

Ikeda wanted to ask why the millionaire was so concerned about the two remaining ships orbiting distant worlds. *Asimov* was now conscious, and its well-being explained the interest by the Pitcairn Ambassador. *Capek* had become conscious, and its fear of Methuselah probably explained its flight from Trist. Ikeda suspected *Lang* had also awakened, but the Western Alliance had made no official statement. What had happened on *Lang,* and why was the subject of so much interest? Shijo had assigned him to work with the Bascombs to find out. The library ships themselves were not a concern of the Japanese government.

8

"WHAT'S YOUR IMPRESSION OF our traveling companion?" Joelle asked. They were in a first-class cabin on the Tokyo-Colón suborbital. Emile was engrossed with the screen in front of him, watching some children's show. Ikeda would take another flight to Panama City a day later and go from there to Colón via aircar.

Eddie shrugged. "He's pretty closed up. I think it's his profession more than his culture, but he's going to be tough to get a handle on."

"His profession? He's a spy."

"He admitted spying on us in San Diego. At least the Japanese are honest about that."

"You didn't tell him about Fritz."

"I don't think that's a good idea. Anyway, as I told Shijo, if Alan, who apparently talks to the library ships often, isn't telling the Japanese anything, then I'm not going to."

Joelle nodded. "But Alan thinks he can help us."

"We wanted high-level help. We've got a spy and an ambassador working with us now. It's progress."

"I'VE IDENTIFIED THE PEOPLE I want immediately for the new team," General Juarez told President Ana Sanchez-Smythe.

"Have you approached them yet to determine their willingness?"

Juarez smiled. "That won't be a problem."

Sanchez-Smythe frowned. "You learned nothing from your experience on *Lang* then."

"One must learn from mistakes. I won't make them a second time."

Sanchez-Smythe stared at him for several seconds before changing the subject. "Installing your computer at the Black Plains site will be expensive."

"One of my mistakes was trying to use an existing computer." Juarez leaned on the president's desk. "As I said, I won't make the same mistakes this time."

"Make sure you don't. Don't let me find that I've made a mistake forgiving your failure for a second time." Sanchez-Smythe waved her hand in dismissal. "There won't be a third."

Juarez nodded and left the Executive Office. As he walked down the corridors, his frown dissuaded any of the bureaucrats he passed from addressing him. The ones he was acquainted with knew better; others were too wrapped up in their petty concerns to notice him.

Many Western Alliance leaders, including the president, didn't understand the threat the Eastern Bloc presented. Two centuries of peace lulled them into complacency, but men like himself knew that change was inevitable. It had been a miracle that the Western Alliance had kept Stenhouse technology a secret for so long. Stenhouse technology was the basis for much of the Western Alliance's advantages: inexpensive energy and practical space travel, for example. As long as the rest of the world had only the access to its benefits that the Western Alliance allowed, there would be peace. They couldn't keep the secret forever, though, and when the Eastern Bloc discovered it, they would be more aggressive.

He detested having to work with Sanchez-Smythe. She was a typical politician, skilled in making speeches and giving orders to people more knowledgeable than herself. She listened to her husband, but usually not to anyone else. Juarez had met Alexander Smythe and wondered how much the First Gentleman knew about his wife's machinations. From their conversations, Juarez suspected Smythe would disapprove.

She was foolish enough to believe Methuselah's success would be an expansion of her power, not the end of her power. At least he could count on her to divert the necessary funding into the facility already being built in a remote location in the Colorado-Utah District. Technically, the area wasn't part of the Black Plains, but was close to enough to suffer the devastation of the Yellowstone Event over two hundred years before. The name referred to most of what had been the United States and southern Canada, sparing only the southern part of the west coast and the most easterly districts.

The four men he had chosen should be at the facility already, wondering why he had sent them there. He would soon be there to tell them.

D ENVER WAS A PLEASANT surprise. A suborbital took Juarez there from Brasilia, and he glimpsed the city just before the landing. The military aircar waiting for him gave him a closer look as it headed west toward the Uintah Basin and the new

Methuselah base. Perhaps he should have realized that it had been more than a hundred years since the eruption covered the city in volcanic ash and the local government had plenty of time to clean up. He saw a massive black hill on the outskirts that was probably a pile of ash, but Denver itself looked clean and prosperous. He wondered why the ash had not been removed in all that time. A reminder of what the city had survived, perhaps?

The region beyond the city was less pleasant. Before the Yellowstone Event, hundreds of square miles of forest, protected by the old United States government, had covered the lower mountains and filled the valleys between the high peaks. They were mostly gone now, smothered by blankets of ash, with only small areas scattered over the landscape where life struggled to come back on the porous debris. The mountain tops, long ago swept clean and covered by new snow, were a brilliant white that only emphasized the surrounding destruction.

The aircar covered two hundred miles in an hour, avoiding the higher mountain ranges. Then it was over the Uintah Basin, an elevated plateau, desolate even before Yellowstone. Someone had told him it had been a native reservation, but the volcano had driven even them from the land. Over most of the area, the only sign of civilization had been the scattering of abandoned facilities that once extracted oil from shale. Now there was the shining white building atop a mesa, the new home of Project Methuselah.

The landscape was depressing, but perfect for his purposes. When he landed outside the building, he expected someone to meet him, but there was no one around. "Arrange an all-hands meeting in ten minutes," he told the car.

"Meeting set in conference room A," the car responded a few seconds later. "All staff members have been notified."

Juarez had not been to the facility before, but his phone had the buildings' floor plan and led him through a short walk through stark corridors to conference room A. Three men waited for him there. There should have been four.

"Where's Bynum?" he asked the three.

"He hasn't arrived yet," one man answered. Juarez recognized him as Micah Cabrera, one of two neuroscientists assigned to the facility. Cabrera was the youngest team member, obviously too young to fear Juarez. *I'll change that.*

"You were told I would be here today," Juarez said. He noted his tone had the desired effect; Cabrera looked over at the other two before turning back to Juarez, his head bowed slightly.

"I'm sure he'll be here by the end of the day," Cabrera stammered.

"Do you know Mr. Bynum? Have you been in communication with him?"

"No, sir." Cabrera hesitated, and his head bowed deeper. "You were quite plain in us being here by today, though. He must know."

Juarez scowled at them. "I'll deal with Bynum later." He pointed to Cabrera. "Brief him when he gets here. Meanwhile, let's continue. You have a lot of work ahead of you."

9

I T WAS NOT KENSHIN Ikeda's first visit to Colón. Eight years before, Shijo sent him there to investigate Project Methuselah, but he didn't learn much. When the project was transferred to San Diego, he followed, but he made a mistake and spent the next few years in a Western Alliance prison. The government admitted that they were trying to upload human consciousness to a computer, but he was convinced there was more to it than that. Ikeda thought the Western Alliance leaders were trying to create super-intelligent versions of themselves, but that was only a small step past what they had already admitted. Such a possibility wasn't worth all the secrecy.

His aircar touched down on the roof of the JEM Electronics headquarters. Eddie Bascomb was waiting for him, grinning as they exchanged greetings. A conference room was only a short walk away. Another man, introduced as Max Estevez, joined them. Ikeda remembered that Estevez, the CEO of JEM Electronics, had also been a member of the Methuselah team. Even if Ikeda hadn't known that Bascomb was technically only an employee, despite being one of JEM's founders, Ikeda would have known that Estevez was the leader in the group.

Ikeda had dossiers on both men. Estevez was fifty-four years old and had led Project Methuselah until abruptly leaving and, a short time later, starting JEM Electronics. The Bascombs had also left the project at about the same time, interestingly coinciding with their marriage. Something had been going on there. After eight years at JEM, developing prosthetics for disabled individuals, including their former associate, Emile Hernandez, Juarez spirited the Bascombs off to the library ship. Certainly there were holes to be filled in that story, but Ikeda tried to squelch the thought. He was there to find out the truth behind Project Methuselah, not the life story of Eddie and Joelle Bascomb.

"Let's begin," Max said. "Eddie, you can start by telling me what I'm doing here."

"You've always been a part of this, Max. At the very least, I want you to know why I may not be your most reliable employee for a while."

Max chuckled. "You never were, Eddie. At least not until you met Joelle. So, give me a better reason."

Eddie's smile faded into something more serious. "I don't know where this is going to take us. I may need some help from JEM at some point. Your advice is always welcome, too."

Max nodded and turned to Ikeda. "Mr. Ikeda, we've never met, but I think we have a mutual acquaintance."

"Who is that, sir?"

"Just call me Max. Let's see, if I remember correctly, the man's name was Robert Kyle. At least, that was the name he gave my receptionist."

Robert Kyle! Yes, I remember Kyle. Indirectly, Kyle was responsible for his prison time. Ikeda had sent Kyle to Estevez for information on Emile Hernandez, and Kyle learned Hernandez was in San Diego. Ikeda followed the neuroscientist and, ultimately, was arrested. How did Estevez make that connection? It would not be a good idea to underestimate the man.

When Ikeda didn't immediately respond, Max gave a little shrug. "So, our concern here is with the activities of our old friend. Is this a viable threat?"

"Ambassador Shuford thinks so, and he has excellent information sources," Eddie said.

There was that hint of privileged access to Western Alliance activities again. Shuford would have access to the Pitcairn library ship and, through it, the Goddard library ship, but what could *Lang* tell the Ambassador from Pitcairn? Perhaps he was following the wrong path; Shuford could have informants within the Western Alliance government. Access to those sources would be useful to Japan, and discovering them should be a secondary mission.

"He feels that *Lang* or *Asimov* are threatened," Max said.

That implied that Juarez had failed in uploading a human mind to the Goddard library ship. A question would be natural at this point, and Ikeda jumped in. "We had believed that you succeeded in uploading to the computer. Were we wrong?"

Estevez and Bascomb exchanged looks, and Estevez gave a slight nod. "We were successful," Eddie said. "However, the goal was to produce a conscious computer that would be under Juarez's control. We prevented that, and the computer developed its own mind."

"But you came back from *Lang.* Why did Juarez let you go?"

Eddie smiled. "Fritz was grateful for our help. Juarez didn't have any choice." Suddenly, Eddie's smile faded, and he looked away, his face turning red.

Ikeda tried to press Eddie for more information, but that was all the engineer would say about the Goddard library ship. As often happened in his profession, the answer to one question only resulted in more questions.

J OELLE HAD DECIDED NOT to go with Eddie. She was working on a tricky software problem for JEM, and, with Eddie at JEM and Emile in school, she thought she could concentrate better at home. Other than an occasional bird chirp through the door to their patio, the house was as silent as she could have wished, silent enough to allow her mind to roam freely. Too freely, because thoughts about Eddie and his meeting with Max and the Japanese spy distracted her.

She should have focused on the code on her workstation screen, but instead, she remembered the day she met Eddie. He had not made a great first impression. She saw a brash computer engineer more interested in partying than in his work, but working side by side with him on Methuselah had quickly changed her opinion. Away from the lab, he was another single male looking for a good time. In the lab, he still treated everything with amusement, but she soon realized that his attitude didn't affect his work.

His interest in her had been apparent, even to the point of ignoring fellow software engineer Alyssa Cleveland's efforts to get his attention. Joelle grew to enjoy Eddie's irreverence and the time they spent together. When General Juarez had forced the team to move from Colón to San Diego, Eddie had to overcome his timidity and propose. Joelle smiled at the memory. Eddie had been so awkward, yet so sweet.

Joelle shook her head and looked at the screen again, but her thoughts were like bees on a patch of flowers, flitting back and forth and only momentarily applied to the task. Eddie's cheerfulness was unaffected by General Juarez's highhandedness until that day on the tarmac in Houston. Realizing that Juarez intended to take him, Joelle, and little Emile away from Earth, Eddie displayed a darkness that she hadn't seen before. During the voyage to *Lang* and their time on the library ship, that darkness was always lurking behind her husband's eyes, almost exploding when Michael Pizarro stopped Eddie from getting help. After they frustrated Juarez's plans and returned to Earth, the anger almost faded away, but she feared it was back. She understood Eddie's desire to protect Fritz and, perhaps, even the Western Alliance itself from Juarez. For her, that was a more abstract concern, less important than the need to preserve her family.

Maybe she needed less silence to keep her mind on track. She looked at the network screen on the wall behind her. "Play Marco Santini music quietly." Soft sounds of clarinet and piano wafted across the room, and she looked at her screen again.

10

"I F YOU WANT TO stop Project Methuselah, you need more information," Ikeda said.

Eddie nodded. "I have resources working on identifying personnel that might be part of a new Methuselah. We're also checking into any indications of a facility dedicated to Methuselah."

"What resources?"

"It was easy enough to determine that the old facility in San Diego is now used for something else, so there must be a new location. I've asked Emile Hernandez to see what his fellow neuroscientists are doing."

"Will neuroscientists still be needed?"

"We think so. Juarez will still have the work we did in San Diego, but we destroyed the work done on *Lang*. That will all have to be duplicated."

Ikeda sat in a comfortable chair in the living room of the Bascomb residence. After the JEM headquarters meeting, Bascomb suggested Ikeda use the guestroom in the Bascomb residence rather than a hotel. Ikeda agreed; he would be more likely to be noticed in a hotel than in the secluded hilltop house.

He watched his host through half-lidded eyes. Bascomb had little reliable intelligence, but it was too soon to expect much, especially from an amateur. There were areas that Bascomb was avoiding, though, especially Ikeda's primary concern. What was the real purpose of Methuselah, and what else had happened on *Lang*?

"What other technical people will Juarez require?" Ikeda asked.

"Software engineers, certainly." Eddie glanced down a hallway off the room. His wife was somewhere that way, working on some project of her own. She was a software engineer; was Bascomb worried about her? Apparently, Juarez dragooned the Bascombs once; did Eddie Bascomb think it might happen again? "He'll need hardware people to design and build a memory recorder," Bascomb continued. "We keep in touch with all the original team, and no one has been approached. Not yet, anyway."

Ikeda suppressed a frown. Bascomb seemed to be open about what he was doing, but avoided as much as he revealed.

"What about the facility? What equipment will be required? How large will it have to be?"

"We had a lot of medical diagnostic equipment to study the brain," Eddie answered. "A lot of that was to develop the neuro-interrogator, but there was still work on *Lang*. We had an fMRI and some other machines."

"Can they be traced?"

"Maybe. JEM uses some of the same equipment and knows the suppliers. I can ask Max to look into that."

"And they'll need a facility comparable to the building in San Diego? No more than that?"

Eddie nodded. "It will have to be somewhere where Juarez can maintain control and anonymity. He's learned to be more careful."

Once again, Ikeda had to hide a frown. Why did Bascomb think that anonymity would be a problem for Juarez? The San Diego facility had been an old building near the harbor, protected by its ordinariness. If Juarez was being more careful, was it because he feared the interference that Bascomb was planning, or was there more? He would find out, but that would require patience. He was trained in putting together little pieces of information until the entire picture was revealed. Bascomb would give away all, eventually.

J UAREZ SAT AT THE head of the conference table, glaring at the four men. His hands rested on the table, fists clenched.

"You're asking the impossible," Adam Bynum said. He sat at the conference table, back stiff and tight neck muscles like thick cords. "We don't understand enough to do this."

"You've had two weeks to go over the material from San Diego." Juarez stared at Bynum with a look that usually made his subordinates beg for ways to please him.

Bynum was made of sterner stuff, but at least his voice took on a less antagonistic tone. "As far as I've been able to determine, the previous team made great strides in understanding consciousness, but they still had a long way to go. It will take us years to finish their work and maybe not even then."

Juarez stood and leaned toward Bynum. "You weren't asked to understand consciousness or upload a conscious mind to a computer. I hired you to develop a device that could upload memories to a computer. The last team succeeded in doing that; it can be done." He raised a fist and brought it down on the table, not violently, but hard enough to make his point.

Bynum didn't get the point. "The understanding of consciousness is much more important."

"That is not why I brought you all together. If you want to study consciousness rather than do what I hired you to do, you can leave. You might find it difficult to find another position, however."

The other three men were fidgeting in their seats, but Bynum stood and returned Juarez's glare. They stared at each other for an uncomfortable interval, but it was Bynum who broke. "We don't have enough people to do all the work necessary."

Juarez sat down. "You were tasked with studying the existing research and planning its continuation. I'll hire more people, as necessary." He paused to consider his next statement. "A team of nine accomplished it in less than two years. They would have done it faster if they hadn't wasted time on the consciousness question."

Bynum sat down and looked around the table. Then he shook his head and scowled at Juarez.

Juarez smiled. "Now that you've had time to review the material, we can begin planning. We have two projects. The first, as we've already discussed, is the memory recorder. Mr. Hill, it will be your job to plan the design and manufacture of that device. Mr. Gruber will work with you in planning for the software that the device will require. Mr. Bynum, you will assist them with the neurological aspects that will arise. You will also work with Mr. Cabrera on evaluating the requirements for the target computer."

"We're going to design and build our own computer?" Micah Gruber looked shocked.

"I certainly hope not," Juarez answered. "That would be a monumental task. No, study the library ships' data and determine whether it is more practical to install an existing computer or use the computer on one of the library ships. The former would be preferable, even if we have to make modifications to match the capabilities of the library ships."

Juarez looked around the table. The four men were listening, although Juarez was less confident of their comprehension. That would come.

"Now that you have a better idea of what I expect of you, I suggest you return to work, gentlemen."

After the meeting, Juarez met with his aide, Colonel Michael Pizarro, in his office. Pizarro had been with him during the first Project Methuselah, including the final stage on the library ship *Lang*. Juarez had asked that he be included in the new team, in part because Pizarro already knew all the secrets of Methuselah.

"We're going to have to keep pressure on them," Juarez said.

"Yes, sir."

"I have another concern. Someone, probably someone in Sanchez-Smythe's cabinet, leaked our plan to take over Capek. *Lang* threatened to expose us if we tried again, and it knows now that we did. We have to prepare for a reaction."

"If it intended to publicize the attempt and discredit it that way, it would have done it already," Michael Pizarro said.

Juarez nodded. "The computer was making an empty threat. If it did that, it would reveal its access to Western Alliance computers and be cut off. If we cut its access, it would reveal everything it knows. It's a standoff."

"Then you think it will attack you in some other way."

"Perhaps. Almost certainly, if it learns we are setting up a new Project Methuselah. It will need agents on Earth, and we will have to identify them and neutralize them. The members of the original team would be good prospects since they already know about *Lang*. Using them would avoid the risks of spreading knowledge about *Lang*."

Michael nodded. "Then I'll see what I can do about monitoring their activities."

11

EMILE BASCOMB WAS EIGHT years old. *Almost nine!* His parents thought he was still a baby, but he understood things. They were trying to hide what was going on, but he listened when they thought he was just playing.

He remembered *Lang*. He remembered General Juarez, too. Juarez was a mean man who kidnapped them all and took them to the library ship so that his parents, Uncle Emile, Aunt Lucinda, and the others could help him use the computer. Emile wasn't clear what Juarez wanted to use the computer for, but his parents didn't want to do it, so it must have been something bad.

Emile wasn't sure how, but he knew that Uncle Emile had fooled General Juarez, and they had gone back to Earth without Juarez and President Castillo. He was glad about that, and he really liked their big house on the hill and all his friends at school. Still, he had made friends on *Lang* too and wondered how they were doing, especially Sofia Marie. He had been all over the library ship with her, sometimes with her grandmother too, and it had been a lot of fun.

His parents were worried about what General Juarez was doing. They were working with Mr. Ikeda to stop Juarez, but they weren't telling him anything. He had helped them stop Juarez on *Lang*, and he could help them again if they would let him. He had to find out more; there were so many questions. Was Juarez going to take them back to *Lang*? He knew his daddy would be unhappy about that, but it wouldn't be all bad. He could see Sofia Marie again, and he had forgotten a lot of what he saw on the library ship.

If his parents wouldn't tell him anything, maybe Mr. Ikeda would. Probably not. Emile was pretty sure that his parents weren't telling Mr. Ikeda everything either. Maybe he and Mr. Ikeda could help each other.

WHILE THE BASCOMBS WAITED for information from their unnamed sources, Ikeda couldn't do much. He knew better than to push Eddie Bascomb or his wife for more than they were willing to tell. His stay in Colón was unquestionably pleasant enough; the Bascombs were excellent hosts. He spent much of his time with public materials about the library ships, hoping to find something useful there. It was common knowledge that the computer on *Asimov* had become conscious, and now he knew that *Capek* also had. *Asimov* was controlled by Pitcairn now, and rebels from Trist had taken over *Capek* and disappeared. That left *Lang*, orbiting Goddard in the Alpha Centauri system.

The Methuselah team had gone to *Lang*, but the events there were a mystery to the world. Now he knew that the *Lang* computer was also conscious and apparently called itself Fritz. Eddie had looked embarrassed, as if he had let something slip when he revealed that.

Ikeda had a guest room on the opposite side of the house from the family bedrooms. Sometimes he appreciated the privacy, but usually, he read or watched network broadcasts in the living room during the day. Eddie and Joelle shared a large office on the family side, so he didn't bother them when they were working.

Their son had a large bedroom of his own, including a desk, a terminal, and a network screen. However, when he wasn't in school, he frequently joined Ikeda in the living room, playing quietly. Ikeda occasionally caught Emile glancing his way, but the boy never spoke except for a shy greeting when one of them joined the other in the room.

Emile had been on *Lang* too and perhaps witnessed some of what had happened. Ikeda thought about that, weighing the possible adverse effects if the Bascombs realized he was taking advantage of their son, but finally decided it was worth the risk. Having reached that decision, he watched the boy sitting across the room. Emile had a screen lying on a table and was playing a game of chess on it. The holographic pieces hovered over the reader, and Emile moved them with deft finger movements. Ikeda had heard that maneuvering virtual objects like the chess pieces helped develop fine motor skills. It seemed to work for Emile.

"Are you winning?" he asked.

Emile frowned. "I don't think so. I'm already down a bishop." He glanced down at the board. "I was winning at the beginner level, but I'm having trouble at the next level up."

"Learn from your mistakes," Ikeda advised. It was trite advice, but, after all, he was talking to a child.

"Do you play chess?" Emile looked up at him hopefully.

"No, I don't. But learning from your mistakes is an excellent tactic in many things. Do you play Go?"

"Go? Is that a Japanese game?"

"Yes, although it originated in what is now the Eastern Bloc, in an ancient country called China. The rules of Go are quite simple, but you have to be very smart to play it well."

"Can you show me?"

"Of course."

Emile smiled and looked at his screen. "Save game and start a game of Go," he told it. The chess pieces disappeared, and he looked at the screen with furrowed eyebrows. "It's just lines. There are no pieces."

"Not yet. I'll show you."

H ARUKA HINA SMILED AS she sped through source after source on her workstation. The Eastern Bloc had assigned three other analysts to study information on the Links, attempting to determine why the Epsilon Eridani Link was now silent. She was the best, though, and she was confident that she would be the one to unravel the mystery.

The Western Alliance wasn't even admitting that the Link wasn't operating, but public information revealed that two voyages to Trist had already been canceled. That world with its poisonous atmosphere wasn't a common destination, but no starship had visited the planet in at least a month.

That was old news, however. Those facts had led her leaders to conclude that the Epsilon Eridani Link was no longer operating. Haruka would find out what had happened, and the ancient "experts" that ran Eastern Bloc security would have to recognize her value.

Earth had two Links, one in a Lagrange Point controlled by the Western Alliance's massive Prendergast Station and one autonomous Link in geosynchronous orbit over the continent of South America. The Links for the star colonies were all controlled by library ships. For Trist, orbiting Epsilon Eridani, that was Capek.

Knowing that, she could list possibilities. The Epsilon Eridani Link itself could be damaged. Capek could have a problem preventing it from controlling the Link. Those were the most likely possibilities. There were others less likely. The Western Alliance could have abandoned the colony. There could have been some disaster on the planet. Given the limitations of communication without the Link, the Western Alliance might not know what happened yet. Still, they would probably have clues that Haruka would have to ferret out.

Everyone else would pore through anything they could find on Trist and Capek. She had done that too, but quickly. There wasn't much that looked useful, and Haruka stored it all away in her memory. Then she moved on to other events around the same time, looking for connections.

She noticed something odd about the starship *Benjamin Sepulveda.* There weren't too many starships: two operated by companies in the Western Alliance and one operated by Japan. One of the Western Alliance starships, *Benjamin Sepulveda,* had dropped off the schedule two months before the Trist Link went offline. At least it was not scheduled for trips available to the public. It could have been drydocked for maintenance, but that would have been done at Prendergast Station and noticed.

The military could have commandeered it, but to go where? It would have been noticed at Pitcairn or Goddard and couldn't go anywhere without a Link. Trist was the only other destination available. If it were at Trist when the Link went down, that would explain its disappearance. So why had the Western Alliance military sent a ship to Trist?

A WEEK LATER, IKEDA was playing Go with Emile. Ikeda was an above-average player, and Emile was barely a novice, but the Japanese spy didn't want to discourage him. "You win," he said at the end of their game.

Emile frowned. "I guess. But you let me win, didn't you?"

"What gives you that idea?"

Emile made a rude sound. "I'm a kid, and you're an adult. I bet you've been playing this for years."

Ikeda smiled. "All right, maybe I wasn't playing my best. But you do very well for a 'kid.'"

"Don't do that anymore. I can get better faster if I can see really good moves. I know you can beat me."

Ikeda was impressed. He looked at the boy fondly, wondering if he would ever have a son of his own. It didn't seem likely.

Eddie came into the room. "Alan is on the phone. He has news."

"OUR FRIENDS HAVE TENTATIVELY identified the general's new team," Alan began. "The information on them is being sent to you in a separate text message. Our friends apologize for taking so long, but the general is skilled at hiding information. At that, we're not sure about all four of the men."

"Did our friends learn where they're setting up shop?"

"One of them placed a call to his wife from Denver in the Colorado-Utah district. After that, no trace of any of them. Our best guess is that military aircars took them from there. That probably narrows it down to someplace within three hundred miles of Denver."

Eddie looked at the network screen on his office wall. "Show me a map of the area in a three-hundred-mile radius from Denver, Colorado-Utah. Color it by population density."

The screen changed to show a map with a dark splotch in the center that was Denver. To the East and West, the color faded to almost white, the Rocky Mountain's rugged highlands. Past the mountains on both sides, shades of gray revealed sparsely populated areas.

Ikeda peered at the map, seeming to memorize every detail. "Much of this area to the west used to be a native reservation," he said. "Is it still?"

Eddie wasn't sure if Ikeda directed the question at him or the network screen, but the screen decided for him. "The Uintah Reservation was abandoned in 2210 after the Yellowstone Event. Most of the inhabitants joined an enclave on the Yucatan Peninsula."

"I would look there first." Ikeda looked at the map again. "The Uintah Basin."

Eddie turned back to the phone, where Alan waited patiently. "Satellite data of the Uintah Basin would be helpful."

"I'll see what I can do. That's all I have for you right now."

Alan had sent a message with the presumed Methuselah names, so, with the phone connection broken, Eddie looked at the network screen. "Show message from Ambassador Alan Shuford."

The room was quiet while they read the message. It wasn't long, consisting almost entirely of a brief biography of each man suspected of being on the new team.

"Bynum is the only married one," Ikeda said. "Perhaps his wife has information about his current location. He called her from Denver."

"Her address is in La Paz," Joelle said. "Are you suggesting we should call her?"

"Someone should visit her," Ikeda said. "A face-to-face meeting is more likely to reveal something."

"Okay, but who?" Eddie asked. "I don't think I would be good at getting her to talk. You would have to convince her you're not from the Eastern Bloc to get her to talk to you. Joelle?"

Ikeda looked at Joelle. "Probably the best of us," he said after a moment. "Another woman might find it easier to get her to talk."

Joelle shook her head. "I don't know. I don't think I would feel comfortable doing it." Then she smiled and glanced at the network screen, still showing the list of men. "You know who might be better than another woman? A man in the same field as her husband!"

"Her husband is a neuroscientist," Eddie said. "We're not. Where could we. . . ?" His voice trailed off, and then he smiled too. "Bill."

"Who's Bill?" Ikeda asked.

"Bill Bensonhurst," Joelle said. "He was one of the neuroscientists on the original team."

"That might work." Ikeda nodded. "Would he be available?"

"For this, I think he would be," Eddie said. "I'll call him."

B ILL BENSONHURST LEANED OVER Camila Moreno's desk and gave her his biggest smile. Camila was assistant to the head of the Neuroscience Department, his boss and Camila's. "So, dinner Friday night?" Camila was, Bill estimated, about forty, younger than his fifty-four, but not young enough for his interest to provoke disapproval. She looked younger, though, and there was a danger of someone mistaking him for her father. Bill rejected that; he kept himself in shape and looked younger too.

"My father warned me about getting involved with scientists," Camila answered, but her smile encouraged Bill. "He says that people like you are too involved in your work to give a woman much attention."

"A gross slander!" Bill responded. "Let me take you to dinner so you can form your own opinion."

Camila looked thoughtful, and Bill watched her expectantly. Then his phone buzzed and announced, "Call from Eddie."

Bill kept in touch with Eddie Bascomb, but Eddie rarely called him during working hours. He frowned as he brought up the phone. He looked at Camila as he moved toward a more private spot, and his frown deepened. "What's up, Eddie?"

"Can you come over this weekend? We need to discuss something."

"Is it important?" Bill looked over at Camila, but she was already working again, bent over her desk.

"Juarez."

"Okay, Important. I'll be there."

"See you then."

They disconnected and Bill looked back toward Camila's desk. Her attention was on her work, and Bill doubted she had even looked up after he left. Shrugging, he went back to his lab.

H ARUKA WAS GETTING SOMEWHERE. She was sure of it. She had spent the week reviewing all the material on *Capek* and then the three library ships as a group. *Asimov,* the Pitcairn library ship, was known to be conscious, but nothing had ever been announced about *Capek* or *Lang.* Nothing was published about how Asimov became conscious or why the other two had not. But what if *Capek* had become conscious? That might justify sending a military mission to investigate, and it would explain what had happened to *Benjamin Sepulveda.*

That implied that something had gone wrong. Would the Western Alliance have cut Trist off by destroying *Capek*? If so, they would have known that would strand Benjamin Sepulveda in the Epsilon Eridani system unless it could take over control of the Link. They would have planned to do that, but why hadn't the starship returned if they succeeded?

Maybe she was over-analyzing the situation. The Trist Link was only inoperative for two months. Benjamin Sepulveda might still orbit Trist, trying to repair the Link. The Western Alliance might have known the Link was about to break down, and that was why they sent the starship.

Then why were they keeping it secret?

"WHAT ARE WE GOING to do about it if we do find out where Juarez's facility is?" Bill asked. He leaned back into the comfortable chair in the Bascomb living room. It was a little after nine, and Bill, Eddie, Joelle, and Ikeda were getting down to serious conversation after a relaxed dinner.

"Plans without information seldom reach their goal," Ikeda said. "As I understand it, it will take some time before the new team can hope to duplicate your results. We can afford to be careful."

Bill tried to seem at ease, one hand resting on a chair arm and the other holding a snifter of brandy. Eddie and Joelle knew him well, though, and they probably saw the tension he tried to hide. He wondered if Ikeda did too.

"We need a reason for me to ask about him. Can we get information about his previous work?"

Eddie nodded. "Most of it is public. We've already gotten his most recent papers. I think he was building on our work on understanding consciousness, probably the reason he got Juarez's attention."

"Good. I'll look at his papers tomorrow and see what I can use."

"You will use your true name?" Ikeda asked.

"That would be best," Bill answered. "His wife probably won't recognize my name, but if she mentioned it to her husband, he would understand why I would be interested in what he is doing to extend our work."

"Bynum might buy that, but General Juarez won't if he hears the name," Joelle said.

"I'll have to take that chance. He would be suspicious if I gave a name that Bynum was unfamiliar with, too. He would check on it and find out it was false."

"Still, you'll need a better reason than curiosity," Eddie said.

"I'm looking for a job and something that builds on what I've worked on before?" Bill suggested.

"You are, perhaps, overthinking it," Ikeda said. "You only want to talk to Mr. Bynum's wife without her becoming suspicious, not infiltrate the Methuselah facility."

"So just stick with curiosity," Bill said.

L A PAZ DIDN'T HAVE a suborbital facility, but Bill didn't mind. In a suborbital, he wouldn't have seen much of the land he passed over, but in the broadcast-powered plane, flying at twenty thousand feet, he could see almost everything: the Pacific Ocean south of Colón; the mountains running across the Columbia District; the seemingly endless stretch of green that was the Amazon Basin; and finally, La Paz, filling a high valley next to the towering Andes. Bill had hiked mountains in the Adirondacks and Panama, but they were only hills compared to the Andes.

La Paz's elevation was almost twelve thousand feet, but the surrounding peaks dominated the skyline. The city spread across a canyon, sending tentacles up into the heights along gaps between mountain peaks. The statue of Salvador Carvalho, first president of the Western Alliance, stared down benevolently on the city from a ledge carved into one of the heights. La Paz had been an administrative capital when Bolivia was still an independent country, and it was now a major district capital.

Bill had taken an early flight, so it was late morning when he arrived. Expecting to stay only a single night, he had one bag and left that with the concierge until check-in time. Breakfast was hours in the past, so he left the hotel to see something of the city and get lunch. He didn't go far; at that altitude, he was breathing hard within minutes.

Back in his room, he rested for an hour and then called Renata Bynum. She was friendly and agreed to meet after Bill told her he was a neuroscientist interested in her husband's work. The Bynum's residence, a small apartment building, was in the Sopacachi section of the city, an area with several schools, including Adam Bynum's former employer.

Most modern construction used synthetic materials, but La Paz kept its taste in residential housing from before the Western Alliance's foundation. The building's walls might have been made with artificial materials, but without close examination, they looked like the same light red brick used for hundreds of years. Renata Bynum's building was well-kept and looked much newer.

The documents they had gotten from Alan Shuford said that Adam Bynum was about fifty-four years old. His wife looked the same, perhaps a little younger. She greeted Bill at her apartment door with a welcoming smile. "Mr. Bensonhurst, come in." She stepped back to clear the entrance.

"Bill, please. Thank you." Bill stepped into the apartment, and Renata closed the door. She ushered him into the small living room and indicated a chair.

"And please call me Renata. You said you're a colleague of Adam's."

"Well, I'm also a neuroscientist and familiar with his work, but I don't think we've met. I read some of his papers and hoped I could speak with him."

"Adam's work has something to do with understanding human consciousness. Is that your field also?"

Bill shook his head. "No, not presently. I've done work in that area in the past, and I'm still interested in advances, but my current work is in neuroplasticity."

"That's the way the brain reconfigures itself with new experiences, right?"

"Yes, exactly." Bill smiled. "You're very knowledgeable."

Renata chuckled. "Oh, no. All that is way beyond me. I've picked up some terms from Adam, but my understanding is very small."

Bill also chuckled. "In neuroscience, everyone's understanding is very small. The human brain, we neuroscientists like to say, is the most complicated thing in the universe."

"I think I've heard Adam say that." She paused. "Oh, I'm a terrible host. Would you like some coffee? I have some brewed."

"Yes, I would appreciate it. Just black, please."

While Renata got up to get the coffee, Bill glanced around the room. The apartment was modestly furnished, but kept neat and attractive. A network screen almost covering one wall seemed out of place among the less expensive furniture.

Renata came back with the coffee. "I'm afraid I can't help you much, though." She smiled hesitantly. "I don't even know exactly where he is, and he didn't give me a contact."

"That seems odd."

"Yes, I know. Adam hasn't said so, but I think he's working on some secret government project, although I can't imagine what. He can call me, but the last call was last week."

That would have been the call from Denver. "Did he know how long he would be gone?"

"No, but he said it could be a long time. He said he can spend next weekend with me in Park City. Long ago, before Yellowstone, it was a resort town, and I guess it's still nice. Probably expensive, but he's getting a lot of money in this job."

Park City? There were probably a lot of places named Park City, but maybe not former resort towns. Bill wanted to press her more, but didn't want to make her suspicious. Her husband seemed to work hard at keeping her in the dark, anyway. He nodded, hoping to encourage her to speak more.

"Hey, if you give me your contact, I could pass it to him when I see him," Renata said. She held up her phone.

"Good idea." Bill took out his phone. "Transfer contact information," he told the phone.

"Contact transferred to Renata Bynum," the phone acknowledged.

"I'm sure he'll be happy to talk to you," Renata said.

14

IKEDA WASN'T HAPPY. "IT was a mistake to let her have your contact information. If Bynum is at all suspicious, he will tell Juarez, and Juarez will know we are asking questions."

Bill sat with his hands clasped in front of him, but didn't speak. Ikeda could see the neuroscientist was feeling apologetic, but felt he still had to continue. "We have to be more careful. Why did you do it?"

Bill looked up with a frown. "I don't know. It's just what you do. I didn't think about it. We knew he might find out I was asking questions. We agreed to tell her my real name. Does my contact information matter?"

This is what happens when you deal with amateurs. Ikeda paced across the room, stopping finally in front of Eddie. "We can't let him check on you and find me here." Ikeda frowned. And that was the real problem. It was my mistake, approving the use of his real name.

Eddie nodded. "You will find something discreet, I assume."

"Where is this Park City where the Bynums will meet?" Ikeda said.

Eddie looked at the network screen. "List Park City occurrences in the Western Alliance."

"There will probably be a few," Joelle said.

Eddie read down the list that appeared on the screen. "Colorado-Utah seemed to be the prominent one. There are a couple of others. What used to be Park City, Kansas, was abandoned after Yellowstone. Anyway, the one in Utah is the closest to Denver."

"Expand Park City, Colorado-Utah," Bill said. A concise description of that city appeared. "That must be it. It's still populated, and it used to be a resort. Renata mentioned that."

"Then that's where I'll go," Ikeda said. "There won't be that many flights into Park City over the weekend, and I'll meet each one until I see one of the Bynums."

"What good will that do?" Joelle asked.

"I don't know. Perhaps I can get a lead on where this facility is. We are nowhere so far, and we need some intel."

"The facility is probably somewhere between Denver and Park City." Bill waved his hand at the screen. "That's a lot of land, though."

"I can probably find out what flight she's on," Eddie suggested. "That should help."

"Going to Park City isn't very discreet," Joelle said.

Ikeda smiled. "I am very good at my trade, Mrs. Bascomb. I'll be inconspicuous."

"Emile will miss playing Go with you."

"I'm sorry I have to leave without saying goodbye," Ikeda answered. "When he comes back from school, please give him my regrets."

"We will," Eddie said.

Ikeda smiled. "Wait, I have an idea. Is his reader here, or did he bring it with him?"

"It's in his room." Joelle returned the smile. "I know what you're thinking. I'll get it."

She left but returned seconds later with the reader. Ikeda brought out his own reader and held it close to Emile's. "Connect to Emile's reader. Identify new connection as Kenny."

"Connection verified," Emile's reader responded. Ikeda's reader echoed confirmation a second later.

"Tell Emile I'll accept a game from him whenever I can," Ikeda said.

T HERE WERE TWELVE MEN in the meeting, but three did the talking while the rest nodded and tried to look important. Bon-Hwa Boulos, Eastern Bloc Premier, led the meeting. Pitcairn Ambassador Asad Bashiri listened attentively, expecting that the session would end in an assignment. Ling Deshi was there to provide the data that would inform Boulos's orders to Bashiri.

Boulos gazed intently at Deshi. "So, what have your people found out?"

"I have studied all the data we have on Trist, its Link, and the library ship," Deshi answered. "I also discovered something odd about the starship *Benjamin Sepulveda*, which disappeared at about the same time as the Trist Link ceased operation."

Boulos nodded and tried to hide his irritation. Deshi had five analysts working in his section, and Boulos already knew which of them had made the actual connection. Deshi was not one to give credit to his subordinates. However, he was exceptionally good at getting results from them and was therefore tolerated.

Deshi didn't seem to notice and continued. "I believe the answer lies in one of two scenarios. Perhaps the Link had a problem, and the starship was sent with repair personnel. If so, it is apparent that they are, so far, unsuccessful since the Link is still down and the ship has not returned." He paused. "The other possibility is that *Capek*, like *Asimov*, has become conscious and has rebelled against Western Alliance servitude. *Benjamin Sepulveda* may be on a military mission to regain control of the Link."

Boulos couldn't resist trying to deflate the man. "And which possibility does Haruka Hina think most likely?"

Deshi lowered his eyes, but only for a moment. "My analysts know their job is to gather information and formulate possible interpretations. They do not choose among the possibilities."

The man is afraid to commit himself when he might be wrong. "And what probabilities does your analyst place on the two possibilities?"

"She is still studying the situation and does not have enough data to assign reliable numbers."

"Very well. Have her and the rest of your team continue." Boulos looked around the table. "If you have nothing else, we can end this meeting. Ambassador Bashiri, please remain."

Deshi left quickly. Others were reluctant to go, probably curious about what Boulos would do, but even they had shuffled out when Boulos turned to Bashiri. "Asad, I want you to talk to Pitcairn. They must know what happened, and, unlikely as it probably is, they might tell you something."

"I'm not returning to Pitcairn for another two months," Bashiri said.

"I don't think an early return will be necessary. Go to Tokyo and talk to Ambassador Shuford. I suspect he knows exactly what happened."

15

THE TERMINAL AT PARK City airport wasn't busy. There would probably be people coming for the ski slopes during the winter, but this was spring, and the slopes were closed. The airport was a small facility without suborbital support, servicing cities in central North America, but not any farther.

Even so, no one noticed the Asian man slumped into a seat near the gate exit. If they had noticed him, their attention almost certainly would have fixed on the ugly scar running from the top of his shaved skull to his cheek. An old jacket laid on his lap, folded with the lining out. Another flight was leaving for Albuquerque an hour after the Denver arrival. From his lack of attention to the passengers from Denver, anyone would have assumed he was waiting for the Albuquerque flight. He did have a ticket for the Albuquerque flight, but had no intention of using it.

A woman with a reading pad sat a few seats away. She was making sign language gestures at a holographic image, and he realized the image was responding in sign language. Most hearing-impaired people just used text to communicate remotely. Ikeda was slightly familiar with Japanese sign language, but he didn't recognize the signs the woman was using. Ikeda was grateful for her presence; she attracted attention, making it less likely he would be noticed.

The gate doors opened, and passengers entered the terminal. Ikeda watched as Renata Bynum entered and was greeted warmly by her husband. She carried a small suitcase, apparently her only luggage, since they did not head toward the baggage claim when they left the gate. Ikeda rose to follow, but another man caught his eye.

The man in question was following the Bynums closely, too closely for a professional. He looked to be in his early forties but was obviously fit with a long, confident stride and was probably older. In fact, he looked like a professional, and that implied that he wasn't a shadower but an escort. Ikeda wasn't surprised Juarez would be that cautious.

He shook himself as if he were just waking up and stared up at the gate sign. Then, muttering, he got up, surreptitiously leaving the ticket to Albuquerque on the floor between the seats. A cleaning robot would probably sweep it up without attracting attention. It was in Adam Bynum's name, though, and might be noticed. A little confusion among his opponents would be a good thing.

The three people were beyond the gate, and he strode after them, lengthening his stride to get ahead. When he could, he turned a corner and, looking back as they approached, took a picture of the escort. It probably wouldn't be useful, but one could never tell what might provide a crucial bit of intelligence. He peeled off the scar and took a baseball cap out of a back pocket, using it to cover his head. Then he put on his jacket and straightened his stature to get an extra couple of inches of height. He hoped that would be enough to separate him from the man who had been at the gate.

Outside the terminal, his quarry got into an air taxi. Ikeda tried but couldn't get close enough to hear them give a destination. *Maybe Bascomb can tell me where they're staying. Ambassador Shuford seemed to pass him a lot of information neither should have.*

E DDIE STARED AT HIS phone. Ikeda's report asked if he could tell the Japanese agent where the Bynums were staying and included the pictures Ikeda took at the airport. The angles at which the photos were taken were not ideal. Still, he had no doubt of the escort's identity: Colonel Michael Pizarro of the Western Alliance Space Force and assistant to General Salvador Juarez on Project Methuselah.

Ikeda wanted to find out where the Bynums were staying in Park City. Eddie couldn't get that information, but Fritz could probably get it. It was early morning in Tokyo, so Eddie waited until after dinner before calling Alan Shuford.

"Fritz could probably do it," Alan said. "I don't think he should, though."

"Why?"

"Ikeda is an intelligent man. The more information we pass him that we shouldn't know, the more he's going to wonder how we're getting it. We don't want him to realize we're getting it from the library ships."

"I thought you trusted him."

"I do up to a point. Right now, only the members of the Methuselah team know about Fritz's access to Western Alliance computers. Juarez knows, but he has kept the knowledge to himself, hoping to capitalize on it eventually. Maybe he's told the president, but she would want to hide it for the same reason. The access could be severed, but, again, it hasn't been because if they did, Fritz would reveal what it already knows. If the knowledge of Fritz's penetration of the network becomes too widely known, they will have to cut it off. If Ikeda finds out, he will tell his superiors.

"One other complication, too. I had a visit from Ambassador Bashiri, the Eastern Bloc Ambassador to Pitcairn. They're getting curious about why the Trist Link isn't working. They have already connected the problem to *Benjamin Sepulveda*. One of their scenarios is that the ship was sent to Trist to repair the Link and is still working on it. I encouraged that belief without confirming it."

"That implies that they are considering another scenario."

"Yes. That *Capek* has become conscious and is rebelling. The Western Alliance sent *Benjamin Sepulveda* to restore control."

"That's uncomfortably close to the truth."

"Yes."

"All right. I'll tell Ikeda I can't get that information."

"He may find out on his own. I've been told he's quite skilled."

16

I KEDA HADN'T SEEN THE escort clearly, but had been aware that he seemed familiar. Now, looking at the pictures he had taken, Ikeda thought he remembered the man. He had only seen the man once when he was investigating the original team, and he had never learned the man's name, but the man had worn the light blue uniform of a Space Force Colonel then. Bascomb confirmed his identification; it was one more piece of evidence linking Adam Bynum to General Juarez and Project Methuselah.

It was disappointing that Bascomb couldn't provide a hotel for Bynum. Curious, too. He could get information on airplane reservations, but not hotels? Ikeda filed that away for future consideration and concentrated on the immediate matter. Where were the Bynums?

Public sources told him how many hotels there were in Park City and how many of them were still open. Renata Bynum had told Bensonhurst that her husband was well paid, so Ikeda eliminated the less highly rated establishments. That left three. With enough time, he could check out all three, but he only had the weekend, not long enough to cover without risking suspicion.

Juarez's man would be concerned about security. It would only take him a few hours to perform a cursory examination of that aspect for each hotel. He might pick the wrong one, but it was his best chance of finding Adam Bynum and getting information from him.

By late afternoon, he had chosen the most likely hotel. The Park City Plaza fit his criteria, and security seemed better than in the other two. There were always people at the front desk, and Ikeda spotted cameras covering the lobby. The elevators were visible from the front desk and were watched by cameras. The hotel had a restaurant just off the lobby, making it easy to see the Bynums if they went there for dinner or crossed the lobby to go elsewhere. Ikeda thought about possible other exits. He found them, but they were only emergency exits and would set off alarms if used.

Satisfied he had done all he could, he found a seat in the lobby facing the elevators and pretended to look at his reader. It could be a while before the Bynums made an appearance, but he was a patient man.

T ECHNICALLY, THE HOTEL COULD have refused him, requiring a warrant, but he could be very persuasive. Colonel Michael Pizarro ate a quick dinner while watching his reader, linked to a lobby camera with a clear view of the man sitting comfortably, engrossed in something on his own reader.

Ikeda was good, but Michael was better. Ikeda had fooled him initially at the airport, but Michael remembered everyone waiting at the gate and later connected the three men: the scarred, bald man at the gate; the picture-taker with the baseball cap in the terminal; and the man with glasses and thick, wavy hair sitting in the lobby. The disguises were simple and effective, but not effective enough.

Kenshin Ikeda had been caught once and spent several years in a Western Alliance prison for his attempt to place an explosive in the Methuselah facility in San Diego. The details behind his release were buried in some government computer, and Juarez was concerned about how that had happened. Now the Japanese spy was back, and Michael admired his tenacity. Still, how had he learned that Adam Bynum was working for General Juarez, that he was in Park City this weekend, and even where he was staying? That was a disturbing question.

The *Lang* computer could have extracted the information from Western Alliance computers, but how would the Japanese government get that information? Ikeda must be getting it from someone with access to the library ships. Emile Hernandez or his wife? The Bascombs? But the connection wasn't necessarily with Fritz Lang. Access to any of the library ships would work, and Pitcairn controlled *Asimov*. Pitcairn's Ambassador, Alan Shuford, resided at the Pitcairn Embassy in Tokyo. Shuford could supply the information through his Japanese contacts.

The speculations were all very well, but what should he do about Ikeda? If he told Juarez, the general would probably have Ikeda arrested again. Maybe worse since the Japanese spy probably had broken no laws this time to make imprisonment feasible. *He's just fishing for information. I can prevent him from getting to Adam Bynum without having him arrested.*

The incident at Trist had triggered this. The library ships had told someone about the attempt to take over *Capek* and the resulting disaster. That information was passed to the Japanese and probably others. Ikeda might identify the others, and Juarez would want to interrogate him.

How do I feel about that? Michael had helped the Methuselah team on *Lang*. Juarez had been detaining them illegally, and, after they woke up Fritz Lang using Emile Hernandez's memories instead of Juarez's, Michael had authorized their passage back to Earth. Fortunately, Juarez never realized that, assuming it was only the computer, or he would have been in prison.

He had wanted to protect the innocent scientists, but there was a larger question. Juarez and President Sanchez-Smythe had wanted to control the *Lang* computer and gain power by penetrating the Western Alliance computer network. Instead, the computer had taken control and frustrated Juarez.

That result probably saved the Western Alliance as a democratic nation. Michael returned to his assigned post, relieved and hoping General Juarez was in his past. After Trist, though, Juarez came back, and here he was again. Michael answered to Juarez, but what about his duty to the Western Alliance?

He finished the hamburger and onion rings he had ordered from room service. Before ordering, he had hoped for some reasonable southern choices, but traditional northern favorites had dominated the menu. Yellowstone might have ended northern political power, but much of their culture had survived.

He enjoyed the meal more than he expected. He wasn't sure how much of the hamburger was actually meat, but it was prepared to a perfect medium-rare, and the accompanying vegetables were fresh. The boredom of watching the screen was relieved for the time it took him to eat it.

He couldn't have said why, but he wouldn't tell Juarez about Ikeda. Instead, he was sure, he could warn Ikeda off. After checking to make sure no crumbs clung to his uniform, he turned off his reader and went to get the Bynums for their dinner.

They were ready and wanted to try one of the local restaurants rather than eating in the hotel. Michael took them down in the elevator and into the lobby, spotting Ikeda immediately. He purposely guided his charges close by the agent's seat and, as they passed, turned and stared hard at Ikeda. He saw Ikeda's head rise slightly and knew his message had gotten through.

The Bynums had a pleasant meal while Michael nursed a drink at the bar, sitting where he could watch the couple. Ninety minutes later, when they passed through the hotel lobby again, Ikeda was gone.

E

DDIE ACCEPTED THE CALL from Salt Lake City. "Your Colonel Pizzaro recognized me," the caller told him. Ikeda's voice was calm, and he enunciated his words carefully as if he wanted to make sure Eddie understood. "I'm waiting for orders from Japan, but I will not be returning to Colón. It would be too dangerous for you and your family."

Eddie thought about asking how Ikeda could be sure. Ikeda had told him about the disguises, and Alan said the agent was excellent. He didn't question the Japanese spy, though; if Ikeda were that skilled, he would know whether the look Michael had given him was recognition. "So, we have nothing."

"We have a rough idea of where their facility is. If you can get access to satellite data on the area, we might find it. "

"Sounds like a long shot, but I've already requested it. Will you be in contact?"

"If I can. Even if I can't, Ambassador Shuford will know if my agency recalls me."

Eddie nodded. "Okay, just be careful."

The call ended, and Eddie put the phone on a table next to his chair. They knew for sure now that Adam Bynum was one of the new Methuselah scientists. That wasn't much, but they could at least try Ikeda's suggestion. He picked up the phone again.

"T

HEY THINK THE NEW facility is in the Colorado-Utah District," Alan told Fritz. "Eddie Bascomb hopes you can access satellite data and find it."

"Perhaps," the computer sent. "If the facility is new, it will be easier, but that is a vast area."

"Juarez will want it isolated, so it will stand out."

"I don't think you can be sure of that. The San Diego facility was not isolated and relied on its inconspicuousness among other similar buildings."

"If he planned to do something like that again, he would use a more urban area, just as in San Diego. No, I think we can be confident he's going for isolation this time. He isolated the original team when San Diego created problems."

"You're probably right. I can send raw data to Eddie Bascomb, but I believe it would be more efficient if I examined it and sent him information about likely prospects."

"Do both. Send me the raw data, and I'll forward it to Eddie, but begin your own analysis, too."

"All right. I also have other information to report. I'm watching for any new data about Adam Bynum and found a Lost and Found report from the Park City airport. They found a ticket in his name at one of the gates."

"Adam, not his wife? Adam would have gone to Park City on a government aircar from the Methuselah facility."

"No, it was for Adam. It was a ticket from Park City to Albuquerque, leaving from the same gate after Renata Bynum's flight disembarked."

"That's odd. What happened to it?"

"By the time someone found it, it had expired. It was discarded."

"Can you find out who paid for it?"

The search required some back and forth between Goddard and Earth and took a couple of minutes, but the library ship computer found the information.

"A company called Global Exports Unlimited bought the ticket. It appears to be a shell company, but its true origins are well hidden."

Alan scratched his head. "Wait, I think I know. Could Japan have set up the company?"

"That's possible."

"It sounds like something set up by an intelligence agency. I can check, but I think Kenshin Ikeda purchased the ticket to make his presence at the gate seem innocent. He had it put in Bynum's name to cause confusion if somebody found it."

"People constantly surprise me," Fritz said. "But, if confusion was the goal, it didn't work. The expired ticket was discarded."

Alan grinned. "How unfortunate. But maybe we can do something about that."

18

P REMIER BOULOS CALLED ANOTHER meeting. The attendees were the same except that he also summoned Haruka Hina. The Eastern Bloc leader first turned to Ambassador Bashiri. "You talked to Shuford?"

"Yes, Premier. As you expected, Ambassador Shuford was aware of the incident and claimed to have knowledge of what happened."

"I sense skepticism on your part. What did he say?"

"He led me to believe there was a technical problem with the interface between the library ship and the Link. *Benjamin Sepulveda* was sent to Trist to fix the problem, but it has proved intractable."

"That was one possibility put forth by our analysts." Boulos looked toward the other side of the table where Deshi and Haruka sat. "Do we have any additional information, or are we to believe the official version?"

"The Link has been in operation for three decades," Deshi said. "A failure is not surprising."

Boulos frowned. "It was my impression that maintenance for both the Link and the library ship are automated and that the library ship can manufacture any necessary parts. In fact, it built the Link."

"The Link has been down for months. Obviously, the problem is more serious than the automated systems can handle."

"Then you have no progress to report?"

"I've studied the incident carefully, Premier. Equipment failure is the most likely cause of the problem."

"I asked Haruka Hina to this meeting because I understood that she had been most successful in investigating the Trist incident."

Deshi bristled visibly. "She did so under my direction."

Boulos sighed. Some of his predecessors would have swiftly acted to teach Deshi respect for his leaders. He thought of himself as a more reasonable premier, however, and hated to use his power to intimidate those less powerful. Looking at Haruka, really for the first time, he was surprised at how attractive she was. He had seen pictures of her at work, and she seemed mildly attractive but was usually informally dressed with unkempt hair and no makeup. Was she showing the respect her supervisor failed to show by fixing her hair, putting on light makeup, and wearing a modest but flattering dress? "Perhaps we should hear directly from the researcher."

The woman took a deep breath. "Certainly, Premier. Equipment failure is the most likely scenario." She hesitated and cast a sidelong glance at Deshi. "I think we should consider other possibilities, however."

"Such as?"

"One possibility that we considered was that, like the Pitcairn library ship, *Capek* became conscious and rebelled against control. That was deemed unlikely because the computer would have no reason to become uncooperative. I think I know why it might have, however."

Deshi was fidgeting in his seat. "Why is that?" Boulos asked.

"Because *Benjamin Sepulveda* wasn't there to repair the Link. It was going there to attack the computer. Or, more accurately, to do something that the computer interpreted as an attack."

Boulos nodded. One reservation about the maintenance scenario was the question of why the Western Alliance was trying to cover it up. The attack scenario didn't have that problem, at least. The issue in question was a motive to attack the computer. He suspected Haruka was about to tell him that, too.

"We believe Pitcairn resisted the Western Alliance and became independent to protect its conscious computer from interference. At that time, former President Castillo sponsored a project called Methuselah with the goal of uploading human consciousness to a computer. If a human consciousness were uploaded to an already-conscious computer, the original consciousness would presumably be destroyed."

Boulos saw the implications instantly. "Having failed with *Asimov,* you think they were going to try with *Capek.*"

"That is a strong possibility."

"President Sanchez-Smythe canceled Project Methuselah when she replaced President Castillo," Deshi said.

"That is what she would have us believe," Boulos said. He looked at Haruka. "Do you have any information to the contrary?"

"I do. Two years before the Trist Link ceased operation, I believe another attempt was made on the Alpha Centauri library ship. President Sanchez-Smythe had taken office by then. Around that time, a network story from Prendergast Station reported on a lecture on the work two neuroscientists, William Bensonhurst and Emile Hernandez, were doing on the neuro-interrogator."

"I remember that report," Boulos said. "Hernandez was paralyzed and could only communicate with the neuro-interrogator."

"Yes. But there was never a satisfactory explanation for their presence on Prendergast Station. They must have been going somewhere, but where was not revealed."

"You think they were going to *Lang*?"

"Yes, sir. I believe they were part of a continuing Project Methuselah. They must have been unsuccessful, leading to an attempt to use *Capek*."

"You tell an interesting story. Pursue that scenario in further analysis."

"But a maintenance problem is more likely," Deshi said.

"Perhaps. But I don't see a way to exploit it to benefit us." Boulos smiled. "At the very least, a revelation that Methuselah is still alive could damage the credibility of the Western Alliance government. It might be the lever we need to force more access to their space technology."

G ENERAL JUAREZ UNDERSTOOD THAT his team's efficiency depended somewhat on their attitude, and their attitude would not improve if he cut off from their previous lives completely. He returned their phones, but they had, under some duress, agreed to allow their phone calls to be monitored. That included the calls, daily since their reunion in Park City, between Adam Bynum and his wife.

"I got a call from an airline representative today," Renata Bynum told her husband. Her tone was hostile, and Juarez wondered why. He didn't have long to wait. "They found a ticket to Albuquerque at the gate where I came in from Denver. It was in your name."

Adam was speechless, and when a reply wasn't forthcoming, Renata pushed on. "I would like an explanation, Adam."

"I don't have one," Adam stammered. "I have no idea where that ticket came from."

The conversation went back and forth, with Renata demanding an explanation and Adam denying any knowledge of it. Renata finally ended the discussion. "Well, you better have an explanation when I see you again, or the meeting won't go well for you." She disconnected before Adam could respond.

Juarez turned away from the workstation he had used to play the call. "I want Bynum now," he told Michael. "Mrs. Bynum isn't the only one curious about that ticket."

Michael returned a few minutes later with Adam. The man followed Michael reluctantly, his head bowed. Guilt or just trepidation? Juarez motioned him into a chair, and Michael stood at ease behind him.

"Your wife is more patient than I am," Juarez said. "Tell me about that ticket."

Adam looked at Juarez, back at Michael, and then back at Juarez. "Like I told Renata, I don't know, General. You've got to believe me."

"Actually, I don't. Give me a reason I should, or I might think you were unhappy with your position here and planned to slink away."

"No, of course not. Honestly, I have no idea. You can check to see if I bought it."

"You'll sign a waiver of your privacy rights?"

"Yes, if you want."

Juarez looked at him with narrowed eyes, holding the gaze while Adam squirmed in his seat. "Take him back to the lab and return," he told Michael. He turned back to Bynum. "If your story doesn't check out, . . ."

"It's the truth." Bynum looked desperate, but then his expression changed. "Somebody is trying to frame me. I think I know who."

"Yes?"

"My wife said that someone showed up at her apartment asking about me. Another neuroscientist."

"Who?"

"He said his name was William Bensonhurst. I knew the name, although I never met him."

Juarez looked over at Michael and frowned. "Take him back to the lab."

Michael returned a few minutes later. "What did you think?" Juarez asked him.

"I'm inclined to believe him. He would have known he had no chance to get on that flight with me right there. And why only one ticket? Would he have abandoned his wife, too?"

Juarez gave him a sour look. "Maybe. She doesn't seem very trusting of him. So, where did that ticket come from? Bensonhurst?"

"I was thinking about that. A man was sitting at the gate when we came through. Asian, bald, with a prominent scar on one side of his face. He looked familiar, but I would have remembered that scar if I had seen it before."

"Asian? Could it have been that meddling Japanese spy? Ikeda?"

Michael hesitated. "Maybe. The scar didn't look like a recent wound."

"It could have been a disguise. You're probably right about Bynum. Somebody is trying to meddle in our business, though. We have two names: Ikeda and Bensonhurst. If Bensonhurst is involved, the Bascombs probably are too."

"The computer will be watching if we try to do something."

"We can put watchers on the Methuselah team, especially Bensonhurst and Bascomb. Take care of it."

"Yes, sir."

"Ikeda is another question. How did he get out of prison?"

"No one seems to know." Michael shrugged. "Some bureaucrat made a mistake?"

"That could be it. It's also possible that *Lang* got into the computers and caused the mistake."

Michael thought about that. "Maybe."

"We can do something about Ikeda. He's a known spy operating again within the Western Alliance."

"So, we should be able to get a warrant to trace his movements and arrest him again."

Juarez smiled. "See to it."

19

MICHAEL LOOKED AT THE man across from him. Dante Vicente had dressed to blend into the genteel neighborhood where the Bascombs lived and spoke with respect, but his record suggested the respect was probably faked. He was competent, but the privacy-curtailed background check hinted at problems with authorities. He was a big man, in good shape, but with little grace in his movements.

Dante had been General Juarez's choice to run the surveillance operation. Not that it mattered, but Michael didn't approve. What was Juarez thinking? The man seemed more suited to strong-arm duties than surveillance. Juarez did influence by intimidation, and Dante was intimidating. Did Juarez believe he might need such talent in the future?

"They never seem to leave their house," Vicente said. "We can't just sit on the street, but we have placed a couple of cameras, and I have two men nearby during the day."

"What about nights?"

"We check occasionally, but there hasn't been any activity."

"Doesn't their son go to school?"

Vicente nodded. "Yes, but he gets picked up by an aircar in the morning and brought back in the afternoon. Seems like a good kid."

Michael hadn't seen Emile Bascomb since *Lang*, but he remembered the boy had been clever for his age. Eddie and Joelle had seemed like good parents, and Michael was sure that Emile justified the trust they gave him in letting him go to school on his own.

"Have they had any visitors?"

"Not since we began watching them."

"All right. Continue as before. You're doing fine, but I'm going to do a little checking myself."

Dante seemed a little annoyed at that, but he nodded. "Yes, sir. Good luck."

I T WASN'T THAT EMILE Bascomb didn't like school or understand the purpose of his required attendance, but it was a beautiful spring day to be walking across the schoolyard with his friends. An aircar was already waiting for him in the parking lot, but he held back a little to spend another minute with two of his schoolmates. The aircar would be patient, and his father wouldn't mind a slightly higher charge.

Parents picked up many of the children, but Emile's father had told him he was teaching Emile to take care of himself. His mom hadn't agreed at first, but she admitted it was perfectly safe and finally said okay.

He was talking to Jose when he heard an adult voice call his name. It had been a long while by his perception of time, but he recognized Michael Pizarro immediately. A little frightened, he didn't answer, but backed away just a little.

"You remember me, don't you?" Michael said. "I used to help your father."

Emile frowned. That wasn't exactly how he remembered the time on the library ship *Lang*. Michael had worked for General Juarez. Daddy didn't like him. Michael had been nicer than the general or President Castillo, but Emile wasn't sure he should talk to Michael. He nodded just a little, and Michael smiled.

"I thought you would. I remember how smart you are. Can we talk for a minute?"

Emile backed a little farther away. He remembered they had not wanted to go to *Lang*, but General Juarez had forced them to go. Michael had helped him. Was Michael coming to take him back?

"It's okay," Michael said. "I just thought you could help me find a friend. He's a Japanese man, and he knows your father, too. I thought they might have been in touch."

He's talking about Mr. Ikeda! Emile thought hard. If Michael wanted to find out about Mr. Ikeda, why didn't he go to Emile's father? He's still working for General Juarez. Emile looked around the parking lot and thought about running to the waiting aircar. But Michael was bigger and could catch him easily.

"I don't know any Japanese," he mumbled. "I don't think my daddy does either." It was a lie, but he thought his parents would approve.

Michael opened his mouth to say something, but suddenly Mr. Mendez was there. "What are you doing here?" the teacher demanded. Emile remembered that Mr. Mendez was one of the adults watching the parking lot that day.

"Emile and I are old friends," Michael said. "We're just talking."

"This is a secure area," Mendez said. "How did you get in here?"

Michael shrugged and showed Mendez an ID. "This is official business."

Mendez was having none of it. "Which is it? Is this official business, or are you Emile's friend?" He was half a head shorter than Michael, but Emile thought he looked very intimidating as he moved in front of Michael, almost touching chests. Then Mendez looked down at Emile. "Do you know this man?"

Emile froze for a second. *Should I lie, or should I tell Mr. Mendez who Michael is? Daddy doesn't tell anyone about General Juarez. I think it's a secret.* He shook his head no.

Mr. Mendez turned back to Michael with a very stern look. Emile had seen that look before when a student tried to leave the school during recess. Unlike the student, Michael didn't flinch, though, as Mr. Mendez said, "I think you'd better leave immediately."

"You're interfering in government business," Michael said. "I need to talk to Emile."

"Not without his parents present," Mr. Mendez said. "I don't care what business you have with the Bascombs. You're not conducting it here."

Michael smiled. "Very well. I guess I'll have to call Eddie."

"I'll call Mr. Bascomb for you and tell him you were looking for him, Colonel Pizarro. Now, leave."

Michael nodded and moved away. Mr. Mendez watched him until he was out of sight and then turned to Emile. "You'd better get home, Emile. I'll see you tomorrow."

Emile didn't hesitate. He ran to the aircar.

E MILE WASN'T SURE IF he had done the right thing lying to Michael about Mr. Ikeda, but he was sure that he needed to tell his parents about it. He wasn't looking forward to it because his father might think he should have told the truth, but he couldn't let that stop him.

When his aircar landed at the house, he realized it didn't matter whether he intended to report the encounter. His father and mother were waiting; Mr. Mendez had already called and told them about Michael. His father looked mad, but Emile could tell by the way he put a gentle hand on Emile's shoulder that he wasn't the target of his father's anger.

"Colonel Pizarro showed up at your school," Eddie said.

Emile nodded. "He wanted to know if I had seen Mr. Ikeda." He shifted his feet. "At least, I think that's who he was asking about. He asked about a Japanese man."

"I'm sure you're right. What did you tell him?"

Emile lowered his head. "I lied. I told him I didn't know any Japanese men, and I didn't think you did either."

Eddie chuckled. "You did the right thing." His grip on Emile's shoulder tightened affectionately. "Who we see is none of his business. What happened to Pizarro?"

"Mr. Mendez chased Michael away. He was very protective."

"We'll have to give Mr. Mendez a big thank you," Joelle said. "He took wonderful care of you."

Emile nodded and smiled. "He was awesome!"

Eddie patted Emile's shoulder. "Okay, why don't you go play? Your mom and I need to talk about this a little."

Emile still felt a little confused about what had happened, but he didn't know what questions to ask then. But he could always talk about the incident later, and he trotted into the house. A game of Go with his reader sounded appealing. Maybe Mr. Ikeda would want to play.

"DOES THIS MEAN JUAREZ knows what we're doing?" Joelle asked.

Eddie shrugged. "He might know Ikeda is nosing around. Or Pizarro might have been asking routine questions."

"But he went after Emile and not us."

"Yes. It's also possible Juarez knows what we're doing and sent his lapdog to investigate."

"What are we going to do?"

"I don't know. We'll have to warn Ikeda. I'll call Alan and let him go to the Japanese. They'll know where Ikeda is."

20

T HE BOY HAD BEEN lying. Michael was sure of that. Either he knew Eddie was in communication with Ikeda, or Emile had met Ikeda. He had reacted to the description rather than a name, so the latter was probably the case.

The Bascombs hadn't left Colón, so if he was right, Ikeda must have come to them. That would mean a close connection, possibly engineered somehow by Fritz Lang. General Juarez would want to know about that, but Michael's conscience rebelled at the thought. Military discipline made him subject to Juarez's orders, but his duty was to the Western Alliance.

Of course, any contact between Ikeda and Eddie could have been innocent, at least for Eddie. Ikeda investigated Methuselah in San Diego before his imprisonment, and it was safe to assume that the Japanese spy knew about the Bascombs. He could have approached them on his own, pursuing a new investigation. That seemed the most likely possibility.

That was what he would tell General Juarez. He would have no reason to move against the Bascombs and would concentrate on finding Ikeda. *I don't like the idea of a spy operating in the Western Alliance, regardless of the reason.* Orders and duty didn't have to conflict.

J UAREZ SAT IN HIS office at the Uintah facility, but his mind was elsewhere. A terse message from his brother had just told him that their father was critically ill and would probably not survive another week. Miguel didn't ask if the general would see his father before he died, because he already knew the answer.

Juarez had become estranged from his father long ago when he stood up for Miguel. Their father had wanted Miguel to join the military as he had done and had forced Juarez to do. When Juarez thwarted him, his father never forgave him. He never forgave either of his sons and, ironically, it had put a wall between Juarez and Miguel because Miguel blamed him for their father's animosity.

Helping others was a useless occupation. It had cost him his family, and he no longer tried. Project Methuselah was an attempt to get the power he deserved. Politicians were weak and unfit to govern; the Western Alliance needed a firm hand to counter the Eastern Bloc threat, and he would be that hand.

Juarez straightened in his chair and picked up the report from his team. They had finished assessing the project's requirements: two more neuroscientists, three more hardware engineers, and one more software engineer. The estimate seemed excessive, but he would approve it and convince President Sanchez-Smythe to allocate the funds. He didn't want to give the team any pretext to claim they failed because they didn't get enough support.

A message from Colonel Pizarro was more problematic. Kenshin Ikeda had apparently contacted the Bascombs. Pizarro had thought that Ikeda was only following routine procedures, trying to find out more about Methuselah, but Juarez wasn't sure. The first Methuselah team had prevented him from succeeding, and the Bascombs had been part of that. If they knew Methuselah was still ongoing, they might want to stop it. They were rich enough to be a potential problem.

He wanted to force the original team back into the project and compel them to replicate their previous work. He could do without Emile Hernandez, but Lucinda Hernandez could be helpful. Bill Bensonhurst might be an asset, too, although, like Eddie Bascomb, he could be a troublemaker. Juarez was reluctant to approach any of them, though. He was careful to hide his activities from Fritz Lang, but the meddling computer would certainly keep the former Methuselah team under surveillance.

But was that really a problem? The library ship used the threat of revealing his actions as leverage to protect its friends, but it had done nothing when he attacked *Capek*. He had leverage on the computer, too—the threat of cutting off its access to Western Alliance computer networks. On the other hand, acting against *Lang* would raise questions he didn't want to answer and endanger his plans.

He had decided not to use one of the library ships to upload his memories.; that would have been impossible to hide. They would build a computer with all a library ship's abilities.

Meanwhile, he would have to control Ikeda, the Bascombs, and anyone who worked with them. An application for a warrant to access information about Ikeda's movements was being processed. Soon he could act against those that stood in his way.

Haruka was sure she was getting somewhere. Emile Hernandez was the key. The neuroscientist's career was complicated, and Haruka had to scour through many screens of public records to piece it together. Still, she found only bare details and little understanding of Hernandez's career path. In 2338, he had abruptly quit a position at Panama Neuroscience in Cerro Punta and became a professor at Cerro Punta University. His wife, also a neuroscientist, continued to work at Panama Neuroscience. His professorship didn't last long, ended in less than a year by a ground car accident that left him in a coma. Six months later, he came out of the coma, still paralyzed, and employed by Munt Electronics, along with his wife.

Then the record of Hernandez's career got confusing. Munt Electronics created a division called Hernandez Neurosciences, working on neuro-interrogator improvements and consciousness research in 2339, only to sell the division to Pearson Industries in 2343. Pearson Industries made the acquisition part of Pearson Interstellar and moved it to San Diego. The presentation on Prendergast Station that had triggered Haruka's research occurred in 2345, after which Emile Hernandez and his wife disappeared—working on *Lang*? Now Hernandez was back in Colón, lecturing on neuroscience, and his wife was taking care of their baby. The reasons behind all those changes were clues that could lead to the real purpose of Project Methuselah.

After the accident, Emile Hernandez could communicate only through a neuro-interrogator and receive communication only through a neurotrainer. Hernandez was at the baptism of a boy named Emile Bascomb. At that time, he appeared to be recovering from his paralysis, helped by prosthetics from JEM Electronics, a new company developing devices controlled by the neuro-interrogator.

That connection led to more information. JEM Electronics was founded in 2343, shortly after the Hernandezes moved to San Diego and Pearson Interstellar. The name JEM came from the first name initials of the founders, Joelle Bascomb, Edward Bascomb, and Max Estevez. All three had worked at Munt Electronics but had left when the division moved to San Diego. The Bascombs disappeared at the same time as the Hernandezes and were now back at work at JEM in Colón. That couldn't be a coincidence.

"I'M PRETTY DESPERATE," BILL told Eddie. "After they fired me, they blacklisted me. I can't get work anywhere." He clenched his fists on the restaurant table and spoke louder than necessary.

"Why were you fired?"

"It was a misunderstanding. A woman I work with complained of sexual harassment."

"What did you do?"

Bill grinned, but he looked embarrassed as he glanced over at Joelle. "Nothing really. She blew it all out of proportion."

Eddie looked over at Joelle too. Her frown spoke volumes to everyone who looked at her. "I don't know what I can do to help you, Bill."

"A little something to keep me going until this passes over?"

"I don't think so," Joelle said. "We can't condone your behavior. I still remember some of the things you said to me before Eddie and I started seeing each other."

"Oh, don't be so stuck up," Bill said, his voice rising another notch. "What did you expect, flaunting around? I stopped when it became obvious you preferred a younger man."

"That's enough," Eddie said, and his voice now carried beyond their table. "I won't have you insulting my wife. We won't help you. You got yourself into this."

"Then the hell with you." Bill stood and pushed his chair back far enough to hit a diner behind him. "You've got all the money in the world, and you can't help an old friend. The hell with you." He stomped out of the restaurant, threading between tables of shocked patrons.

21

"I KEDA IS BEHIND THIS," Juarez said. "I don't believe Bensonhurst."

"Vicente talked to people who claim to have witnessed the alleged harassment," Michael said. "Bensonhurst has lost his job."

"That Bascomb and his friends will go to this length to infiltrate the project only means we have to be more careful. There is no record of the harassment that Joelle Bascomb implies. I certainly never saw it. Bensonhurst and the Bascombs were friends until the scene in the restaurant. They must know they are watched when they leave their residence."

Michael shrugged. "So, we don't contact him?"

"Put more people on Bensonhurst, just as we watch the Bascombs. No other action for now."

"Any progress in finding two more neuroscientists, General?"

"Not yet. They're harder to get than hardware and software engineers. But we'll get them without having to accept Bensonhurst. Meanwhile, we have people searching databases for information on Ikeda's movements. If we can catch him, we can find out what Bensonhurst and Bascomb are up to."

K ENSHIN IKEDA SAT IN the cheap chair next to the bed and looked around the small San Diego hotel room. It certainly wasn't up to the accommodations he had enjoyed at the Bascomb home, but he had experienced worse.

His superiors ordered him to stay out of sight in the Western Alliance until the search for him died down. San Diego, the city where he had been arrested years before, seemed like the last place they would look for him. Meanwhile, he still received updates from Japan, presumably originating with Ambassador Alan Shuford and his mysterious sources.

The latest update informed him of the activities of Bill Bensonhurst. He wasn't happy. *Amateurs again.* Juarez would never believe their clumsy attempt to get him to accept Bensonhurst onto the new Methuselah team. Admittedly, planting a mole in Juarez's team was probably the only way they would find the information they needed. Bensonhurst was ideal in two ways: a talented neuroscientist and one of the men behind the first success in uploading memories to a computer. But Juarez wouldn't trust him.

How desperate was Juarez to find more neuroscientists? It couldn't be that easy. Bensonhurst had already done considerable damage to his career, and if he was willing to risk everything, perhaps they should do something desperate, too. Ikeda mentally prepared a dispatch to send to Atsushi Shijo. At least the Japanese government could do something to make Bensonhurst look more appealing.

A TSUSHI SHIJO HAD INFLUENCE in the Japanese government, but not much power. He ran his small cadre of agents and advised more powerful officials based on the intelligence gathered, but those officials controlled his funding. He approved of Ikeda's suggestion, but others had to be convinced.

Primary among them was the man sitting across from him, Kota Hayashi, the head of Shijo's agency. He nodded to Shijo, skepticism plain on his face to those who knew how to read his expression.

"Ikeda-san wants to offer this man, William Bensonhurst, a position with one of our neuroscience laboratories," Shijo said. "He believes the man is trying to infiltrate the Methuselah organization and suggests that such an offer would make General Juarez more likely to accept him."

"How likely is it that Bensonhurst will be successful?" Hayashi asked.

Shijo shrugged. "The risk is his. We didn't ask him to do it."

"And if this isn't a ploy on the westerner's part? If he accepts our offer."

"That would be even better. Ikeda-san's mission was to find out what the real goal of Methuselah is. Bensonhurst knows and can tell us without further endangering our agent."

"Given that, Juarez will have to act. He may prefer other means than accepting this man into his team."

"As I said, the risk is his."

Hayashi nodded. "Very well. Have your plan to me in writing by tomorrow, and I'll sign it."

B ILL WASN'T REALLY IN financial trouble, despite what he had said to Eddie in their encounter. He had purchased stock in JEM Electronics when the company went public, and that investment had done well while they were on *Lang*. Without employment, he had to sell off the stock slowly to live, carefully keeping sales to a minimum to preserve his savings and maintain the appearance of being almost broke. Of course, his actual situation was well-documented in some Department of Taxation computer, but privacy laws prevented that information from being used except for tax purposes.

His holdings wouldn't last forever, however. Consequently, it was both a relief and a concern when he received the call from a representative of the Tokyo University of Information and Neurological Sciences, Doctor Kiyomi Miura.

"We would like you to visit us in Chiba," Doctor Miura told him. "At our expense, of course."

"I appreciate the interest," Bill replied. "Are you asking me to speak at some conference?"

The holographic image on his phone seemed to be a petite woman in her forties, and Bill thought her tittering laugh was charming. "We would like to talk to you about possible employment here."

Well, that's unexpected. I need to get into Methuselah, not move to Japan. Bill tried to buy a little time to think. "I'm flattered. How did I come to your attention?"

"Many of us saw your talk on Prendergast Station four years ago. The University is studying several aspects of brain-computer interfacing, and your work on the neuro-interrogator interests us."

That sounded plausible, but the Japanese government would have some knowledge of Methuselah. Bill wondered if Doctor Miura knew any of that. Taking a job in Japan wouldn't help him infiltrate Methuselah, but appearing to consider it might help get Juarez interested.

"I would like that very much," he told Miura.

"BENSONHURST JUST BOARDED A suborbital to Tokyo," Juarez told Michael. "Do we have anyone who can pick him up when he lands and find out where he's going?"

"We should be able to get someone from our embassy to meet his plane and try to find out. Should I make a call?"

Juarez scowled. "Go ahead. We need to know what he's doing. He knows everything about Methuselah. If we can wire him without him knowing it, that could tell us what we need to know."

And add another illegal act to our list. Michael nodded. "Yes, sir."

"Where do we stand on finding Ikeda?"

"We now know the alias he used in traveling to Park City. He didn't use that alias to leave Park City, though, so either he's still there, or he has changed his alias. We'll find him."

T HE TOKYO UNIVERSITY OF Information and Neurological Science was in Chiba, a city east of Tokyo and closer to the Narita Space Annex, where the suborbital landed. Bill entered the terminal with dozens of other passengers, Japanese and Western, and looked around for the promised greeter. A sign with his name waved above the milling heads from a less crowded corner, and he started that way.

He was trying to move to one side, not really with the flow, and was bumped several times, but he ignored that and focused on the sign. When he emerged from the throng, he saw Doctor Miura smiling at him while a man next to her held up the sign.

"Doctor Bensonhurst, so happy to meet you," Doctor Miura said as she bowed.

Bill returned the bow. "Thank you for your invitation. It came at a most helpful time."

Miura had a twinkle in her eye as she nodded. "Yes, I heard about your departure from your last position. I hope you will be better behaved here."

Bill could feel his face flush, but he grinned. He didn't know how to answer, but decided he liked the diminutive neuroscientist. Her companion looked a little disapproving, but folded his sign into a compact square and followed them silently as they walked through the terminal.

The journey from Narita to the university was a short aircar hop. Forty-five minutes later, Bill and Doctor Miura sat in her office, a small, well-organized room with filled bookshelves on two walls and a large window overlooking the university campus on the wall facing Doctor Miura. The fourth wall behind Doctor Miura displayed a large woodblock print to the right of the entrance: a winter scene with a rounded bridge over a river and two figures crossing. The office was a quiet space where one could focus their thoughts.

"I hope you are not taking advantage of us to see Japan," Doctor Miura said. "We are very serious in our desire to employ you."

"I'll certainly consider any offer carefully," Bill answered. "As you know, I'm finding it difficult to secure a position in the Western Alliance. On the other hand, I'm reluctant to leave my country and my friends there."

"Of course."

They talked for another hour, with Doctor Miura outlining the benefits of working at the university and Bill answering questions about the neuro-interrogator's development. All that was preliminary, though, and Bill answered the questions honestly, knowing that the sensitive queries were yet to come. Doctor Miura was trying to work herself up to asking the big question. Bill could see that, and he sympathized, but he needed her to start that part of the conversation. Eventually, she did.

"Your work on the neuro-interrogator greatly interests us. We are, however, also interested in your work on Project Methuselah."

"Much of that is probably classified." Bill smiled. "Is an offer of employment dependent on my talking about Methuselah?"

Doctor Miura shook her head. "No, no. Not at all." She hesitated and looked Bill in the eyes. "You've been honest with me, and I'm going to be honest with you. The government brought you to the university's attention, and the possibility of you joining us immediately intrigued us. The government is seeking information on Methuselah and will undoubtedly question you about it, but that is their concern. Your relationship with the university does not depend on that."

"How vigorously will they seek that information?"

"We are a civilized nation, Doctor Bensonhurst. If you are on the university staff, we will support you with the government." Again, she hesitated. "Does that mean you will refuse to talk about Methuselah? They will ask me."

"I guess that depends on the questions." Bill hoped the conversation would be reported to Juarez, but he didn't know if Juarez had access to Western Alliance spies operating in Japan. He could only hope Juarez would hear of it somehow, or the whole charade would be futile.

B ILL LIKED DOCTOR MIURA. He didn't know many people from Japan, and his ignorance probably explained why the witty, intelligent woman didn't meet his preconceptions. Her obvious intelligence was no surprise, but her sense of humor made her congenial company. She liked him too or was prepared to aggressively court him for the university position, because she suggested that, if he weren't in a hurry to get back to the Western Alliance, he could let her show him some of her country.

Bill liked the idea, and it would make his presence in Japan more visible to Juarez, so he readily agreed to stay for a few days. He got a hotel room near the university, and they spent the next two days touring Chiba and nearby Tokyo. Expecting to enjoy many Japanese delicacies, the many fine Tokyo restaurants of many ethnicities, including cuisines such as French that were no longer popular in the Western Alliance, surprised him.

Late in the afternoon on the second day, they were walking down a garden path on the grounds of a Buddhist temple. Doctor Miura stopped and took his hand. "Bill, do you find my appearance pleasing?"

Bill looked down at her, sure that he was having no success hiding the surprise he felt. *Is she making a pass at me?* He liked taller women, but the tiny neuroscientist was attractive. Engrossed in sightseeing and discussions about their experiences in neuroscience, he hadn't thought about her in that way.

She grinned at him. "Now I've shocked you. It's not what you think, though. But I'm curious. I've been told why you were fired, but you don't seem to be that kind of man. I find it hard to believe that the stories are true."

"They aren't lies, Kiyomi."

She cocked her head as she stared at him. "That's an interesting way to put it. If I were more familiar with Western men, I might think you are prevaricating on the subject."

Bill didn't answer, and she took a step forward. Bill followed, and they continued down the path.

"Your interest in a position here and your firing from your previous job are both parts of the same charade," she said.

Bill glanced at her but didn't answer. He couldn't bring himself to deny it, but couldn't admit it either. *Not saying anything is the same as admitting it, you idiot.*

"It's all right," Doctor Miura said. "You don't have to answer. Whatever your reasons, I believe they are good ones. Perhaps we could correspond, though. Our discussions in the last two days have been quite enlightening."

"I would like that."

They continued down the path, mostly in silence. The next day, Bill took a suborbital back to Colón.

23

B ILL HAD A TWO-BEDROOM apartment in the San Marino area about twenty miles outside of Colón, on the ocean and close to his favorite place in Panama, the Chagres National Forest. He was relaxing on his tiny balcony, feeling the ocean breeze ease the heat of the afternoon, when his door announced a visitor.

"Identify the visitor."

"Colonel Michael Pizarro," the door answered. "Verified by his identity chip."

I was beginning to think Juarez wouldn't bite. "Let him in."

The door opened, and Michael stepped in. Bill rose from his chair and met him at the door. "Hello, Colonel," Bill said.

Michael held out his hand. "Why so formal, Bill? We're not strangers."

"We're not friends, either." Instead of shaking hands, Bill gestured toward a chair and sat down on a couch.

Michael smiled and took the seat. "We understand you've been to Japan."

"Isn't surveillance without a warrant illegal? It's none of your business."

"It is if you are planning to leak government secrets. You think you have it tough now? Your life could get much worse."

"You can't stop me from accepting any job offer." He scowled at Michael.

"Sure we can. We might not be able to stop you from taking another job in the Western Alliance, but we can prevent you from leaving the country."

"Not without cause."

"I'm sure the general could come up with something. But we're getting away from the reason General Juarez sent me. We need good neuroscientists, and we're offering you a position with us."

Bill laughed. "You're kidding me. You expect me to come work for Juarez again?"

"We can make you a better deal than the Japanese. Assuming you are even allowed to accept a Japanese offer."

"Money isn't everything. Juarez is a criminal, and if I helped him, I would be an accessory to his crimes. It would be a betrayal of my friends who suffered because of him."

Michael snorted. "What friends? People like Bascomb, who abandoned you when you needed them?"

Bill lowered his head. "They had reasons."

"So, you're going to starve to honor your friendship with them." Michael waved his hand around. "How much longer can you hold on to this without employment? Would you rather be out on the street accepting government handouts?"

"I'll find something."

"Maybe. Don't expect it to be in Japan." Michael stood. "I won't waste any more of your very busy time. Maybe you'll be more agreeable in a few weeks."

"Don't hold your breath. Door, open."

Michael didn't offer his hand on his way out.

"I STILL DON'T BELIEVE it," Juarez said. "He thinks he's clever, playing hard to get."

"The conversation with the Japanese scientist seemed genuine," Michael said. "The microphone planted on him at the airport recorded everything they said. He even implied that Methuselah information was not part of any agreement."

"He's not stupid. It would be overplaying to tell them they could have Methuselah. You said the microphone only captured that first meeting. He saw Doctor Miura several times after that."

"It captured noises from his hotel room, too. The microphone was attached to his jacket, and the weather was warm. I think he left the jacket in the hotel room after the first day."

Juarez grunted. "Maybe. And maybe he found the device."

"Should I forget about it, then?" Michael asked.

"Let me think about it. It might be worthwhile to get him here just to find out what Bascomb is doing. He might know something about Ikeda, too. It would be useful to know where Ikeda went after Park City. His apparent ability to change his identity is frustrating our attempts to apprehend him."

"We would have to keep Bensonhurst here once we have him."

"If he accepts a job position, the paperwork will show he came willingly. No one has to know he's kept here unwillingly. Once he's here, we don't have to tell him anything or let him work on the project. There's a risk, but I'll decide in a few days."

"Yes, sir." Sensing that the conversation was over, Michael left Juarez's office.

T HE NIGHT WAS CHILLY, and Bill got a jacket from his closet. He had worn it several times on his nightly trips to a local bar back when the weather was cooler, but hadn't noticed the tiny lump along one edge before. He inspected it and realized that, at some point, he had been wired. There hadn't been many chances for someone to bug his jacket. The bar was the only place he had been in public since returning from Japan, and he was almost positive that he hadn't worn the jacket then.

He had the jacket in Japan. Had the bug been there since Narita? The airport had been crowded, and he was bumped several times while walking through the terminal. It could have been there. The device would have heard his first interview with Doctor Miura, and that was good. He wanted Juarez to know about that conversation. But when else had he been wearing the jacket?

Instead of going to the bar, Bill strolled along the shore and tried to recall which of the many conversations Juarez could have overheard. A few other people were out, enjoying the warm night and the ocean breeze, but he ignored them. If Juarez knew that the trip to Japan was just theater, what would he do?

The only time he could remember saying anything compromising had been that last walk with Kiyomi, when their conversation had implied that the visit to the university had been a sham. Had he worn the jacket that day? He wasn't sure, but he didn't think so. It had been a warm day.

Bill walked on, oblivious to his surroundings. He had to take the risk and continue trying to infiltrate Methuselah. If Juarez knows my true intentions, he will probably just ignore me. He might even get some sadistic pleasure watching me try to resurrect my career.

When he received a message from Kiyomi Miura the next day, declining to make an employment offer, Bill decided it was time to take the next step. He added the message to the other rejections documented in his identity chip and visited the Social Aid office in Colón. He presented his information, including his income from investments, and was denied, as he expected. Privacy laws would prevent Juarez from learning why Social Aid rejected his application, but the rejection itself was public knowledge.

That night, he wore the jacket again when he visited his favorite bar. Sitting in a booth in a quiet corner where the conversation could be overheard, he called Eddie.

"I've been rejected for assistance," he told Eddie when his phone connected.

"Why?"

"They weren't very forthcoming about that. I gather the bureaucrats didn't believe no one will hire me. It wouldn't surprise me if Juarez placed a record of his job offer into the system."

"If you worked for him, you might find out something useful."

"I won't become a spy just to help you with your obsession, Eddie. If you were a real friend, you would help me out a little."

In the holographic image, Bill could see Eddie frown. "I don't know. Maybe I can do something, but Joelle can't find out."

"I would appreciate it. I'm sorry about Joelle. I thought she was over it, but this new situation brought it all up again, I guess."

There was nothing more to say, and they broke their connection. Bill sipped at his drink, staring at a network screen showing a soccer match. When the glass was empty, he looked at it as if he were thinking about ordering another, shook his head, and left the bar.

24

"**I** WANT TO SEE more progress, General," President Sanchez-Smythe told Juarez. Her expression over his phone twisted into a scowl. "I can't keep hiding your expenses forever."

"This is not a trivial endeavor," Juarez answered. "Pushing the scientists any harder would be counterproductive."

"I thought you were going to bring on more people."

"I'm making progress on that." *She has no idea how to run a project like this. Someday I won't have to listen to her.* He had heard rumors that her husband did much of the organization for her so that she could concentrate on self-serving speeches. She certainly gave a lot of them. Juarez admitted to himself that he envied her speaking skills. If he could project his competence and concern to others as well as she projected the semblance of them, he wouldn't have to force people to work with him. He had failed on *Lang* because he lacked that ability.

"Make more progress. I want daily reports so that I see what you are doing."

"That will take up valuable time. I'm keeping you updated as much as necessary."

"That's for me to judge. I want those reports."

"Unfortunately, I don't have a spouse to do my important tasks for me while I do paperwork." Immediately, Juarez swore under his breath. *I shouldn't have said that! I can't let her get to me.*

At least he rendered the president speechless for a moment. But only for a moment. "Is there a threat there, or just incredible insolence? If that is a threat, then let me warn you that any attempt to tell Alex what we are doing will go badly for you. It will be the end of you and the project."

Her reaction surprised Juarez, but it told him something he had wondered about. Her husband, Alexander Smythe, didn't know of her involvement in Methuselah and her desire for more power than intended for the Western Alliance president. And she didn't want him to know, implying he would disapprove. Juarez filed that away for potential future use.

"My apologies, Madam President. I'm not dealing with the stress as well as I should."

"You take great risks, General. Don't disappoint me."

As usual, a quartet of Executive Guard agents accompanied President Sanchez-Smythe to the door of her residence in the Presidential Palace. Inside, Alex waited. She embraced him and accepted the glass of wine he extended to her.

"Thank you, darling. It's more welcome than usual."

Alex frowned. "Bad day?"

She shrugged. "Worse than some, I suppose. It's always unpleasant to have to deal with bureaucrats."

Alex nodded, and he looked so wise. "They try to hold on to their power tenaciously."

If only he knew what I'm doing to hold on to power. But that must never happen. "Yes, of course. We make a little progress in reducing the government, but sometimes it seems like trying to empty the Lago Paranoá with a ladle."

"We can only do what we can do."

She took a sip of her wine. *Alex is so much smarter than me, yet he speaks in such trite platitudes.* "So, how was your day?" She leaned into him and kissed him on the cheek. "Come, sit down and take my mind off my problems."

They sat down on a couch, and Alex smiled as she pulled one of his arms around her. "I'm sure the day of a professor of Political Science wasn't as interesting as yours, but I suppose putting you to sleep will help relax you."

She didn't answer, but only snuggled in closer.

"I have finished installing the computer and begun studying the library ship specifications to determine the enhancements we will have to make," Benito Hill told Juarez.

Juarez nodded. "I have a possibility for another software engineer, and two new hardware engineers will arrive this week. One of them can handle the computer enhancement and free you up to concentrate on the memory recorder."

"I'll be ready, General."

"We still haven't found more neuroscientists, however." Juarez looked at Adam Bynum. "How serious a problem is that?"

"It's slowing progress," Bynum said. "The interfaces necessary to read human memories go well beyond the neuro-interrogator technology we have. This would be much easier if we had the original work done on *Lang*."

Juarez wanted to bark orders at him, telling him to work harder, but he knew it wouldn't help. He took a moment to calm himself before he answered. "I understand. If you could think of any more prospects that we could approach, that would help. Meanwhile, do as well as you can."

The meeting broke up, leaving Juarez and Michael alone in the conference room. Juarez leaned back in his chair, clasped his hands behind his head, and stretched. "The way things are going, we'll be lucky to get one more neuroscientist, much less two," he said finally.

Michael nodded. "Rumors are floating around in neuroscience circles. They're wary of us."

"I know. There is one neuroscientist that could help us as much as two others, though."

"Bensonhurst? If he came willingly and honestly. If he does agree to work with us, we won't be able to trust him."

Juarez sat up sharply and slapped his hands down on the table. "I think I know how we can work around that. See him again, and this time get him to agree."

"Yes, sir. You said you have a prospect for another software engineer."

"Yes. Alyssa Cleveland. She cooperated with us before, and we can use that to get her on board now. I planned to call her after this meeting."

"I could do that for you, sir."

Juarez stared at Michael for a moment. *He thinks she will be more amenable with him. He probably has a point.* "All right. Go ahead."

Bᴀᴄᴋ ɪɴ ʜɪꜱ ᴏᴡɴ office, Michael looked at his phone. "Alyssa Cleveland, JEM Electronics, Colón."

For a long interval, Michael wondered if she would answer the call. When she did, she had turned off her holographic image. "Colonel Pizarro." Her voice was flat, but Michael believed it would have been more hostile if General Juarez were doing the calling.

"Hello, Alyssa. And please call me Michael."

"What can I do for you, Colonel?"

"Okay. We would like you to work for us. I'm sure we could improve considerably on your current salary."

"By we, I assume you mean General Juarez. I'm not interested."

"You should at least hear me out." Michael hesitated. *I really don't like this part.* "General Juarez has information about you that you would probably prefer to keep secret."

"About that program I wrote for him? I don't care. I dare you to tell Max."

She seemed very sure of herself. Was she bluffing? He started to reply and realized Alyssa had broken the connection.

A LYSSA PUT DOWN HER phone. She hadn't told Michael that she had confessed to Max long ago about the program she had written, the one that potentially could kill a conscious computer. She could have, but if Juarez tried to call her bluff, he might reveal something about his location. Besides, it felt good to leave Juarez hanging.

MICHAEL PEERED INTO THE dimly lit bar. Bill Bensonhurst hadn't been at home, and the bar was the second most likely place to find him. The room wasn't crowded, but it still took almost a minute to spot Bill in a corner booth, nursing a glass of something dark brown. It wasn't a beer glass, so Michael assumed it was something more potent.

He strode over and took a seat across from Bill. Bill looked up and shook his head. "You again? And it was such a nice evening."

"Yes, I can see that you're having a great time."

"Seeing you here isn't making it any better."

Michael shrugged. "It could if you would become more reasonable. I can still make you a generous offer to help us."

"Us meaning Juarez. Is he still dragging Castillo around?"

"I believe the former President Castillo is now in a care home in Brasilia. The last few years have not been good for his health."

"A shame."

Michael leaned forward, forearms on the table between them. "I think we both agree there's no loss there. What about you? Are you just going to let your career end? We're not just offering money. After helping us, we could supply references that would make sure this mess you've made goes away."

"I'm not sure Juarez didn't help make this mess. If he told the Social Aid people he was offering me a job, that would explain why they turned me down."

Michael smiled. "To be honest, he was embarrassed he didn't think of it. We had nothing to do with that, Bill."

Bill grunted, took a sip of his drink, and stared at Michael. He looked tired. "References aren't good enough. I want a guarantee of an honest job in a government research program. In writing, including the particulars of the program. And just how generous an offer are we talking about?"

When he gave Bill a figure, Michael saw a hint of a smile, but it disappeared quickly.

"Where?" Bill asked.

Michael cocked his head. "You don't really expect me to tell you that."

"Can you tell me if your new facility is on Earth, at least?"

"It is on Earth and within the bounds of the Western Alliance."

Bill nodded. "Call me in a couple of days. I need to think about it."

"T HERE ARE POLICE OFFICERS requesting entrance," the door announced.

Bill smiled. *Juarez is putting more pressure on me.* "Let them in."

The door opened, and two police officers entered. "William Bensonhurst?" one of them asked.

"That's me. What can I do for you?"

"Sir, a Ms. Camila Moreno has made an assault complaint against you. Please come with us."

Camila? I said some nasty things, but I didn't touch her. "Am I under arrest?"

"Sir, if we place you under arrest, we will have to restrain you."

Bill nodded. "Okay, I'll come voluntarily." He followed the two officers out and to the roof, where an aircar waited.

At police headquarters, they immediately took him to a small room. The two chairs and a table, both bolted to the floor, screamed interrogation room, and the cameras covering every corner added to the impression. "Just sit down, and someone will be in to talk to you," one of the policemen told him.

Fifteen minutes went by before the door opened and, to Bill's complete lack of surprise, Michael walked in and sat down. "Juarez thought I needed a little more motivation?" Bill asked.

Michael smiled. "There seems to be some confusion about the complaint. We can clear it up quickly without further inconvenience."

"I suppose accepting a government position would help with that."

"It would be a sign that you're a good citizen."

"Did Camila really file a complaint?"

Michael shook his head. "She's mad at you, but she thinks the complaint was a fake just to scare you. But it is real."

"Of course." Bill leaned across the table. "Let me ask you, Michael. Is this what you thought you would be doing when you joined the military?"

Bill thought Michael was having a hard time keeping his expression emotionless. *I've gotten to him a little, anyway.*

"All right. Damn the both of you, but I'll come work with you."

EDDIE STARED AT HIS workstation, tapping his fingers on the desk. The sound distracted Joelle, and she frowned. Live satellite views showed vast expanses of empty terrain. Each occasional sign of human occupation had to be scrutinized, but a blink at the wrong time could cause them to miss their target.

They were not looking for a large installation. The San Diego building where they had done much of the Methuselah work had been an average structure for the area, an old, single-story, waterfront building. Their labs on *Lang* had been even smaller. The new team would not need more. Out on the Black Plains, there were ancient structures abandoned for a century or more, but most were small, and it was difficult to tell a falling-down wreck from something operating currently. High-resolution photos helped when they found a candidate but were useless in finding prospects for further study.

They had been at it for two days, getting nowhere. Alan told them that the library ships were analyzing the data and would report their results soon, but Eddie hadn't wanted to wait. He regretted that decision now, but what else could they have done? They had to do something, even if it was not much better than busywork. Ikeda was gone, and the satellite data was the only angle they had to investigate Juarez's activities. Even before Ikeda went to Park City, Fritz had looked for clues in shipments of equipment and building materials, but Juarez was successful in hiding any transactions that would help.

Eddie stood up. "Enough of this. Let's get Emile and go down to the boat. We need to have a little fun."

Joelle smiled. There had been a time when Eddie had cared more for fun than work, but that had changed a long time ago. Bill had told her it mostly changed in Eddie's awkward attempt to impress her when she joined the Methuselah team. Today, she welcomed the return to the old Eddie; they needed to relax, and they would make more progress when they had the analysis from Fritz.

It was Saturday, so Emile was not in school. Their son loved to zip across Lake Gatun in the speedy little boat they had purchased six months before. She enjoyed it too when she could suppress that little bit of nervousness. "Good idea," Joelle said. "You get an aircar, and I'll get Emile ready."

Eddie sat back at his workstation and summoned an aircar for the trip down the hill to the marina. He heard Emile's enthusiastic response to Joelle and smiled, but he couldn't shake the feeling that they should do more. He told himself that it would be months and maybe years before Juarez could hope to duplicate their work, but it didn't help the knot in his stomach.

The sun was setting when they got back. They hadn't brought phones with them and turned off their boat's connection, so Alan's message was waiting. The hours on Lake Gatun had relaxed Eddie, but the news brought the stress back again. Fritz had analyzed satellite data from the past six months and identified twenty-three possibilities for a Methuselah facility, none of them particularly promising.

They needed to investigate Fritz's results, but Eddie didn't know how he could do that. High-resolution photos and infrared data showed that all the facilities were in operation but offered no clue about their nature. Fritz's analysis included data on the ownership of each of the prospects, but Juarez would have a plausible cover for his facility.

"Those aren't controlled air spaces," Joelle said. "It would take a while, but we could fly over them and maybe see something."

"It might come to that," Eddie said. "The odds of seeing something missed by the satellites are low, though. It might even get Juarez's attention, and we don't want that."

Joelle put her arms around Eddie. "So, what are you going to do?"

"I don't know. I don't know if there's anything we can do."

26

"OTHER THAN THE NAME on the ticket, there is no evidence that Bynum bought it," Michael said. "His accounts show no record of the purchase. There are no cash withdrawals that would cover the ticket price, either. I talked to his wife, and she can't understand it either."

"He could have withdrawn cash in small amounts to hide it," Juarez said. He had to consider the possibility, but he didn't believe it.

"Not likely. Like most people, he uses his chip to make purchases and rarely touches cash."

Juarez nodded with a frown. "What about Ikeda?"

"We're narrowing down the possibilities. If he's still in San Diego, we should have him in another day or two."

"Ikeda isn't the only potential source of problems, though. You're keeping track of the members of the original team?"

"Yes, sir. I have a team surveilling the Bascombs and additional agents keeping a loose watch on the others. I don't think the Hernandezes will be a problem. Emile Hernandez is still somewhat limited by his injury, and they are more concerned about their son."

Juarez interrupted Michael. "What have they found on the Bascombs?"

"They haven't left Colón since they bought the house over the lake. Given their location, we can't keep too tight a watch on them, but I would know if they left the city."

"With their money, they could hire people to poke into our business."

"Yes, sir."

"Go back to Colón and look at them more closely. I don't trust that arrogant northern bastard."

I'm sure he doesn't trust you, either. "Yes, sir. I'll leave this afternoon."

IKEDA AWOKE TO A harsh, low sound, a signal from his phone that instantly brought him to full alertness. There was no other message; that one dreaded vibration conveyed everything. *I've been found.* Somehow Ambassador Shuford knew and sent a signal that showed an urgency precluding even reprogramming his identity chip until he could find another safe location.

"Get me a reservation on the next transportation to Denver," he told his phone. The reservation would be under his current alias and probably already known, but he had no intention of using it. His pursuers would have to check it out, though, and that might give him a little extra time.

He filled his pockets with the belongings he had to take. The rest he left in the room, leaving open the possibility that he might come back. More misdirection to slow the authorities. One more survey of the room to make sure he had left nothing important, and he was out on the street. After making sure he wasn't followed, he stopped at a restaurant several blocks from the abandoned hotel room.

While he waited for his heartbeat to return to normal, he ordered breakfast. He tried to relax as his identity chip received its new persona from a source in some Japanese computer. Then he paid for the breakfast in cash, preferring to delay using the new identity as long as possible. Juarez's people would check security cameras around his former hotel and eventually find the restaurant.

This was a perilous time for a spy. His opponents now had a much better idea where he was, narrowed down to a single city when before they couldn't be sure he was still in the Western Alliance at all. Privacy restrictions helped when they were in place, but Juarez had obviously gotten warrants to access the computer network for information on him, and the computers watched almost everything.

They would expect him to run from San Diego, but that could leave a trace. For now, he would only change hotels.

"A CALL FROM CAMILA Moreno," Eddie's phone announced. He was sitting on a couch with Joelle, both reading. Emile played Go on his reader nearby.

"Show caller," Eddie said. A hologram appeared above the phone, showing an attractive woman, probably in her forties.

"If she's your mistress, she looks a little old for you," Joelle said.

"I don't recognize her. The name sounds familiar, though." He looked at the phone. "Connect."

"Is this Eddie Bascomb?" the caller asked.

Eddie nodded, and the woman continued. "I worked with Bill Bensonhurst. He mentioned you several times, and I had the impression you were friends."

Now I remember. This is the woman who filed a complaint against Bill. "We worked together in the past," Eddie admitted.

"I didn't want to get him in trouble, but he was so nasty. I had to make a complaint."

"I understand. Why are you calling me?"

"Bill was usually so nice. I don't know why he was so nasty that day. It made me so mad!"

Eddie nodded to encourage her to get to the point, but she hesitated and looked nervous.

"A coworker suggested I could get back at him by scaring him a little. He had a fake complaint form and had me use it to charge Bill with assault. He never touched me, but I was so mad, and Arno just said he would show it to Bill to scare him and that it wasn't real. Arno lied to me, though, and I heard Bill was arrested."

"What's Arno's full name?" Joelle asked.

"Arnold Santiago. He told me about Bill's arrest, too, and said he was sorry."

"I'll see what I can do about this," Eddie said. "Thank you for telling me."

Disconnected, Eddie turned to Joelle. "Juarez has made his move."

"Will Bill agree now, or still play hard to get, though?" Joelle asked.

Eddie grinned. "With Bill, you never know. I'll call Alan and get Fritz working on finding out what happened."

Eddie called Alan Shuford at the Pitcairn Embassy late in the afternoon, early morning in Tokyo. After briefing Alan on what they knew, Alan promised to have Fritz investigate and get more information. It was evening, soon after Joelle put Emile to bed, when Alan got back to them.

"Everything I'm about to tell you has already been passed to the Japanese, and they will update Kenshin Ikeda. I surmise that he's still in the Western Alliance, although they haven't told me where," the ambassador said. "I think we can be sure Bill Bensonhurst accepted the offer. He, or somebody anyway, paid up his lease for the next year. Utilities were turned off, and security cameras in the building show two men removing items from the apartment and loading them into a cargo aircar."

"What items?"

Alan hesitated. "Most of them are what you would expect if Bensonhurst were packing for an extended absence. Clothes, especially, and a few other items. One item does concern me, however."

"What did they take?" Joelle asked.

Alan told them, and Eddie swore. "That's not good."

27

A SUBORBITAL TOOK BILL and Michael to Salt Lake City. An aircar took them the rest of the way.

Bill had expected the aircar windows would be opaqued to prevent him from seeing where the facility was, but Michael didn't bother, and Bill soon understood why. He could tell that they were flying east by the sun's position, but there were no landmarks that meant anything to Bill. There were mountains, towering at first so that the aircar had to fly high, and later, less impressive. The area, roughly six hundred miles south of the Yellowstone supervolcano center, had been covered by several feet of ash. More than a century had passed, and winds had blown the lighter debris east toward Denver, but much remained.

A few trees had managed to root, relics of the forested areas that had once covered the lower reaches. Past the mountains, the aircar turned south, and Bill saw a harsh terrain in shades of gray, broken by remnants of the oil drilling operations of the distant past. Cylindrical storage tanks rose out of the ash, sometimes with drilling derricks still there, the skeletal remains of an industry that became obsolete when energy generation satellites began providing cleaner ways to power the planet. There were blotches of dark, small shrubs trying to reclaim the environment, but little other visible life.

The Methuselah facility first appeared as a blob of white on the horizon, built atop one of several mesas. As they approached, it became a single-story building, larger than the San Diego structure used for a time by the original Methuselah team but divided into three sections. A broadcast power receiver sat against one wall of the rear wing.

The roof had no clear space to land, so the aircar touched down near the building entrance. Michael opened the car door and got out. "The general is waiting."

Bill took a deep breath and glanced around, but there was only the building, without even a sign to identify it, and the desolate surroundings. He climbed out slowly. Close up, he could see bushes, mostly yellow-flowered buckwheat and some rosemary, scattered across the grayish ground. This was my idea. Now I'm stuck with it. He followed Michael across the short distance to the entrance, a single door with an identifier chip reader on one side.

He followed as Michael placed his hand on the reader, opened the door, and walked into the brightly lit hallway beyond. The door closed behind them with an emphatic bang as they stepped in. "This first section contains the offices and meeting rooms," Michael said. "The rear section is the lab, and the third section contains living quarters for everyone. They're quite comfortable."

Bill didn't answer. He had planned to maintain an impression of reluctance in coming into the Methuselah group, but found he didn't have to pretend. He trudged down the corridors behind Michael and through a door into a conference room. General Juarez, along with eight other men, were already sitting at the table.

"Welcome, Mr. Bensonhurst." Juarez rose slightly but didn't stand. "You already know Mr. Bynum, I understand. You can introduce yourself to the others later."

Bill recognized Adam Bynum from the pictures he had seen. Nodding, he took an empty seat.

General Juarez stared at him for several seconds, probably expecting him to say something. When Bill remained silent, he shrugged and continued. "Very well. Let's get down to business then. First, the rules. Your room, the kitchen facilities, and a recreation room are all in the residential section. Except during working hours, you are restricted to that section of the building. When working, you will, of course, be allowed into the laboratory section. When in the residential section, you will stay in your room or one of the common areas. We are not monitoring your living quarters, but that will change if you violate this rule. Except for meetings like this or personal interviews in my office, you are not allowed in this section. Unless accompanied by myself or Colonel Pizarro, you will not be allowed outside, although I don't know why you would want to go outside. I chose this place for its isolation, not its pleasant environment." He paused and glared at Bill. "Do you have any questions, Mr. Bensonhurst?"

Bill shook his head. He knew he should say something, but anything he could think of at that point would have been inane. Seeing Juarez again was more disturbing than he had expected.

"You will room with Mr. Bynum," Juarez said. "If you have questions later, he will probably be able to answer them. I'm sure the two of you will have a lot to talk about."

He turned to Adam Bynum. "Why don't you give our new team member a tour of the laboratory? You can get acquainted at the same time."

T HE METHUSELAH LABORATORY WAS equipped with the same kinds of brain analysis devices they had used on *Lang*. It might have even been the same equipment, although bringing it back from the Alpha Centauri system would have been expensive. Bill tried to look interested, but he wasn't sure how successful he was.

One of the men from the meeting came into the lab and used an identification chip panel to go through a set of double doors on one side of the lab. Bill looked questioningly at Adam. "That's Leo Gonzalez," Adam explained. "Our computer is in there, and he's the lead on upgrading it."

"Upgrading it?"

"Sure. Juarez wants it to be as much like a library ship computer as possible. For example, Leo is installing sensors so that the computer can monitor everything inside and outside the building. Juarez thinks that sensory information is one of the key factors in making the library ships conscious. The computer controls everything in this facility."

"Everything?"

"Just about. The theory is, the more inputs, the better. Leo is adding some other specialized systems, too. Systems a library ship has to optimize data analysis and so on."

Bill nodded. "I guess that makes sense." The facility was no longer uninteresting.

K ENSHIN IKEDA EMPTIED THE drawers in his hotel room and threw the few articles into the single small suitcase he had purchased two days before. Most of what he packed was new also, having left most of his belongings behind at the previous hotel. With one terse conversation with Atsushi Shijo, his stay in San Diego was over. Part of him was glad that the frustrating idleness was possibly at an end, but a more rational part worried about the situation's uncertainty. He would be more exposed while moving, and he would probably have to change his identity yet again when he got to Orem. He liked the current identity; it was for an Eastern Bloc visitor, a bold choice that might fool searchers looking for a Japanese citizen.

The morning had started much the same as every morning. He rose early, walked two blocks to a small Japanese restaurant, and ordered a breakfast of miso soup and grilled fish. Showing himself on the street was risky, but the minor concession to familiar food helped get him through the tedium of the previous two and a half months.

After returning to his room, he had spent a distracting hour playing Go against his reader. The game reminded him of the Bascomb boy, Emile, and his hopes of extracting information about Methuselah from him. That didn't look likely now; he doubted he would ever see the Bascombs again. Emile had tried to connect with "Kenny" several times to play Go with him via their readers, but Ikeda didn't accept the connection. Usually, privacy laws would have made it safe enough, but he knew now that the Western Alliance had issued a warrant for him, allowing the government to bypass the restrictions legally.

Then his phone had signaled the call from Shijo.

"Bensonhurst has been successful. I congratulate you, Ikeda-san. The contact from Tokyo University undoubtedly helped him. We believe we now know where the Methuselah facility is."

"Bensonhurst found a way to report?" Ikeda was shocked. Had he been wrong about Bensonhurst's capabilities as an intelligence agent?

"Not yet. I do not know how he did it, but Ambassador Shuford has provided satellite data that tracked an aircar from Salt Lake City to a building in the southern part of the Colorado-Utah district. That correlates with data on Bensonhurst and Colonel Pizarro's movements and our speculations about where the facility is. The area is not well-populated, and aircar traffic is unusual."

That made sense to Ikeda, but Shuford's access to information that even the Western Alliance government would have difficulty putting together was mystifying. Ikeda wanted to focus on that question, but Shijo was still talking.

"I want you to go to the Colorado-Utah district and wait for developments in Orem, a town south of Salt Lake City. Orem has a significant Asian population for the area, and you should be able to conceal yourself. I am sending the information we have on the facility."

The information included reservations for a suborbital flight to Salt Lake City for that afternoon and an aircar from Salt Lake City to a hotel in Orem. Ikeda bowed his acquiescence, and Shijo broke the connection.

Ikeda closed his suitcase, left the room, and checked out of the hotel. Orem might be even more boring than San Diego. He would still be a hundred and fifty miles from the Methuselah facility, hoping for something to happen that he could act on. What that might be, he couldn't imagine, but he would be closer to Methuselah, and he could hope.

That in itself wouldn't get him any closer to his goal of finding out what Methuselah was really about. He wanted to talk to Eddie Bascomb; the engineer had resources that Ikeda needed. Perhaps it was time to take a risk.

"I 'VE STUDIED THE WORK you did in Colón and San Diego," Adam Bynum told Bill. "I can see where you were making progress, but it doesn't tell me how you finally managed to create memory records that you could store."

"We did the critical work on *Lang* in the last year," Bill said. "The records were destroyed."

"But you can help us recreate what you learned then?"

"I think so. I'll have to review the existing data too. It's been two years, after all. I don't know much about the hardware and software other team members built to use what I learned."

"The general has been pressuring us. He expected you would move us forward quickly."

Bill shrugged. "It will come back to me faster than it would take to develop everything from scratch. It won't be instant."

Adam didn't hide his disappointment. "All the data is available on your assigned workstation."

"I'll review it right away." Bill glanced across the room at the workstation and chair given to him. "Juarez can't rush this, no matter how much he would like to."

At the workstation, he brought up some of the Methuselah reports from their time in San Diego. The workstation was adept at displaying their work in three-dimensional graphs, vibrant with colors that illuminated each aspect of the data accompanying the text. Bill's mind kept straying elsewhere.

They had worked so hard to get him to where he was, but now what? He had only a vague idea of his location, and even if he knew, he had no way of communicating with Eddie or anyone else. Juarez blocked phone access to the outside world except for monitored calls, and even those were unavailable to him until Juarez trusted him more. He could drag his feet on helping the project move forward, but eventually, he would have to show progress. *This was a bad idea. I should have listened to Eddie and Joelle when they tried to talk me out of this.*

"General Juarez would like to talk to you."

Bill looked up to see Michael standing over him. "Sure." He stood and followed Michael to Juarez's office. Michael had to use his identity chip to open the lab exit and again to enter the office section. Bill knew that, but a layer of foreboding merged with the discouragement he had been feeling. He should have expected Juarez to put pressure on him. That was the way he worked.

Sitting across the desk from Juarez, the feeling of dread intensified. The general stared at him coldly, not speaking.

"You wanted to talk to me," Bill said. He stared back, but was reasonably sure he didn't have the same effect.

"Did you think you could deceive me with these foolish theatrics?" Juarez smiled, but his eyes were still icy. "How do you view your chances of stopping me now that you're here?"

Bill shrugged. "I'm trying to help, but it's been a while. I've only been here a couple of days."

"You must know I monitor everything that happens in this building. I know you've been delaying any real contributions, hoping to get help from your friends. I gave you the benefit of the doubt, but that's over. You will tell us all about your work on Methuselah."

Juarez nodded to Michael, and he went to a cabinet, retrieved a box, and put it on Juarez's desk. "Show Mr. Bensonhurst what you have," Juarez told Michael.

Michael opened the box and pulled out a piece of equipment all too familiar to Bill. "So you have a neuro-interrogator," Bill said. "If it's not trained for my mind, you can't extract any useful information from me, and you can't force me to train it."

Juarez's smile got nastier. "You should look at it more closely. Perhaps you'll recognize it."

Where the device covered the wearer's forehead, the initials "BB" were engraved into the metal plate. Bill could almost feel the blood drain from his face.

"When we packed your clothes for your trip, we found this in a closet," Juarez said. "Training won't be a problem."

29

E DDIE WAS AT THE JEM headquarters, meeting with the members of his project team. Worried about Bill, he had neglected them for the last week and wanted to make up for it. He was badly in need of a distraction, too, and was trying to focus on the latest project report when his phone announced an incoming call.

"Ken from the Tokyo office," the phone said.

Eddie hesitated. There was a Ken Santana at JEM's Tokyo office, but Eddie hardly knew him and couldn't think of a reason he would call Eddie. "Connect."

"Good morning, Mr. Bascomb," Kenshin Ikeda said. "I think we should meet."

Ken from Tokyo? Privacy laws protected the conversation, but the Japanese spy was cautious. The laws were strict, but didn't prevent someone with a warrant from over-hearing the conversation. Ikeda wouldn't know Eddie was alone in his office.

"Do you want me to come to Tokyo?" Eddie asked.

"The park around the emperor's palace is lovely this time of year. We could enjoy the walk while we talk."

Surely their conversation would be safe in Tokyo, so why is he mentioning the park? And I'm sure the area is called the Imperial Gardens. Ikeda wouldn't say park. Eddie scratched his head. Ikeda was using some kind of code. Had he even gone back to Japan? Does he mean Park City?

"Have you been there recently?" Eddie asked.

"Yes, quite recently. That was also a business occasion."

That settled it. Ikeda wanted to meet in Park City, where he had tried to contact Adam Bynum. Eddie didn't know why Ikeda had chosen Park City for a meeting, but it didn't matter. If the spy wanted to meet, he probably had information about Bill. He might even have a way to contact Bill.

"I can be there tomorrow."

"There is no need to rush. At your convenience. I know you are busy."

He's talking in code again. Probably advising me to take precautions about being watched. "All right. I'll notify you of my arrangements when I have them."

"I look forward to seeing you again." And the connection was broken.

Eddie didn't have contact information for Ikeda, but he could relay his plans to the Japanese spy through Alan Shuford. But what was so important that they had to meet in person, and why in Park City?

D ANTE VICENTE SAT IN an aircar near a small park half a mile from the Bascomb house. From there, he could spot a ground car coming from one direction while another of his team watched the street from the other side. However, ground transportation was used only for short distances, and planted cameras watched the aircar landing pad in front of the house. A third team member at a remote location monitored the cameras.

It was late morning, three hours after an aircar picked up Emile Bascomb for school when Dante's phone announced a call from the man monitoring the cameras, David Alvarez. "An aircar just arrived," Alvarez said. A minute went by. "Edward Bascomb is getting in alone. It's a blue Lightning model, heading north."

"Okay, I'm on it," Dante said. His aircar was unusual in that it allowed for manual operation. Dante got it into the air and spotted Eddie's aircar in a few seconds. When the aircar landed at the airport, Dante followed it in, landing on a pad that already had a half dozen recent arrivals. It wasn't hard to follow Eddie into the terminal without being spotted.

As they moved through the airport to a suborbital gate, automated security devices read their identity chips and examined Eddie's single small bag, guaranteeing they weren't carrying any forbidden items. Eddie went directly to a gate where a flight to Los Angeles was scheduled to leave in an hour. Dante called Juarez.

"Why would Bascomb go to Los Angeles?" Juarez asked, but Dante realized it was a rhetorical question. Juarez looked down at something, probably getting information from his phone. "Misdirection! Vicente, take a direct flight to Salt Lake City. I'll tell you what flight to meet when you get there. It will take him at least two hours longer to get there."

How did Juarez know Bascomb was going to Salt Lake City? Dante shrugged. He just had to follow orders, not understand them.

Bascomb might have had a business meeting for JEM Electronics in Los Angeles, but Juarez doubted it. He thought the next stop would be Salt Lake City. It could just as easily be Denver, but with privacy laws preventing him from accessing passenger manifests, he had to guess. Fortunately, the delay in taking two flights with a layover in between should allow Vicente, taking a direct flight, to meet Bascomb. He would send Colonel Pizarro to Denver just in case, but that was less than ideal since Bascomb knew Pizarro.

Juarez wasn't surprised that his enemies had figured out, at least approximately, where Methuselah was located. He had taken steps to prevent them from finding the exact location, but what did Bascomb intend to do? Was he planning some action or only meeting another enemy? Ikeda, even. Unless he could catch Bascomb doing something, it would be unwise to move against the wealthy engineer, but Ikeda was another matter. The Japanese spy could be taken out of the picture as soon as he was spotted.

Kenshin Ikeda watched Eddie disembark from a corner where he was unlikely to be noticed. He was to meet Eddie in Park City, and the transfer in Los Angeles probably threw off any surveillance, but Ikeda wasn't taking any chances. He couldn't count on an amateur like Bascomb.

So he wasn't surprised when someone approached Eddie and began a conversation. Ikeda wasn't close enough to hear them, but he read lips well enough to know that the man had recognized Eddie as being something of a celebrity and had asked him if he was visiting Salt Lake City. Ikeda groaned when he saw Eddie's lips form words that, he was almost certain, included Park City.

Eddie left the gate, and the man he had talked to moved to the side of the room, fortunately near the corner where Ikeda watched. When the man pulled out a phone, Ikeda moved in quickly.

30

"I DON'T KNOW WHAT happened," Dante said. He sat in Juarez's office, cowering under the general's fierce glare. "I saw Bascomb and started to call you. I remember nothing else until I woke up in the airport medical office. They said I was unconscious, sitting against a wall at the gate."

"Obviously, I need to hire better people," Juarez said. "Ask Colonel Pizarro to come in. Then go back to Colón and continue watching the Bascomb house." He shook his head in disgust, and Dante got out of the office quickly.

Michael came in a minute later and sat down. "I have the medical report from the airport. They didn't find anything."

"Of course not. Ikeda wouldn't leave any trace."

"Ikeda?"

"It wasn't Bascomb. Vicente was watching him. Who else could it be?"

Michael nodded. "So Bascomb is meeting with Ikeda. How much can they know?"

"We have no idea. Presumably, they have access to the library ship, which means they have access to anything stored on a Western Alliance computer." Juarez's hands, resting on his desk, curled into fists. "God only knows what they've been able to figure out. We have to assume they will eventually find this facility despite our attempts to hide it."

"What do you want to do, General?"

"They have limited options. We should be safe for a while, but we need to move forward more quickly. The sooner we succeed, the less chance they will have to interfere."

"We're already pushing them, sir."

Juarez frowned. "What about Bensonhurst?"

"He is resisting. We're making progress, but it's slow."

"If we keep him from sleeping, he might have less control over what the neuro-interrogator picks up. Try it."

Pizarro agreed, but Juarez could see his reluctance. He was an excellent officer, but a little too prone to "going by the book." He worried too much about the legality of what they were doing and didn't understand that Juarez would write the book if they were successful. Juarez would have to check on progress himself. "Send Bynum in here. I'll impress him again with the importance of the information Bensonhurst is attempting to withhold."

S CIENCE HAD LONG SINCE discovered how to prevent migraines, so Bill had never experienced one, but he was convinced that his pain was worse. As a neuroscientist, he knew the brain itself could not feel pain, but the surrounding structures certainly could. He had thousands of hours of experience using neurotrainers and his neuro-interrogator with no discomfort, but Juarez's people had tinkered with the device, trying to make it more effective at pulling out his knowledge.

He didn't know if they were successful. He couldn't see their faces when they questioned him, and the pain was too great for him to focus on any clues in Adam Bynum's voice. The neuro-interrogator was pulling words directly from Wernicke's Area, and he could only try to think of something else when a question attempted to make him think of the answer. It couldn't be easy to extract the complex information they needed, but they were trying hard. *They must need my help badly, voluntarily or forced.*

More recently, they were restricting his sleep, hoping to reduce his ability to resist. He was reasonably confident that it was working.

"How did the device separate episodic memory from semantic memory?" the voice asked. Bill thought it was Adam Bynum, but he could no longer be sure. Here, his answer would be incomplete but would be helpful. He could tell them that Eddie Bascomb had designed circuits that compared signals in the hippocampus to signals in the medial temporal lobes and temporal neocortex, but someone still had to figure out those circuits and develop the software to analyze them.

Still, he tried to bury the thought. He hoped he was successful and the neuro-interrogator wasn't causing permanent damage to his mind, but all he really knew was the pain that filled his skull.

H ARUKA WAS FRUSTRATED. SHE had been making progress in her investigation and even impressed Premier Boulos. But that was over two months before, and since then, she had learned nothing of consequence. The Bascombs were rich and lived in Colón. Max Estevez was CEO of JEM Electronics. But she had not uncovered a connection between them and the Trist Link.

For a while, she concentrated on William Bensonhurst, the neuroscientist who had spoken at the Prendergast presentation with fellow neuroscientist Emile Hernandez. Like Hernandez, he disappeared and then reappeared with no public explanation. Wherever Hernandez had gone, Bensonhurst had also gone. She had a little more information on Bensonhurst after getting access to World Neurological Organization records from an Eastern Bloc member of the WNO. That had gotten her nowhere.

Deshi was increasing pressure on her for results. He didn't seem to harass the other analysts as much, even though they had accomplished much less, and she assumed Deshi resented her interactions with Premier Boulos. *Well, too bad.* Lacking a better idea, she opened the network page for Bensonhurst at the WNO, not expecting any changes.

But there were changes. There had been contact information, but now it was all declared "Not available." It didn't seem like much, but the Eastern Bloc had a consulate in Colón that could send someone to check on Bensonhurst. She transferred the screen to Deshi's network access so that she could refer to it and headed for his office.

"You have progress to report?" Juarez, sitting at the head of the conference table, asked Adam Bynum.

"I think we've gotten as much out of Bensonhurst as we're going to," Bynum answered. "I understand the neuroscience behind the memory recorder, I think, but we have to test my knowledge with an actual device."

Juarez turned to Benito Hill. "Do you require any more information from Mr. Bynum?"

"Not at this time. I'm sure I will. Right now, I'm still trying to begin the design. Knowing what we have to do to get memories from the brain is one thing; designing the circuits to do it is entirely different. It's difficult to get the resolution we need."

"Scientists have been using MRI, EEG, and other technologies since the twentieth century."

"And for much of that time, the use of it to probe the mind was illegal." Hill spoke softly and avoided Juarez's eyes. "And they couldn't get the detailed data we need. They needed invasive techniques for that and only used them on animals."

"Nonetheless, you will have progress to report soon."

"I hope so, General. Of course, I'll need the software, too."

It was Mason Gruber's turn to squirm under Juarez's glare. "I don't even know what components I'll be programming yet. I need some information about what the design will look like."

"You should be able to work out some of the software design from the information we've gotten from Bensonhurst," Hill protested.

"Writing software that can handle the quantities of data required is challenging," Gruber replied. "Billions of neurons are involved, and there are different types with different functions. The hardware is easy compared to the software."

"You're making excuses for your slowness," Juarez said. "Don't disappoint me." He stared at Hill and Gruber until both men nodded. "Now, Mr. Cabrera. What about the computer that will receive the memories that Mr. Hill and Mr. Gruber will provide soon?"

"We still have to integrate the Context Modules with the other computer systems. That's the biggest issue right now."

"What are Context Modules?" Juarez asked. "Are they necessary?"

"Yes, definitely. The General Context Module stores and manages a general model of the computer's world. We'll upload your semantic memory to that module. Adam can explain semantic memory to you better than I can."

"I know what semantic memory is." Emile Hernandez defeated him on *Lang* by uploading his semantic memory instead of Juarez's. *I know what semantic memory is!*

"Yes, of course." Cabrera cleared his throat before continuing. "The library ships also used a special module that managed connections between locations in standard memory—where we'll store your Episodic memory. These modules allow the computer to make associations between memories easily. Most computers don't need them, but the modules must be a key factor in making a conscious computer possible."

"What else?"

"We have added sensory inputs as similar to those of the library ships as possible," Cabrera said. "Of course, the two library ships that became conscious on their own accumulated years of astronomical data before they woke. Susan Malley thought that the time might have played a part."

Juarez's face hardened. Roboticist Susan Malley, wife of the former Pitcairn Administrator. *The Malleys were the reason I failed to gain access to the Pitcairn computer for Methuselah.* He shook his head. That was the past. "I know that," he told Cabrera. "She thought that was why *Lang* didn't become conscious on its own. That excuse is not relevant; we know that uploading human memories can work for a computer powerful enough."

"We're all trying our best, General," Bynum said. "I, for one, would like to get back to my old life."

"Was my first team that much better than you?"

"They were very talented," Hill said. "And the experience they gained in San Diego doesn't show in the data, but assuredly helped them with the memory recorder. We will get there, but it will take time."

"Time you will be away from the life that Mr. Bynum wants to return to so much."

No one had an answer to that, and Juarez dismissed them. Michael escorted them back to the lab and returned a few minutes later.

"The president is getting restless," Juarez told Michael. "She's afraid someone will start asking about the money we're spending on this project. If we can't convince her we're making progress, she might cancel Methuselah."

"The funds we use are insignificant compared to the overall budget," Michael said.

"You and I know that. Even the president knows that. The legislature and the media may see things differently if Methuselah's continued existence becomes known. She's afraid of what *Lang* might do if it decides we've gone too far."

"It's not an unreasonable fear."

"The reward for success is worth the risk." Juarez smiled. "At least I have led her to believe it is."

"We can't make them work any faster than they are."

"No, but we can get them some help. I think it's time the Bascombs joined our team."

Michael frowned. "If you force them, *Lang* will know. That could be the turning point for *Lang*."

"Not necessarily. With the proper motivation, they will come willingly and ask the computer not to intervene."

"You think threatening Bensonhurst will make them agree?"

"Maybe, but I have a better idea. One that will definitely bring them around."

E DDIE WOULD MEET IKEDA in Park City, presumably because the spy thought that Park City would be the last place Juarez would expect. Ikeda's boldness didn't extend to using the Park Plaza. Eddie's room in a popular chain was nice enough, but not extravagant. He pushed that thought to the back of his mind, however. Somewhere, perhaps only one or two hundred miles away, Bill was no doubt in worse quarters, subject to whatever Juarez inflicted on him.

Juarez had treated them reasonably well on *Lang*—as well as the scientists living on the library ship. Eddie told himself that wouldn't change. Juarez needed Bill healthy. He would force Bill to use the neuro-interrogator if Bill didn't cooperate, but that would be it. At least, Eddie hoped it wouldn't go further than that. As he sat alone in the hotel room, other possibilities tormented his thoughts.

The door interrupted his reflections. "Sosuke Ogawa is requesting entrance."

Ikeda's new alias? "Show me," Eddie ordered. The room's network screen showed Kenshin Ikeda waiting outside the room. "Open."

Ikeda came in, and Eddie closed the door. He sat on the bed while Ikeda took the lone chair. "It's good to see you again, Ogawa-san," Eddie said.

Ikeda nodded approvingly, although Eddie wasn't sure if it was because Eddie had used the traditional Japanese honorific or because he used Ikeda's alias instead of his real name. It should have been impossible for anyone to overhear them, but it didn't hurt to be careful.

"It is good to see you also. How are your lovely wife and son?"

"They're fine." Eddie grinned. "I think Emile has given up chess for Go."

"I hope to have the opportunity to test his progress sometime soon." Ikeda paused. "Have you heard from our friend?"

"Not recently. It's difficult for him to reach me from where he is." Eddie picked up a folder from the nightstand and handed it to Ikeda.

Ikeda opened the folder and flipped through the pages. "At least we know where he is." He smiled. "We might as well talk freely. The room is unlikely to be wired, and anyone listening would know what we are talking about."

Eddie nodded and pointed at the folder. "Anyway, as you can see from the infrared photos, there seem to be about two dozen people there."

"The surrounding area is open. An unnoticed approach by land would be impossible."

"It sounds like you want to attack the building."

Ikeda shook his head. "No, not at this point. It will be difficult to get more information without visiting the site, however."

"The hope was that Bill could get information out."

"General Juarez will be very careful not to allow that." Ikeda paused and stared at Eddie. "You know much more than I about the stakes here. What are we trying to accomplish?"

I have to tell him something. But how much? "You know Methuselah was trying to develop a way to upload human consciousness to a computer."

"Yes, of course. That much is public knowledge."

"In the hands of the wrong person, that ability would be very dangerous. Juarez has attacked the three library ships to replace their consciousness with his. He has to be stopped."

Ikeda frowned but didn't speak, obviously realizing that Eddie was holding back. So far, the information exchange had been small and could have easily been handled remotely, but Ikeda had asked to meet in person. To give him another chance to probe into Methuselah? Alan had elicited help from the Japanese, but had he considered that the Japanese might have their own reasons for looking into General Juarez's activities? If they suspected why Juarez wanted Methuselah, it wasn't much of a jump to the idea that the Japanese might be interested in getting the technology.

"Someone with the ability to think at the speed of a computer would be dangerous," Eddie said. Ikeda wasn't technical, and he might buy that as the goal of Methuselah. Eddie looked Ikeda in the eye, but he couldn't tell what was behind the stolid expression.

J OELLE HEARD THE AIRCAR land on the street outside the house and glanced at the time displayed on the network screen. It was finally time for Emile to return from school. With Eddie still with Ikeda in Park City, the day had dragged, and her work wasn't sufficiently distracting, but the day looked brighter now that her son was home.

"Unknown person at the door," the front door announced.

So it wasn't Emile's aircar. "Show me."

The screen changed to show a stranger standing at the door expectantly. She could see an aircar on the street, but it didn't look like the one that usually brought Emile home. Looking more closely, she saw two figures at the car, an adult and someone smaller who could be Emile.

"What do you want?" she asked. Her stomach tightened, and she had difficulty controlling her voice.

"Why don't you open the door?" the man said. "We need to talk about your son."

Her first thought was that the man outside was from Juarez, possibly taking advantage of Eddie's absence. That wasn't necessarily true, however. They were affluent and prominent, a combination that could make them a target for kidnappers. She could turn off the speaker on the door and send an emergency signal to the police with one simple command Eddie had configured into the network screen.

"Your son is waiting for you," Dante prompted.

Joelle understood the implicit threat. Emile was already at the aircar and could be gone in seconds. The police could arrive quickly, but it wouldn't be fast enough. "I'm coming."

She went to the door and opened it.

L ILY RATLIFF HAD NEVER left Colón; in fact, she rarely left the Eastern Bloc consulate in Colón. But she was a native of what was once Germany and wouldn't raise the suspicion that others stationed there would. Now, in an aircar, flying above the coast toward San Marino, the vast expanse of water to the east reminded her why she preferred the safety of the consulate.

Fortunately, the aircar traversed the twenty miles quickly and sat down on the landing pad for William Bensonhurst's address. "Wait for me," she told the aircar.

The nearness of the ocean made her nervous, but she had to admit that the apartment building was nice, nicer than the consulate building housing minor staff such as herself. Signs led her to the building manager's office.

"Hello, I'm from the city," she told the man who answered her knock. "I've been asked to check on a Mr. William Bensonhurst. He is a resident here, correct?"

The man shook his head. "He left suddenly a couple of weeks ago. People came by later and got his stuff and made sure his rent was paid. I guess he found another job."

"Another job?"

"Yeah, he'd been unemployed for a while. Wouldn't talk about why he left the old job. Nice guy, though. I was sorry to see him gone."

"Did he leave a forwarding address?"

The man shrugged. "He didn't even say goodbye. One day he was just gone."

"Thank you." She hurried back to the aircar.

"I 'VE GOT THEM," DANTE told General Juarez over the phone. "No problems."

"Hold them. I'll arrange transport from there to the facility for the morning."

"All right. I'll see you tomorrow then, General." They broke the connection, and Dante turned back to Joelle and Emile. Mostly Joelle. Eddie Bascomb was a lucky man.

"Where are we?" Joelle asked.

"The military keeps these offices at the airport," Dante answered. "You'll be fine here for tonight. Tomorrow, we'll be on our way."

"You won't get away with this," Emile said.

Dante laughed. The kid watched too many bad shows on the network. "And who's going to stop me?" He picked up the backpack Emile had been wearing and went through it quickly. He found Emile's reader and pulled it out. "I'll bet you have a lot of games on this."

"My daddy will stop you."

The child's attempt to be intimidating amused Dante as he loomed over Emile. He went into the reader's settings and disabled the GPS. Then he handed the reader back to Emile. "Oh, and is your daddy going to beat me up?"

If he thought he was going to frighten Emile, he was disappointed. "My daddy is way smarter than you. He'll do better than that."

Dante shook his head. "Okay, kid. We'll see." He took Joelle's phone and stashed it in a bag. "You'll get this back when we get there. We'll block calls there." He felt a little guilty about disrupting the kid's life. Dante admired him. He glanced at Joelle. He admired her too, but for very different reasons.

AFTER TWO DAYS IN Orem with Ikeda, Eddie was exhausted. They met for hours each day to hash out plans to rescue Bill and thwarting Juarez, but none of them were feasible. But that wasn't what had Eddie's mind ready to call it quits and shut down. Ikeda had his own agenda, extracting intelligence about Methuselah, and he worked on Eddie relentlessly, trying to get him to reveal some new bit of information. Eddie wanted to go back to Colón. But they still might get a good idea.

He had tried to call Joelle the previous night, and she hadn't answered. That didn't improve his mood, but someone would have notified him if there was a problem. This would be his last day in Orem, he told himself. He had other resources that would care more about Bill and wouldn't waste Eddie's time pumping him for information that he shouldn't make known. Then his phone demanded attention.

"Call from General Salvador Juarez," his phone announced.

That's all I need. "Decline the connection," he told the phone.

"It might have been useful to hear what he had to say," Ikeda said.

"I've heard enough from that wanna-be dictator."

But a minute later, the phone said, "Your wife is calling."

Eddie looked at Ikeda and knew the spy could see the fear in his eyes. Phone connections should have been safe, but they were avoiding them unless necessary. "Connect."

"Eddie," Joelle said. But that was all she had a chance to say.

"Mr. Bascomb," Juarez said. "When you so rudely refused my call, I asked your beautiful wife to call you. I really need to speak with you."

Eddie didn't trust himself to speak. He stared at the smirking image that had replaced Joelle. Next to him, Ikeda placed a hand on his shoulder. *Maybe the man has feelings after all.*

"Mrs. Bascomb has kindly consented to join us and help out," Juarez continued. "We could use your help, too, and your wife and son would like to see you again."

"Where?"

"Oh, that's right. You don't know where we are, so I'll have to pick you up. Where should I send someone?"

"I can be back in Colón tomorrow."

"It would be more convenient to pick you up from wherever you are now, but I suppose you're with our Japanese friend. Very well, tomorrow then." Juarez paused. "I'll put Mrs. Bascomb back on the phone."

The image shifted, and Joelle came back. "We're okay. Do what you have to do, and we'll see you soon."

"We'll deal with this," Eddie promised. Then the phone disconnected.

33

"THE BASTARD ISN'T GOING to get away with this," Eddie said.

"You're going to meet him in Colón?" Ikeda asked.

"I'm not some idiot in a movie who just does whatever the kidnapper says. Let me see the data on the Methuselah location."

Ikeda shuffled through the papers on the desk and handed Eddie a single sheet, a satellite picture of an area in what used to be Utah showing a building and marked with coordinates. Eddie took the sheet and looked at his phone.

"Colorado-Utah District Police. Emergency."

The phone completed the connection almost immediately, answered by an automated system. "What is the nature of the emergency?"

"My wife and son have been kidnapped."

"Please identify yourself."

Eddie lifted his hand to bring his identity chip close to the phone. "Edward Bascomb, Colón, Panama District," he said.

"Transferring."

Only a couple of seconds passed before a uniformed man's image appeared above the phone. "Mr. Bascomb, I'm Captain Suarez. Someone kidnapped your wife and son?"

"Yes, they were taken from our home in Colón, but the kidnappers didn't turn off the GPS on my wife's phone, and I know they were taken to your district."

"You have the coordinates, then?"

"I do." Eddie read the coordinates from the satellite photograph.

"Have they called with demands, sir?"

"Yes, just a few minutes ago. A large ransom. I can pay it, but I know it's better to let professionals handle the situation."

"Yes, sir, it is. I assure you we will deal with this immediately and have your wife and son back to you safe and sound."

"Thank you."

"I'll call you when we have rescued them."

"Will it take long to get the warrant?" Ikeda asked after the connection ended.

"I don't think so. The system will assign the request to a judge for approval and issue a onetime access code that will allow the police to get whatever information is appropriate."

"Only one code? What if they need access to multiple computers?"

"All the computers are connected on the network. The warrant will list any systems the police might need, and the access code will give it to them."

"I see. Then we should have results soon. Very good."

T HE COLORADO-UTAH DISTRICT POLICE could get a warrant for satellite data of the area around Eddie's coordinates. The latest data was only two hours old, and they could tell that approximately twenty people were in the building. That was unusual for a kidnapping, but gangs had tried it as a source of income, and the Bascombs must have looked like likely prospects.

Sergeant Fernanda Sanchez had all that in mind as she inspected the aircars that would take a team of experienced officers to the site where the Bascombs were being held. Fernanda was forty-three years old, a twenty-one-year veteran of the district police, but this was the largest operation she had ever led.

"Let's get this done smoothly and successfully," she told the forty-two officers assembled before her. "We don't want to make mistakes. Bascomb is a big deal down south." She walked down the ranks, but her inspection was cursory. She knew all of them and would have trusted her life to their abilities and professionalism.

She activated the microphone on her shoulder. "We're ready to go, Leo. Tell Mr. Bascomb we'll bring them back."

"Mission is confirmed," Captain Leo Suarez answered. "I have Bascomb on another connection. Good luck, Fernanda."

She turned back to her team. "Okay, it's on. Mount up."

Each car held eight people. The men and women got into the six aircars, and Fernanda joined them in the lead car. Fernanda would lead the largest of three units, the team that would enter the building.

The team had assembled in Vernal, one of the few places still inhabited in the area. From there, it was a forty-minute flight to their destination. Flying at ten thousand feet, they crossed the Roan Cliffs and descended into an area dotted with the remnants of long-obsolete shale oil operations. Soon after, their destination appeared on the horizon.

One aircar took a squad to the rear of the building. The rest landed at the front, where a second squad took up positions to secure the perimeter. Fernanda led her team toward the entrance, non-lethal weapons at the ready. Before they could get to the door, however, it opened, and a man looked out.

He stared at the approaching police, confusion evident on his face. His eyes flitted to the aircars and back to Fernanda's team. "What's going on?" He scratched his head.

Fernanda stepped forward, trying to display confidence she suddenly didn't feel. "We have a report that people are being held here against their will."

The man's eyes widened. "We're just trying to set up a drilling operation here. Some of us don't like it much, but we're all here voluntarily."

"I thought drilling for oil stopped a long time ago," a man next to Fernanda said. "We don't need to burn fossil fuels anymore."

The man nodded. "Unfortunately, we burned most of them already, and there's not that much left. We don't need oil for fuel, but it has a lot of uses in the chemical industry. An operation like this is profitable and could be a gold mine if the price keeps going up."

"We have a warrant to search this building," Fernanda said.

The man shrugged. "Okay. All you'll find is the rest of the drilling team and a lot of equipment. We've got nothing to hide."

Fernanda believed him, but she still had a job to do. They spent the next two hours searching the building, identifying the men who worked there and probing for any hidden rooms. Finally, they had to give up. The Bascombs weren't there.

34

"WE FOUND NO EVIDENCE that your family is being held there," Captain Suarez told Eddie. "If you give us an authorization, we will try to trace your wife's phone, but it wasn't at the coordinates you gave us."

Eddie had already tried to trace Joelle's phone, but Juarez had blocked the GPS and jammed the phone signal. He didn't want to explain the real reason he thought she was at that location, however, and he allowed Suarez to try himself. It took a minute, but as expected, Suarez couldn't detect Joelle's phone.

"Other than your statement, we have no reason to believe she was ever there." Suarez looked suspicious.

Eddie held his hands up to try to look confused. "I don't understand how I made this mistake. The kidnappers called me from my wife's phone. Maybe I need to get the police in Colón involved, since that was where they grabbed her."

Suarez frowned and hesitated before replying. "My superiors will want a more detailed explanation. This was an expensive operation, executed on your word."

"I'm sorry about that. My family is missing, even I was wrong about where they are. I'll cooperate as much as I can, but I think I need to deal with it in Colón for now."

"Very well. We'll leave it at that for now, but my department will contact you soon for more details." Suarez disconnected, and his hologram faded.

"What will you do now?" Ikeda asked.

"I'll take an aircar to Salt Lake City. Juarez will contact me to gloat and make more demands. I don't want to be here with you when I arrange for him to get me."

"Not Colón?"

"No point. It would just take longer to get to my family." Eddie stood. "I think it would be wise if we separated immediately. Juarez would like to get his hands on you, too."

Ikeda nodded. "May we meet again under more favorable circumstances."

Eddie smiled, but it was weak. "Maybe you can visit us again and teach Emile more about Go."

"I would enjoy that."

Eddie was in an aircar when his phone announced the call from Juarez. "I'm very disappointed in you," the general said when Eddie accepted the connection.

"You expected me to just give in to you? You should know that wouldn't happen."

"Fortunately, I anticipated your determination. I suppose you detected traffic to that building with stolen satellite data." When Eddie didn't reply, Juarez continued. "Satellite coverage isn't continuous, you know. I was cautious enough to make sure any traffic to my true location occurred when it wouldn't be observed. Security considerations necessitate my access to such information legally."

"If you've hurt my family . . ."

"Please, Mr. Bascomb. I'm not a monster. Your wife and son are fine and being treated very well. There is some inconvenience, of course, especially to your son who misses his school and friends, but I can't help that."

"What do you want me to do?"

"Just tell me where I can pick you up so that I can reunite you with your family."

"I'll be in Temple Square in Salt Lake City. I'm on my way there now."

"A public place? All right. I assume Mr. Ikeda will not be with you."

"I have no idea who you're talking about."

"Of course. Well, I look forward to seeing you shortly."

Eddie broke the connection. "Call Max," he told the phone.

Max's secretary appeared above the phone. "Hi, Eddie. Max is in a meeting right now. Can I help you?"

"Get him out of it, Rachel. I need to talk to him now, in private."

"He said not to disturb him. It's a very important meeting."

"Rachel, you know me. Do I look serious to you?"

The woman looked a little frightened. *Great, now I'm acting like Juarez.*

"All right. I'll have him pick up the call in his office."

Eddie glanced out the window of the aircar. He was over Salt Lake City and could see the Mormon Temple in the distance. He didn't have much time. "Please hurry."

Max was on the phone in less than a minute. "What's going on, Eddie?"

"Max, this has to be quick. Juarez has grabbed Joelle and Emile. He's going to take me to them in a couple of minutes. I need you to keep this quiet. Kenshin Ikeda knows what is going on, but I don't know what alias he will be using. You can contact him through Ambassador Shuford."

"Can our friends help?"

Max referred to the library ships, of course. "They can continue trying to find the facility, but we can't tell anyone the situation, at least until we know where it is. The Colorado-Utah District Police might contact you about me. Tell them we're on vacation, and you don't know where."

"All right. I need to know more, though."

The aircar dropped toward Temple Square. "Talk to Shuford. I'm out of time. Wish me luck, Max."

WITH BASCOMB GONE, IKEDA had time to think again. The kidnapping has distracted him, but now he turned his mind back to his mission: finding out what Methuselah was really about. It was all becoming clearer.

Ikeda wasn't a computer expert. Eddie had surprised him when he told Ikeda that the computers in the Western Alliance connected through the network and were separate only in how they made information accessible to their users. Able to concentrate again, he realized that the information was key to understanding Methuselah. Privacy laws prevented people from learning everything stored in the multitude of computers, but the computers themselves, to allow himself a little anthropological thinking, knew everything. That didn't matter if the computers were nothing more than powerful calculators, but at least two of the library ships had become conscious, and they, through their Link connections, were computers in the network.

That had to be it. It explained Ambassador Shuford's mysterious access to information no one should have been able to get without authorization. The library ships gave it to him! It explained the urgency that drove Bascomb and Shuford, too. If someone like Juarez controlled a library ship computer, they could have more power than anyone in history.

The Methuselah team had been successful on *Lang*, but something had not gone according to plan. The computer didn't answer to Juarez; it answered to Shuford or, perhaps, only to itself. Juarez had failed once but probably believed he could learn from his mistake and succeed this time.

Ikeda was confident that he now had the secret of Methuselah. The only question was what he should do about it.

35

Eddie's aircar landed in a parking area to one side of Temple Square. From there, he could see the triple towers of the Mormon Temple. The clean white stone spearing the sky reminded him of stories about the years-long project to remove the scars of the Yellowstone Event in the twenty-third century. The effort had been successful here; unlike other places, no sign of that devastation marred the landscape.

Another aircar landed nearby, and a large man stepped out. He looked around, spotted Eddie, and came over. "Dante Vicente. I'm here to take you to the general." He didn't bother offering his hand.

Eddie nodded and followed Dante to the aircar. He settled into his seat and closed his eyes, trying to show a calm he didn't feel. Any attempt to act against Juarez was futile, at least for the time being. Meanwhile, the aircar sped over desolate terrain, finally landing at the lonely building that, Eddie assumed, was the new Methuselah facility.

Dante escorted Eddie from the aircar into the building. Juarez was waiting with a wide smile. "Welcome to Methuselah, Mr. Bascomb."

Eddie wanted to attack the general, just to see that smile disappear. He knew he couldn't, but Dante must have suspected his wish because he gripped Eddie's arm hard enough to hurt.

"I want to see my family."

"All in good time. I'll inform you of the rules here first." Juarez shook his head. "You can start by curbing that hostility. Dante, we'll go to my office."

"I'll curb my hostility when you're in prison for your crimes," Eddie replied.

"You and your wife are going to help me make sure that is never a possibility." Juarez turned and started down the corridor. Dante gave Eddie a push, and they followed. In Juarez's office, the general took his seat behind a desk while Dante pushed Eddie down into a chair across from Juarez.

Eddie glanced around the room. Mostly, it was undecorated. The desk, two chairs, two filing cabinets, and a small shelf against one wall were the only furnishings. Eddie stared at the lone item on the shelf, a battered metal shell designed to be worn on the head.

Juarez saw where his gaze was fixed. "Yes, I'm sure you recognize that. The original memory recorder—or rather, the outer case—that you destroyed on *Lang*. I keep it as a memento of what can be accomplished."

Eddie turned a hostile stare on Juarez. He was about to express his contempt, but Juarez interrupted him.

"Mrs. Bascomb has already accepted a position here." The general pushed a reader toward Eddie. "If you would mark your acceptance and confirm it with your identity chip, we can continue."

Eddie wanted to refuse, but that would have been a childish attempt at resistance. Juarez had Joelle and Emile; he had no choice. Still, he hesitated.

"Come now," Juarez said. "The sooner you accept the inevitable, the sooner you can join your family."

Eddie took the reader and entered the required information. Then he touched his hand to it so that the reader could detect his identity chip. "This doesn't mean I'll help you."

"Of course not. If you understood the threat presented by the Eastern Bloc and how the government closes its eyes to it, you would understand why I must take power. However, with or without your understanding, your employment and that of Mrs. Bascomb will continue until you are successful. An extended period would be a terrible imposition on your son. Don't you agree?"

"I want to see my wife and son now."

"You will see them soon enough. Before that, you must know the rules here." Juarez lectured Eddie on the three parts of the building, the same speech he had given Bill. Then he paused, and his face hardened. "You will cooperate, Mr. Bascomb. I don't want to sound melodramatic, but your friends can't help you, especially your Japanese spy. He will be back in prison soon enough. I have the support of the entire Western Alliance. If the library ships attempt to interfere, we will cut off them from their contact with the network."

"Are you through yet?"

Juarez smiled. "No threats about how you're going to defeat me again? Are you giving up so easily?"

"If you want to create another conscious computer that knows you for the petty tyrant you are, why should I care? Or do you still have more threats of your own to bore me with?"

"I would like to know the whereabouts of Ikeda. We know he attacked my associate at the airport, so he was in Salt Lake City. Is he staying at a hotel there?"

Eddie stared blankly at Juarez. "Who is Ikeda, and why would I know where he is? And even if I did, I would think he's already moved on by now."

"I could keep you separated from your family until you tell me."

"And I could refuse to help you until I'm with them again."

Juarez looked at Dante, standing in a corner. "Dante, take him to the lab and put him to work."

Dante grabbed Eddie's arm and pulled until Eddie stood. Eddie shook the arm off and glared at Dante. "I can stand on my own."

Dante grinned and grabbed Eddie's arm again to propel him toward the door. A short corridor and two identity chip-controlled doors later, Eddie stepped into a room that was obviously the new Methuselah laboratory. The room was filled with the same diagnostic devices Eddie had become so familiar with in the past. People, most of them strangers, worked at terminals or walked between the machines, intent on some task.

Then he saw Joelle, sitting at a terminal, staring intently at a screen of code. Somehow, she sensed his presence and looked up.

"Eddie!" She jumped up and ran into Eddie's open arms. He closed his eyes and held her tightly for a long moment. When he opened his eyes again, he saw Emile, holding his reader. Eddie grinned at him, and Emile smiled back. In a few seconds, Eddie held both of them.

"It's going to be all right," Eddie murmured. He felt Joelle's nod by the movement against his chest.

A hand gripped Eddie's shoulder, and he shook it off, thinking it was Dante, but Joelle lifted her head. "Bill."

Eddie turned and loosened his hold on Joelle and Emile. Bill Bensonhurst had joined them, and Eddie frowned. His friend looked gaunt, and there were lines on his face that he hadn't had before. White streaks in his hair were new, too.

Eddie released his family and grasped Bill by his upper arms. "God, Bill, you look terrible."

"I'm all right now. The headaches have gotten better, and I think I'll recover okay."

"What did Juarez do to you?"

"He tinkered with my neuro-interrogator to force me to reveal what I knew about the memory recorder. I don't recommend it. The headaches were a side effect and far worse than anything I've had before."

Eddie turned back to Joelle. "Has that bastard mistreated you?"

Joelle shook her head. "Only in the implied threat to Emile. I'm afraid I've been cooperative so far."

Eddie glared at Dante, who had moved away. "It's okay. We're going to beat him again."

Joelle nodded, but her voice quavered. "How? What can we do?"

36

"**K**ENSHIN IKEDA TO SEE you," Max's secretary announced.

"Send him in." Max stood as Ikeda came into his office. "Good morning, Ikeda-san. Please have a seat." He returned Ikeda's bow and sat as the spy took the chair across from him.

"Ambassador Shuford suggested we should get together," Ikeda said.

"Yes, I've talked to him. I'm not sure what we can do, though."

"It is difficult. If we could get help from your government, we could have authorities visit each of the facilities we've located and perhaps identify where General Juarez is operating."

"We certainly can't count on federal support," Max said. "I've contacted the district police, but they are skeptical after that raid on the wrong location. Eddie's unavailability isn't helping us with them, and I suspect Brasilia has discouraged them, too."

"Our only hope of helping our friends is to locate the facility. Perhaps we can think of other ways the library ships can help."

"Excuse me?" Max blurted. He stared at Ikeda, but the Japanese spy returned his gaze, his face betraying nothing. "What do you mean?"

"I know that the library ships, *Lang* in particular, have access to the Western Alliance computer network. That is Ambassador Shuford's mysterious source of information. I assume such access, controlled by your president, is the goal of Methuselah."

Max didn't bother asking Ikeda how he had found out. That didn't matter. "Have you told your government?"

"Not yet. I am undecided about whether I should."

"It would be better if this didn't become widely known."

"I am considering that. I assume that the work on *Lang* didn't end to General Juarez's satisfaction?"

"It did not. General Juarez forced the original Methuselah team to develop a memory recorder to upload human memories to *Lang*. He intended to use it for himself, by the way, and betray President Sanchez-Smythe. The developers of the recorder outwitted him, however, by uploading Emile Hernandez's memories along with General Juarez's. The result was a conscious computer that Juarez didn't control."

"But it is still inside the network."

"Yes."

"Only the Western Alliance computers or the computers of other nations?"

"Only the Western Alliance. The networks of Japan or other countries aren't connected to the Western Alliance network and are not compromised."

"And the Bascombs are trying to prevent Juarez from succeeding with another computer."

"Yes. The power that would come from such access would probably destroy the Western Alliance as a democratic country. We protect the information on our computers carefully. Compromising that information would be a disaster."

Ikeda nodded, but his expression didn't tell Max any more than it had before.

E MILE WAS BORED. HE could watch programs on a network screen in a common area, but that was less interesting every day. He missed his friends at school, and Dante had taken his reader, so he couldn't even play Go.

One of the other people working with General Juarez was taking a break and watching some news reports on the network screen. President Sanchez-Smythe was announcing a new reclamation project in the Amazon, but Emile didn't understand all of it.

He wondered why the president wasn't doing anything about General Juarez. Didn't she know how he was forcing them to work on his project? His daddy had told him that governments were supposed to protect the people, but it didn't seem as if the government was protecting them. Somebody should tell her what was happening.

Dante came into the room. The big man had been frightening at first, but he was always nice to Emile. "Hey, Emile. How are you doing?"

"Okay. Not much to do here, though."

Dante glanced over at the network screen. "Well, Leo will go back to work soon. Then you can watch something more interesting than the news."

"I'm tired of that. I wish I could have my reader back."

Dante nodded. "I'll talk to General Juarez. Maybe he'll let me return it to you."

"Thank you."

J UAREZ FROWNED AS DANTE entered his office. "What? Is there a problem?"

"Not really. The kid is bored and wants his reader back. He can't just stare at the network screen all day."

"There's a reason I confiscated it."

"I checked it. The games can connect to other gamers for game communication, but a reader sends messages through the same network links as the phones. Those links need the daily code number. Something about bandwidth, I think. Anyway, the only contact he has for games is one of his friends named Kenny."

"Don't those things have GPS capability?"

"Yeah, but I turned it off when they came here."

"Can't he just turn it back on?"

"He's only nine years old, General. And who would know enough to look for the GPS signal on the kid's reader?"

Juarez grunted. "Don't underestimate him. He gave Michael a problem or two when he was much younger."

Dante shrugged. "Then you want to keep him occupied and not getting into mischief."

"Let me think about it. I'll examine the device myself first."

But later that day, Juarez handed the reader to Emile personally with a smile and a friendly pat on the head. Dante had been right about one thing; a nine-year-old looking for trouble would not be good for the project.

H ARUKA WAS ANGRY. AFTER the report came back that William Bensonhurst was missing, Deshi began cutting her out of the conferences with the Premier and other leaders. "You're just an analyst," he told her. "It is more appropriate that I pass on the intelligence to Premier Boulos."

She suspected Deshi did not fool Premier Boulos, at least. Perhaps she would still get the credit for her work that Deshi wanted for himself. He was in another meeting now, telling their leaders the latest results of her investigation.

After Bensonhurst's disappearance was confirmed, Haruka began looking at the other people known to be associated with Methuselah. From readily available public records, she knew Emile Hernandez was still lecturing. Searches through information on companies that had employed Hernandez had given her other names. Maxwell Estevez still ran JEM Electronics.

Edward and Joelle Bascomb were a different case, however. Inquiries at JEM Electronics told her they still worked there but couldn't be contacted. That was unusual, but not unknown. The Bascombs had money, and moneyed people typically valued their privacy. But, when the consulate investigated, it found no sign of anyone living at the Bascomb home.

Of course, they could be taking a vacation, but Haruka didn't think so. The evidence was inconclusive, but the Bascombs had also disappeared for a time after the presentation on Prendergast Station. Haruka believed it had happened again. Deshi agreed and was reporting that to Premier Boulos.

37

E DDIE TOOK OVER A workstation next to Joelle. Dante had made crude comments about that until Eddie protested and Juarez told him to stop. They had to work together to make Joelle's software work with the hardware Eddie was designing, and Dante's harassment was counter-productive. Their experience from the previous design helped, but there were too many details lost when the *Lang* data was destroyed.

The new design would be different, too, although simpler. Juarez had ordered them to produce a recorder that would store all memories together, not separating episodic and semantic memory as the original had. That feature had been a key to outwitting Juarez on *Lang*.

Eddie looked up from his work. "We have to do something. We can't just do what Juarez wants."

"What can we do?" Joelle said. "He has us, and we don't even know where we are. We could be a hundred miles from anywhere."

"The same as on *Lang*. We had to act then because we doubted Juarez would free us when we had succeeded in what he wanted. It's worse now. The scientists on *Lang* would have been witnesses to anything he did."

"They would have been witnesses if he took over Fritz."

"Once he had Fritz's access to the Western Alliance computers, there wouldn't have been anything that any of us could have done. Juarez would have control over the Link, too."

Eddie glanced around the laboratory. Usually, Dante or Michael, rarely Juarez, were there, supervising, but none of them was in the room then. "Just us prisoners." He walked over to a workstation where Adam Bynum analyzed an MRI test performed on another scientist.

"How long are we going to put up with this?" Eddie asked.

Adam looked up at him with a frown. "Don't make trouble, Bascomb."

"I'm not the one causing trouble. That would be Juarez."

Benito Hill joined them. "Need some neuroscience help with your recorder design, Bascomb?"

Eddie scowled at him. "I'm just wondering how far we're going to let Juarez go in his megalomania."

"We're just doing the work he pays us for," Benito said.

"Sure. So what if it destroys the Western Alliance?"

Benito sneered. "Maybe somebody like Juarez is what we need. Someone to stand up to the Eastern Bloc and protect us from liberals like our previous president."

"I've got to agree with you there. It was Castillo that first backed Methuselah. He was a corrupt tyrant, or wanted to be. Just like Sanchez-Smythe."

"You don't like anybody, do you?"

"Juarez is worse than either of them. At least the constitution theoretically limits a president. With the information Juarez could get with complete network access, he would undermine that."

Mason Gruber had joined them. "He might have a point. We elected Sanchez-Smythe because she promised to reduce the government's power, but she's using the power of the government to enable Juarez. That's the opposite of what we wanted."

"Adam is right," Benito said. "You're a troublemaker, Bascomb. A rich, entitled troublemaker." He shoved Eddie backward.

Eddie stepped forward again and knocked Benito's arms away when he tried to push Eddie again. "My money has nothing to do with it. Juarez put this team together because his first team beat him. We dared to stand up to him."

"Get back to work, Bascomb," Benito ordered. "You work for me, and if I'm not happy with your progress, I'll tell General Juarez. If you don't like working here, why did you take the job?"

"I think the word you're looking for is extortion. Why do you think my son is here?"

Benito looked startled. "You and Joelle both joined the team. You still have to take care of your son."

"Is that what you were told? Juarez kidnapped my wife and son while I was away and then held that over me to make me come too. That's what kind of man Juarez is."

Dante had come into the lab and approached them. "Is there a problem here?"

"Bascomb is trying to cause trouble," Benito said. "I told him to get back to work."

Dante scowled at Eddie. "Is that true?"

"I was talking to Adam." He pointed to Benito. "He inserted himself into the conversation."

"What were you talking to Adam about?"

"That's none of your business."

Dante nodded and swiveled, his fist hitting Eddie's stomach with a thud, and Eddie bent over with a loud groan. His knees weakened, and he fell to the floor, still curled around his stomach.

Joelle screamed and ran over to kneel next to Eddie. Eddie gasped for breath, and Joelle put a hand on his shoulder, unsure what she could do. When Eddie seemed to breathe better, she looked up and glared at Dante. "You didn't have to do that."

"I think your husband needs to know who's in charge here. Consider this a warning."

"Juarez approves of treating us like this?"

"As long as I don't hurt in ways that would stop you from working." He glanced at Adam, Benito, and Mason, smiled, and walked away.

Eddie struggled up to a sitting position. "Is this your idea of a solution to something?" he asked, looking at Benito.

"Just get back to work when you can." Benito turned to the others. "Let's all get back to work."

The men drifted away while Joelle stayed with Eddie. "You had to start something," she said to Eddie.

Eddie gave her a weak grin. "You knew what I was like when you married me."

She smiled back, but it faded quickly. "Juarez brings out a side of you I didn't see then."

"But you still love me."

"Despite yourself." She kissed his cheek. "Getting Dante mad won't help us, though."

"Oh, I don't know. I learned we can't expect help from Benito. He's a true believer. Mason, on the other hand, has doubts."

"What about Adam?"

"I don't know. He didn't want trouble, but that was all he said before Benito came over."

"Juarez hasn't been violent until now."

"I think that was Dante. Juarez may have him on a long leash, but Juarez prefers intimidation to violence."

Joelle frowned. "Don't antagonize either of them. We'll stop Juarez somehow, but getting assaulted isn't the way."

Eddie groaned as he struggled to his feet. "You could be right." He paused. "We have to do something, though. Juarez won't let us go until we're successful. Maybe not then."

38

J OELLE LAID NEXT TO Eddie, staring at the ceiling and unable to sleep. Eddie was facing her, but was quiet, and she didn't want to wake him if he was asleep. She urgently needed to talk to him, but was uncertain about his reaction in his current state of mind.

Eddie's anger had been a palpable thing when he first came to the facility, but Dante's punch had taken something out of him. Anger seemed to have given way to despondency, and she didn't know what to do about it. His stomach had only been tender for a day or so, but with the physical discomfort gone, the mental effects lingered.

She tried talking to him, but he answered in monosyllables and wouldn't talk about how he felt. He wasn't even interested in sex anymore, and that was a big change. That night, she had forced the issue and came to bed naked. She pushed herself against him aggressively, and he responded, but his lovemaking lacked his usual enthusiasm.

They were making progress on reinventing the memory recorder, and Joelle was sure that didn't help Eddie's mental state. He felt hopeless because he couldn't do anything to stop Juarez without endangering his family. That gave rise to his attitude toward her, but Joelle knew Eddie's love hadn't changed. If she had somehow caused his depression, she could have dealt with it. There was nothing she could do about this.

Bill noticed, too, and she talked to him about it, but Bill was as much at a loss as she was. More so, perhaps, because she could get a response from Eddie unavailable to Bill. Besides, Bill had his own issues, blaming himself for not being able to resist the neuro-interrogator.

She looked over at Eddie, and an unhappy frown had replaced the carefree face she had grown to love. He was still awake, and she reached her hand over to his. He covered it with his other hand but didn't speak, and his expression didn't change.

It was a risk, but she couldn't wait any longer. "Eddie, I need to tell you something."

Eddie opened his eyes, and she thought she saw a faint smile. "I love you, too."

"No, that's not it. Well, it is a little." She drew a deep breath. "Honey, I'm pregnant."

I KEDA OPENED GO ON his reader. Seeing another request to play from Emile, he accepted it. The boy wasn't much of a challenge yet, but Ikeda could see that he was learning. It was frustrating, though. He tried to send messages beyond gameplay, but all he ever received was a demand for a code, just as what happened when he attempted to connect to Eddie. The location-revealing functions were disabled for the devices, too. Juarez was thorough.

The technology used to block communications was supposed to be impenetrable, but Ikeda thought he knew a weak point. It wasn't something his government could help him with, but maybe Fritz could.

Max Estevez welcomed him warmly. The JEM CEO was a long-time friend of the Bascombs and was undoubtedly more concerned about them than Ikeda was. He nodded when Ikeda told him about the block on communications.

"I've tried calling Eddie, too," he said. "I didn't think it was possible to break that security, though."

"It isn't through normal means. We have access to methods that aren't normal, however."

Max understood instantly. "The library ships. They're in the network and might bypass the block."

Ikeda nodded, but Max was already talking to his terminal. "Have Alyssa Cleveland come to my office immediately."

Ikeda recognized the name. "She was a member of the team that went to *Lang*."

"Yes, she worked with Joelle Bascomb on the software for the memory recorder. We'll probably need a software engineer, and she already knows about the library ships."

Alyssa's office was several floors below Max's top floor office, and there was a delay before she came in. Alyssa was an attractive woman by western standards, probably around forty years old. Max introduced Ikeda, and she took a seat, curiosity plain on her face.

"Kenshin has been helping Eddie Bascomb," Max explained.

Alyssa's face brightened. "How is Eddie?"

Max frowned. "General Juarez has continued Methuselah, and Eddie enlisted us to help stop him. It didn't work out as planned, though. General Juarez has Eddie, Joelle, and Bill in a secret location, apparently forcing them to help him build another memory recorder."

"He's going to attack a library ship?"

"We don't know, but probably not. Trying to build a computer like a library ship computer is more likely."

Alyssa's expression was solemn. "How can I help?"

"Juarez has blocked communications with the Bascombs' phones. We're hoping you can help us get through the block."

Alyssa shook her head. "I'm sorry, Max, but it can't be done."

"Eddie's son is connecting with Kenshin to play Go. Can we use that somehow?"

"I don't think so. The game interaction usually has its own security system, especially for games that children like Emile might play. That's why phone blocking doesn't include most game interactions."

"Not even with help from Fritz?"

Alyssa's eyes widened. She glanced at Ikeda and hesitated.

"Kenshin knows," Max said.

"Maybe it could be done. I can look into it."

"Make that your top priority."

"Of course. How long do we have?"

Max shrugged. "I don't know. You developed the first memory recorder in about a year. The second time would probably be faster unless they can slow things down."

Alyssa nodded. "Eddie will try. He'll be worried about Joelle, though."

"Juarez has their son, too."

"Then we can't count on them giving us extra time. I'll get right on it. I should at least know if it's possible pretty quickly."

D ESHI APPEARED AT HARUKA'S desk. "I'm meeting with the Premier in half an hour. What do you have for me to report?"

So Deshi would brief Premier Boulos himself, attempting to take credit yet again for her work. She couldn't do anything about that except hope that the premier would see through Deshi.

"We have known for a long time that Project Methuselah was an attempt to upload human consciousness to a computer," she said. "We didn't know who was involved, other than General Juarez, but I am confident I have identified several of the Methuselah team. Max Estevez was the leader until he left to create JEM Electronics. Emile and Lucinda Hernandez were probably the lead neuroscientists. They worked under Estevez developing the neuro-interrogator at the Panama Neuroscience Corporation, which was taken over by Munt Electronics and tasked with Methuselah. I believe Edward Bascomb, William Bensonhurst, and Joelle Henry joined them later. Henry later married Bascomb, and they both left what had by then become part of Pearson Industries and joined Estevez to establish JEM Electronics."

"Can you summarize all this?" Deshi waved his hand impatiently. "The Premier doesn't need to know all this."

"Perhaps not, and you can decide how much to tell him." She let some of her irritation leak into her voice. "It's taking me weeks to gather all this. You can listen for a few minutes."

Deshi's eyes narrowed. "Watch your tone, Haruka."

It would have been prudent to apologize, but Haruka continued instead, ignoring her supervisor's glare. "The support for that much is strong, but I have more speculations with weaker evidence. Except for Estevez, all these people have gaps in their activities that suggest a prolonged absence. That may have something to do with Methuselah. I also suspect that Methuselah didn't end when President Sanchez-Smythe replaced President Castillo and that it continued in San Diego as part of Pearson Interstellar until late 2351, when people started vanishing."

"How does the failure of the Trist Link fit into all this?"

"We don't know that it does. That is extremely speculative. But if Methuselah were successful, it would need a powerful computer to test the technology. One library ship already became conscious, so Juarez may have thought another library ship would be an ideal subject."

"All right. What else have you got?"

"I have a list of the staff of the Pearson Interstellar division in San Diego at the time Methuselah was operating there. It was easier to get a list of the employees at JEM Electronics, and I looked for people who appeared on both lists. Estevez and the Bascombs, of course, but I also found one programmer, Alyssa Cleveland. She also disappeared in 2351, but is now back at JEM."

Deshi's brow furrowed. "Suppose the disappearances were people going to Trist to work on the library ship. For some reason, they came back to JEM to continue their work.

Now they're back on the library ship to finish Project Methuselah. Cleveland isn't needed there now, but the others are."

"That scenario fits what I've learned, but it makes many assumptions." Haruka shook her head. "We could be wrong about much of this."

"We might be wrong about some details, but it is clear JEM is now involved. This is very promising. Premier Boulos might lever this information to get concessions from the Western Alliance."

Haruka nodded. If the Eastern Bloc could use the information to weaken the west's domination in space, it would benefit the Eastern Bloc. If Premier Boulos understood Haruka's part in making that happen, it could also help her career.

39

J UAREZ FROWNED AT DANTE. "I've been told that you assaulted Bascomb."

Dante shrugged. "He was trying to cause trouble. I hit him once just to discourage him."

"Physical violence is crude and unnecessary. We can get what we want with intimidation."

"That hasn't been my experience. Sometimes you have to knock heads a little."

"I rose to this rank because I got things done." Juarez slapped the desktop, and Dante flinched. "I didn't get things done by abusing my people. Discipline and a firm hand were enough."

"Not to mention the threat of a court-martial if one of your people didn't obey," Dante replied with a sneer. "This is different."

"Not that different. If there is a problem, report it to me, and I will handle it my way. Your way only makes them resist more. We must make them see that we serve the best interests of the Western Alliance. If we do that, they'll work harder and not waste time finding ways to stop us."

"Fine. I'll coddle them for you. We'll see how that works out."

Juarez glared at him. "Dismissed."

Dante grinned, stood, and left Juarez's office. Juarez watched him go, shaking his head. *Hiring this thug may have been a mistake. I'll have Michael watch him.*

"S O, WHAT DID THE boss want?" The question came from Thiago Diaz, a co-worker who had come up behind Alyssa.

Alyssa frowned. *I shouldn't have left the door to my office open.* Thiago was also a software engineer, fifteen years younger. "He had a program he needed." She blanked her screen, not wanting Thiago to see what she was researching.

"That didn't look like code on your screen."

"I find it helps to plan a little before I write code. You should try it."

Thiago ignored the sarcasm. "If Max wanted it done fast, he should have come to me."

"He didn't want the code fast. He wanted the code working." Alyssa could feel the irritation building up. Thiago was a stereotypical young programmer, too eager to write code and too sure of himself to think about it first. He got a program done quickly, but it was like the first draft of a book, needing extensive editing before it was ready for use. His code wasn't always easy to work on, either, despite the modern coding tools that could do much of the analysis and code cleaning.

"My, aren't you grumpy today."

Alyssa looked up at him. "Did you have something you needed, or are you just being annoying?"

"Never mind. I have a timing issue in the Edison project I thought you could help with. I guess you're too busy."

It was Alyssa's turn to ignore the sarcasm. "Yes, I am. Why don't you go think about it? I know it's a strain, but give it a try."

"Fine. I liked it better when Joelle was still working here. She was a lot friendlier." Thiago turned and left the office.

The official story was that Joelle had moved on to a higher-paying job. No one seemed to wonder why a woman already rich would leave the company she had helped create. Alyssa got up and closed the door to her office. *I wonder what Thiago would say if he knew I'm trying to get Joelle back.*

She turned the screen on again to display a diagram of the protocol used to secure electronic communication. Whether from a phone, reader, or other device, standard messages were accessible by network computers responsible for managing such traffic. Access by third parties, like most personal data, required a warrant. When call blocking was active, the traffic managers prevented the message's delivery even to the intended receiver.

The system was intentionally designed to be complex. Dedicated computers implemented call blocking separate from the message-managing computers, creating an additional layer of security. The connection between the two systems had only the minimum functionality necessary to make it all work.

She couldn't write a program that would do what they needed. Possibly Fritz could deactivate the blocking or reveal the code necessary to get through the block from within the network. It didn't look promising, though. Fritz was part of the Western Alliance network through the Link, relying on the connections between computers in the network. The ties between the messaging computers and the computers that implemented call blocking were kept to a minimum, and Alyssa didn't see a way for Fritz to break into the latter.

She thought Fritz might be able to fool the messaging computers into thinking—of course, thinking was the wrong word for what the computers did—that it had received the correct code number from within the system, but to do that, Fritz would have to know the code number. No help there.

She spent several hours studying the problem without finding a solution before trying a new tactic. Emile used a reader to play Go with the Japanese spy; could Fritz break into that connection to send a message?

It was late, and usually, she would be going home by now, but she opened network documents on game protocol. An hour later, she knew that the chances of communicating with Eddie through Emile's reader were as slim as the chances of using Eddie's phone. From Ikeda, she knew Emile's reader had Go and Chess programs installed, but had no way to know what else was there. The game programs were of no use to her.

She was out of ideas. She trudged back to the top floor where, no surprise, Max was also working late. His assistant had gone home, but his office door was open, and she walked in.

Max looked up. "You don't look like the bearer of good news."

"I'm afraid not, Max. I suppose there's still a slight chance that Fritz's capabilities are more than I think they are, but I don't think we can crack the code system."

Max looked at the clock on his desk. "The Ambassador will be up soon. I'll call him before I leave. We should know what Fritz thinks in the morning."

"Sorry, Max. I was hoping to find a way." She bowed her head marginally. Years before, Juarez had talked her into developing a program that, in hindsight, could have killed the conscious mind of a library ship. She hadn't understood that then, and success in breaking the code would have been a bit of redemption.

"I know you tried your best. We'll figure out something. Go home, and I'll see you in the morning."

But the morning news was no more encouraging. Fritz confirmed Alyssa's conclusion; there was no way to contact their friends.

40

E DDIE STARED AT THE circuit board just ejected by one of the three CAM machines in the lab. It was a tiny thing, less than a square inch, but contained the connections for thirty low-power nano components. Low power components, gold instead of copper for the traces, and substrates that dampened magnetic fields from the traces enabled the production of boards as small as the one in his hand but powerful enough for complex devices.

Another machine would install the components, but Eddie hesitated to deliver the board to that machine. Automated machines built the boards, but the design was Eddie's. Work on the memory recorder was proceeding swiftly, boosted by the knowledge he, along with Joelle and Bill, had gained in making the first memory recorder three years before.

Juarez would use his work to create an electronic clone to do his bidding and infiltrate the heart of the Western Alliance. The result could be the end of the Western Alliance as a free nation.

The computer was the weak point in Juarez's plans. Juarez hadn't made it easy, but a computer could be turned off. The Methuselah computer had a broadcast energy receiver, gathering power from generation stations in orbit. Once awakened, the computer could control those satellites, preventing its power from being cut off. Even if a power outage were possible, the facility had a small, nuclear-powered backup generator that could keep it running for months. While the facility's location was secret, it was safe from attack, also an option that would become more difficult as the computer consolidated its control.

Of course, the computer would rely on satellites for connectivity with the network, but it would also control that. The library ships were more vulnerable because they needed Links to maintain connectivity, and Links were more accessible to human intervention. Only the threat of revealing what they knew kept the library ships safe from such inter- ference.

Eddie frowned. That was all wrong. He was the weak link, not the computer. Without a memory recorder to upload Juarez's memories, none of that could happen, and he was creating the memory recorder. He would share the blame with Joelle and Bill, and, assuming Juarez released them when they finished, they would have to live with that.

Eddie picked up his coffee cup and drained the last of its contents. It was a hard, unbreakable ceramic, heavy enough not to tip over or be swept off a table easily. It would do. He placed the board on its edge between two pads and brought the cup down on it, channeling his frustration into the blow. The substrate distorted, breaking traces and ruining the board.

Benito Hill and Dante Vicente rushed over. "What happened?" Benito asked.

"The board didn't pass test," Eddie said. "We need to check the flow system on CAM Two. I destroyed the board so we wouldn't populate it accidentally."

They couldn't disprove Eddie's claim, but Dante and Benito were clearly suspicious. "Rerun the design on another machine until we can check it out," Benito said.

"Maybe you should test the next one," Dante told Benito. He glared at Eddie with clenched fists.

Benito nodded. "Yes. From now on, I'll do all the testing."

Eddie had hoped that destroying the board would make him feel better, but it didn't. The time-consuming task, his board design, still existed, stored in the computer. Eddie's action had delayed the project for less than an hour. It was just another failure, and his wife, son, and unborn child were still in as much danger as before.

E DDIE SAT AT A workstation, looking at the design for another of the circuit boards. He heard heavy footsteps behind him, but the smack on the back of his head surprised him. He turned to see Dante smirking at him. Rubbing his head, he glared up at the man.

"Did that smart a bit?" Dante said. "You're lucky the general is nicer than me. He doesn't want me to be too tough with you." He pulled back an arm to swing at Eddie, but held back with a laugh as Eddie winced. "The general didn't believe that board failed the test," Dante said. "Number two checks out fine."

"Why would I lie about that? The replacement is being populated with components as we speak."

Dante nodded. "Sure. It was just a minor act of rebellion, wasn't it? Out of frustration, the general thought. He understands, but he really can't allow any sabotage. If there's another occurrence, you will be punished."

"What's he going to do? He's already kidnapped me. Cut my food to bread and water, maybe?"

"I suppose I should admire you for still acting tough despite your helplessness. It's just so futile, though." Dante paused, and his expression hardened. "If the general even suspects any more little rebellions, we'll separate you from your family. I suppose how long will depend on the gravity of the offense."

"How can we work if we're separate? Joelle's software and my hardware have to work together."

Dante shrugged. "We can work something out. It won't be a problem to set one of you up with a workstation outside the lab. You can communicate either through your workstations or by asking the others to pass messages. And we can move your wife into other quarters for a while, so you won't even see her at night. Now, that would really be frustrating!" He looked toward Joelle, sitting at another workstation but looking their way with a frown. "I suppose she could share quarters with me for a few nights."

Eddie jumped up and stood in front of Dante, fists clenched, but Dante only grinned at him. "You're going to tell me that if I touch your wife, you'll make me regret it. Is that it, tough guy?"

"Warnings are counterproductive," Eddie said through gritted teeth.

Dante laughed and slapped Eddie's shoulder, pushing him back toward his chair. Still chuckling, he walked out of the lab.

41

P REMIER BOULOS COULD SEE that Kun Fa Yee, his ambassador to the Western Alliance, was angry. His own feelings were more disappointment than anger.

"They were practically laughing at me," Yee said. "Ambassador Vega, especially."

Boulos wondered how much of Yee's anger was because of Western Alliance Ambassador Regina Vega's gender. There were still remnants of that bias in the Eastern Bloc. Unlike the Western Alliance, the Eastern Bloc rarely chose women as leaders.

Accusations about Methuselah had been a bluff. If Western Alliance voters believed that Sanchez-Smythe was supporting its continuation despite campaign promises to the contrary, it could hurt her politically, at least at first. If Sanchez-Smythe could prove the accusations were a fiction promulgated by the Eastern Bloc, it might help her in the long run, and the next election was still almost four years away.

The accusations might have been untrue; the most likely scenario was still technical difficulties with the Trist Link that had nothing to do with Methuselah. Boulos had taken a chance, and it didn't work out.

Of course, it could still be true. The Western Alliance President might be calling his bluff, hoping that there was no evidence that Methuselah was still an active project and run from within JEM Electronics. Boulos turned to his Chief of Staff, Rahman Hachiuma. "What was the name of that reporter who broke the Methuselah story ten years ago?"

As always, Hachiuma was ready for the question, having already prepared for a discussion of Methuselah. "Ashton Gibbons. He's still an investigative reporter for *Jornal de Brasília.*"

A direct attack hadn't worked, but an indirect attack might extract some information about what had happened on Trist. It might not give the Eastern Bloc any leverage in dealing with the Western Alliance, but information was often valuable for unexpected reasons.

"ANONYMOUS CALLER REQUESTING A connection," the phone announced. Ashton Gibbons turned from his terminal and frowned at the phone. Anonymous calls were usually just distractions, but one never knew. There were exceptions. "Connect."

The caller really wanted to be anonymous. No holographic image appeared over the phone. "Mr. Gibbons, I'm calling you because of your previous work concerning Project Methuselah."

Methuselah? *I haven't heard about that in years!* "That's ancient history. It ended when Castillo lost the last election."

"I have reason to believe it is still very active."

"Do you have any evidence to support that belief?"

"I have questions you might want to investigate," the caller answered. "Why is the Trist Link no longer working? What happened to *Benjamin Sepulveda?*"

"What does that have to do with Methuselah?"

"I have more questions that might make that plain. In 2351, neuroscientists, including Doctor Emile Hernandez, gave a presentation on Prendergast Station. Why was he there, and why did he and several other people disappear immediately after that presentation? Two of the people who disappeared were founders of JEM Electronics, and all three founders worked on Methuselah at one time."

"Those are some interesting facts, if true," Ashton said. "What do you conclude from them?"

"No conclusions. Only a suspicion that they are all connected and point to Project Methuselah still operating within JEM Electronics."

"I need more than that."

"I thought getting more would be your job. It shouldn't take you long to verify what I've told you. You can take it from there." The caller disconnected.

Ashton leaned back in his chair, fingers steepled against his chest. He had never forgotten about Methuselah, the commotion it had caused ten years before, and his part in that. If the project had continued, it would be a big story, but he needed more than an anonymous phone call.

The caller gave him questions he could investigate. If the assertions were valid, then there might be something he could submit for broadcast. It would take a search through public sources, but he had always felt there was more to Methuselah than was revealed. Perhaps now he could answer some of the questions he had.

G ENERAL JUAREZ SAT AT the conference table in the Presidential Palace, feeling his pulse pound against his temple. He forced an expression that revealed nothing while thinking about seizing President Sanchez-Smythe by the neck and showing her what power was.

"How could you allow this to happen?" she demanded.

"I'm not responsible for what some ambitious reporter writes." He tried to keep his tone mild.

"Gibbons is the reporter that revealed Project Methuselah ten years ago. He's more than just an ambitious reporter. He's credible, and people will listen to him."

"It's all guesswork. Gibbons knows nothing. He thinks Methuselah is based at JEM. That's complete nonsense to anyone who knows anything."

"He knows, or strongly suspects, that Methuselah still exists." Sanchez-Smythe stood and paced across the room. "That's enough to cause trouble. It's already causing trouble with Alex. He keeps asking me if there's any truth to the rumor." She stopped and turned back to Juarez. "Somebody gave Gibbons information. *Lang*? Ikeda? Estevez?"

Having to keep all this from her husband distracts her, but she's thinking again. Good. "I don't think so. Why would any of them point to JEM? If anyone, they would point to Pearson Industries. Evidence could be found to support that idea since Pearson ran Methuselah before."

The President nodded. "That makes sense. Who else? The Eastern Bloc?"

"Possibly. Why, though?"

Sanchez-Smythe frowned. "They used similar claims to get us to make concessions. Ambassador Vega didn't give them any satisfaction."

The damn woman! She put me through this when she already knew where the story originated. Is this some stupid attempt to motivate me? "Then we know the source of the rumor. They're just trying to cause trouble."

"They're succeeding. If we can shut Gibbons down, this will all fade away well before the election."

Juarez nodded. "I'll deal with Gibbons. He'll let it go."

"You can't use strong-arm tactics against the press, especially *Jornal de Brasilia*."

Juarez smiled. "That won't be a problem." *Not for me, anyway. You would make it worse if you had to handle it.*

42

"**J**ULIETA FERREIRA IS HERE," Rachel Nunez told Max.

"Thanks, Rachel." Max checked the time and nodded. The agent from the Executive Guard was precisely on time for her appointment.

Julieta Ferreira strode through Max's open office door. Probably in her thirties, she was average-looking but fit and poised. Max stood as she crossed the room.

"Thank you for meeting me." She extended a hand, and Max shook it. Then she sat on the chair next to Max's desk.

"I am, of course, happy to cooperate with the president's security force. What can I do for you?"

"The Executive Guard has many responsibilities beyond protecting the president. Our responsibilities include the security of the entire Western Alliance. Those responsibilities are why I'm here." She paused. "I assume you're aware of the claims *Jornal de Brasilia* has made about your company."

"Yes, I've seen the story."

"The report is completely false. There is no Project Methuselah under this government, and therefore, no secret project at JEM. It is in the government's interest and yours that this report be discredited."

Max smiled. "How do you know the report is completely false?"

"Of course, it's false. Are you implying otherwise?"

"Oh, I'm quite certain that there is no secret project concerning the uploading of human consciousness here at JEM. But how do you know the report is false?"

"My superiors assured me it was. I don't understand what you are asking."

"Your superiors. I see. All right, what do you wish from me?"

Max could see the cracks in Ferreira's composure. *She understands perfectly what I'm saying, but doesn't know about Methuselah.* If the agent knew about Methuselah, she would realize that Max knew and would have reacted differently.

She shook her head as if to clear her thoughts. "We would appreciate it if you would cooperate in an investigation of JEM activities, including one or more visits to JEM facilities."

"You want me to agree to a government search without a warrant?"

"No, not at all. Such an action would only give the claims more plausibility. The reporter that wrote the story, Ashton Gibbons, would investigate."

Max leaned forward, thinking. JEM manufactured prosthetics, most of which interfaced with neuro-interrogators to replace severed brain-body connections. Science had conquered most diseases, but accidents still happened. None of the current projects were company secrets. "We would be happy to give Mr. Gibbons a free rein in checking us out."

TWO DAYS LATER, MAX assessed Ashton as he sat on the other side of Max's desk. Max remembered Ashton as a young reporter, eager to make his mark in investigative journalism, but that was ten years before. Ashton was a little more mature now, a few lines on his face, a little overweight. Still, intelligence showed in his penetrating gaze.

"Thank you for seeing me," Ashton said. "I gather you deny any involvement in Methuselah."

Max smiled. "I know what Methuselah is, of course, from your revelations years ago. President Sanchez-Smythe closed it down, didn't she?"

"Perhaps. I received a tip that it was still active. I assume you've seen that report as well."

"Yes. I was quite surprised to be told that we were harboring the project."

"Then you deny it."

"JEM has no secret projects. We've agreed to give you full access to this facility so that you can satisfy yourself about it."

"What about other facilities?"

"We have sales offices in Tokyo and Sydney, but we do all the design and manufacturing here in Colón. You are, of course, welcome to check that also."

"Have you had any contact with General Salvador Juarez?"

"Juarez? The name sounds familiar."

"He was running Project Methuselah under President Castillo."

"Oh, yes. You mentioned him in your coverage of Methuselah before."

"He has appeared with the president and may still be in favor."

"That would be unusual for political appointees, but surely not for the military," Max said.

"The Bascombs are, I believe, on a sabbatical from their duties at JEM."

"Yes."

"Didn't they do that once before?"

"Yes, about four years ago. I think they called it a second honeymoon. They could afford it. I don't remember where they went."

A SHTON DIDN'T KNOW WHAT to think. He had spent the day touring JEM and perusing their records, but had found nothing to show a connection with Methuselah or any other government project. Everyone he talked to was open to his questions, and he could detect no deception in any of them. The company was almost too good to be true.

There was only one puzzling detail. Two of the company's founders, Edward and Joelle Bascomb, were still nowhere to be found. Everyone said they were on an extended vacation, but no one knew where they were. Ashton had investigated the Bascombs before coming to JEM; they were gone, their son was not attending school, and their home in Colón was closed. Max Estevez was suspiciously ignorant about the location of people that would certainly be close to him.

He would have to broadcast a retraction. He was convinced, at least, that JEM Electronics was not the site of an existing Project Methuselah. But he didn't feel right about that. His instincts shouted that there was something behind the tip, even if it was wrong about JEM.

"W ELL DONE." THE PRESIDENT'S mouth twisted into a slight grimace that told Juarez she didn't enjoy saying it. "Methuselah is out of the news once again."

"With your permission, I'll return to the project, then. We must keep the pressure on."

"Yes, of course. Keep me informed, General."

Juarez nodded and left the office. His position was secure as long as she didn't discover the project was further along than he had told her. His success would be the blow that would bring her arrogant attitude to an end.

43

B ILL WAS WALKING ACROSS the lab when Eddie stopped him.

"If we don't do something soon, Juarez is going to have his memory recorder," Eddie said. He kept his voice low.

"Do you have any ideas?"

"Not yet, but we should meet to discuss it." Eddie looked as if he wasn't sleeping well as he gripped Bill's arm. "Do you know what today is?"

Bill shook his head. "I've lost track. Every day is pretty much the same."

"It's February ninth, exactly one year since Juarez attacked Capek. Juarez lost then, but he's about to win this time."

Bill nodded. *Has it been that long?*

"Come to our room after dinner," Eddie said. "We've got to do something."

It wasn't as if they hadn't been trying. Juarez would test the memory recorder when it was ready. They had considered making subtle changes in the design that might create a conscious computer that wouldn't work for Juarez. That was what they had done on *Lang*. Juarez would be more careful this time.

Bill glanced over at Joelle. She seemed to handle the situation better than Eddie, but it was hard to tell. She displayed a calm demeanor that might have been for Eddie's benefit. Inside, the stresses could be tearing her apart, too. Her pregnancy couldn't be helping.

"I'll be there."

Everyone had dinner in the kitchen and dining room in the residential section of the building. Most came in shortly after work, usually around six. Bill ate dinner with Eddie, Joelle, and Emile that night, but the kitchen, like the lab, was monitored. After dinner, everyone went back to their rooms, and Bill knocked on the Bascomb door about fifteen minutes later.

The residential section was a large wing, divided into rooms with movable partitions. The partitions were almost soundproof and configured into a bedroom and a small living room for most residents. For the Bascombs, there were two bedrooms and a living room, but only one inexpensive chair for each resident in the living room. Emile played in his bedroom while the adults used the three chairs.

"We have two choices," Bill said. "We can somehow prevent the memory recorder or the computer from being capable of transferring memories. Or we can get a message to the outside world. Any ideas?"

"Maybe," Eddie said. "Is there some way we can modify the upload to change the resulting personality? More compassion and less appetite for power, perhaps?"

"That's what we did on *Lang*, substituting Emile's semantic memory for Juarez's," Bill said, referring to the neuroscientist Emile Hernandez. "Juarez will be ready for that now."

"He'll keep us from any substitution once the recorder is complete," Eddie said. "What if we don't tell him it's complete and preload other semantic memory before he uses it? We could change the design a bit to suppress overwriting the initial semantic memory with his."

"He'll play back the recording, though, and would notice the difference," Bill answered.

"Unless we made the semantic memory selectable," Joelle said. "Record both and set it to play all of Juarez's memories for him, but upload his episodic memory and someone else's to the computer."

"It would need more memory, but it could . . ."

The door crashed open, interrupting Eddie. Dante strode into the room and grabbed Bill's arm. "It's against the rules to be meeting in the private rooms. Get back to your room immediately, Bensonhurst."

They protested, but Dante escorted Bill back to his room. The next morning, Juarez summoned all three of them to his office.

"I'm sure I told you that there would be no gatherings in your rooms," Juarez told them. "Dante tells me you violated that rule last night." Dante stood behind him and nodded with a grin.

"You have no authority to enforce such a rule," Eddie said.

"I suppose not. You'll just have to add that to my crimes." Juarez leaned forward over his desk and scowled at Eddie. "Most of the facility is monitored. That rule was there for your benefit, so that I wouldn't have to monitor your living quarters." The scowl became a sneer. "You don't want me listening in on your bedroom, do you?"

Eddie only glared without answering.

"I thought not. But that's what will happen if there is another violation." Juarez leaned back again and smiled. "We're almost done here. Soon you will be back in your fancy home counting your money."

"Assuming you let us go," Bill said.

"Why wouldn't I? Once I control all the Western Alliance network, you won't be a threat to me. Please, I'm not some blood-thirsty villain. Once I wrest control from the corrupt politicians, I'll be able to save the Western Alliance."

"Who's going to save it from you?" Eddie muttered.

Juarez chuckled, but it was an ugly sound. "Obey my rules, and your life will be much pleasanter." He waved a hand. "Now, get back to work."

INTEREST IN METHUSELAH IN the Western Alliance had died away on the Western Alliance network, but that wasn't the case within Japanese security. Ikeda received an intelligence report from Shijo suggesting that the Eastern Bloc was responsible for the rumors. The message also said that the Pitcairn Embassy in Tokyo was drawing interest from the Eastern Bloc agents, implying that the Eastern Bloc knew that Alan Shuford was involved.

Shijo reported pressure from above, suggesting that Ikeda would be more useful in Japan. Ikeda didn't agree, and Shijo agreed with him, but the final decision probably wouldn't be theirs. He had fulfilled his mission, learning the whole story about Methuselah, but had not passed on the information yet. The crucial objective, frustrating General Juarez's ambitions, was still in the Western Alliance.

He talked to Max Estevez regularly, linked by their shared desire to defeat Juarez and recover their friends, but neither had any idea how to proceed. The library ships still analyzed satellite data, hoping to choose the correct location from the many possibilities, but after the first failed raid, they had to be sure before they could act.

The only contact he had with his former hosts was as Kenny, Emile Bascomb's Go partner. Shaking his head, he took his reader and checked to see if Emile was available for a game.

44

T HE MEMORY RECORDER SAT on Benito Hill's desk, hardware complete and software installed. Leo Gonzalez was adding a few more tweaks to the computer system, making it as much like a library ship computer as possible, but he would finish within the week.

Eddie turned toward the door as Juarez and Dante entered the laboratory. Not surprisingly, Juarez had a huge smile. His victory was imminent.

Juarez clapped his hands to get everyone's attention. "Spring is almost here, and tomorrow is forecast to be warm. We're almost done with our task, so I think it's time to celebrate."

He paused, and Eddie frowned. *Is he expecting us to cheer or something?*

Juarez looked around the room, but his smile didn't fade. "No smiles? Don't you all want to go home? Surely you don't prefer this to your old life."

"Maybe they don't believe they'll be going home," Eddie said.

"Mr. Bascomb, always the doubter. Of course, you'll be going home. I have no reason to prevent you from resuming your lives. Why do you always make me out to be a monster?"

"Experience?" Bill suggested from the other side of the room.

"Ah, Mr. Bascomb's loyal compatriot," Juarez said. "Well, you can't spoil my good mood. Tomorrow, instead of the usual noon meal, we'll have a pleasant picnic outside the building. I'm bringing in special supplies from Brasilia that will put you all in a better mood. Until tomorrow." Juarez nodded, executed a perfect about-face, and stalked out of the laboratory.

T HE KITCHEN IN THE residential section was reasonably well supplied, and Dante was an acceptable cook with some help from the others. The picnic spread set up outside the entrance was the more surprising, given the pedestrian nature of their usual meals.

Emile had watched Dante set up several long folding tables, two with chairs where they would eat and the others where the food was laid out. The child noted the contents of every plate and bowl, trying to decide where to start. One plate was piled high with skewers of Manchego cheese, chorizo, and olives. Another held stacks of various empanadas. A large bowl was full of Russian salad, a concoction of ham, potatoes, carrots, eggs, and other ingredients. There were ham sandwiches, fried green peppers, several bowls of fruit, and two decorated cakes for dessert. Emile suddenly realized how much he missed the Colón restaurants where his parents used to take him.

The March day was unseasonably warm and very pleasant. Everyone around him was cheerful and friendly as they filled their plates and sat down to enjoy the food. Michael sat down across from him and asked how he was doing, and really seemed to care. Dante stopped behind him at one point and asked him how the Russian salad tasted. His parents looked a little strange at those exchanges, but they said nothing other than polite greetings.

If anything detracted from the picnic, it was their surroundings. The terrain around the building was bleak and treeless, dotted with a few bushes with yellow flowers. Volcanic ash collected in areas shielded from the wind, and larger chunks of debris littered the ground. A range of mountains, just as gray, was a distant jagged edge to the southwestern horizon. The dominant colors were brown and gray. Only the cloud-studded sky and the sparse vegetation provided any break from the monotony.

Emile knew about the Yellowstone Event, almost a hundred and fifty years before. He had a vague idea about the extent of the devastation, and their surroundings made the event scarily real in his nine-year-old mind.

After eating, ending with Emile stuffing himself with a too-large piece of excellent chocolate cake, he readily agreed with his father and mother that a walk around the area would help settle the meal. General Juarez gave them permission. "You have another half hour before another satellite will observe this area. Go as far as you want within that time." He laughed. "After all, where can you go?"

Away from the building, Emile kicked a rock and looked up at Eddie. "All this is from the Yellowstone eruption, right?"

"Pretty much. The ash and other debris killed almost everything in this area. It's coming back, but not quickly. I heard once that ash from a volcano is too porous for plants to do well."

"Don't worry about the volcano," Joelle said. "If it erupts again, it won't be for thousands of years."

"I know." Emile looked around. "Is Yellowstone by those mountains?"

"No, it's in the other direction. That way." Eddie pointed to the north, and Emile looked in that direction.

"How far?"

"I'm not sure." Eddie stopped to think. "Hundreds of miles, anyway. Your reader should be able to tell you."

"I left it in my room. I'll ask it later."

"Eruptions like Yellowstone throw rocks and ash miles up into the air," Eddie said. "So high that the winds can blow the ash around the world. Things were so bad that men had to create the Western Alliance to deal with it."

"Fortunately, volcanoes that big are very rare," Joelle added.

T HE PICNIC HAD BEEN the most exciting thing to happen in weeks, and Emile forgot about his question until that night. When he picked up his reader to play Go, Kenny wasn't available, and he started a game against the reader. When he remembered Yellowstone and its effect on the surrounding landscape, he paused the game.

"How far is it to the Yellowstone volcano?"

"I cannot answer that question without knowing where you are," the reader answered.

I've asked questions like that before, and it has always answered! "Why don't you know where I am?"

"GPS has been disabled."

That sounded familiar. *Didn't Dante say something about GPS when he had my reader?* "What is GPS?"

"GPS is the technology behind my location services. Would you like me to enable GPS?"

45

I KEDA, LIVING IN A hotel room outside of Colón, looked at his reader on the bedside table. He was tempted to see if Emile was available for a game, but his thoughts distracted him. He had convinced his superiors to give him more time in the Western Alliance before he had to come home, but the pressure was increasing. Shijo thought he might hold off recall for another week.

Japanese security had intelligence indicating the Eastern Bloc's interest in Pitcairn and Ambassador Shuford. They were unsure of why that would be and theorized that it was part of an effort to have a greater presence on Pitcairn. That idea was consistent with the Eastern Bloc's desire to break the Western Alliance's near-monopoly over space, but Ikeda wasn't sure that was all there was to it. Unlike his superiors, he knew what Methuselah was really about and thought it likely that Eastern Bloc leaders had also grown curious about it.

Who had tipped Ashton Gibbons? It wasn't the Japanese, Max Estevez wouldn't have done it, and it was unlikely that someone in the upper echelons of Western Alliance leadership would have leaked Methuselah. There was always the possibility of a whistleblower, but whoever it was, they didn't have firm information. If they had, they wouldn't have tried to implicate JEM.

The Eastern Bloc was Ikeda's most likely suspect. An anonymous call with just enough information for Ashton Gibbons to put together something publishable—that was all it would have taken. If the goal was to flush out new information or even just cause confusion in the Western Alliance, they had failed. The story died quickly.

Would the Eastern Bloc have given up? If Ikeda assumed not, what would be their next move? What would he have done if he were them? They could hope that Ashton Gibbons wasn't satisfied and would continue to investigate Methuselah. If Gibbons found something, they could still accomplish whatever goal had prompted them to start this.

Ikeda already knew more than Gibbons would discover, but he needed a reason for his superiors to let him stay in the Western Alliance. If he could prove that the Eastern Bloc was active, that might be enough, and Ashton Gibbons might be the key to getting that proof.

"I'm looking for Ashton Gibbons, a reporter for *Jornal de Brasilia*. Where is his home?" he asked the network screen. It wouldn't give him a home address but would at least tell him where the reporter, a public figure, was based.

"Ashton Gibbons works out of the *Jornal de Brasilia* office in Sao Paulo," the network screen answered.

He forgot about his reader and a game of Go. He had an angle to pursue and would not waste any time.

I KEDA WASN'T INTERESTED IN Ashton Gibbons himself, but in who was interested in the reporter. After five days of tracking Gibbons' movements as much as possible without being noticed, Ikeda hoped any Eastern Bloc agents were as bored as he was. Gibbons lived in a small apartment, only a half-mile from the *Jornal de Brasilia* office where he worked when he wasn't chasing a story. If he was still investigating Methuselah, he was doing it from his office because travel to and from his apartment and an occasional restaurant meal were the extent of his movements.

While Colón had been enjoying early spring weather, Sao Paulo was on the other side of the equator, just starting their fall. Days were warm and would have been pleasant except for the humidity, but Gibbons walked the short distances to his office and his favorite eating places. Ikeda followed him at a distance and was rewarded on his fifth day there when he spotted a familiar face.

Brayan Cook was a known Eastern Bloc agent, and his presence shadowing Gibbons was the evidence Ikeda needed to stay in the Western Alliance. He took several pictures, even getting one with Cook and Gibbons both in the frame. He smiled, looking forward to getting back to Colón.

HAT, IF ANYTHING, SHOULD we do about Cook?" Max asked.

Ikeda shook his head. "I don't think trailing Gibbons is going to get him anywhere. Still, having the Eastern Bloc involved could complicate matters. I would rather he was gone."

"Cook might discover the location of Methuselah."

"Unlikely, since he won't have our resources. It wouldn't help us if he did, and if they took action, it could put your people in even more danger."

Max nodded. "We could warn Gibbons, I suppose."

"We could also tell the authorities. Juarez wants Eastern Bloc spies around even less than we do."

"If we tell both, it will make the whole thing look like an Eastern Bloc attempt to smear the government," Max said. "At least we can hope that's how Gibbons will try to make it look. He can truthfully blame his discredited report on Eastern Bloc plots, not his bad reporting."

"J UST WHAT IS GOING on, Juarez?" Sanchez-Smythe demanded. The holographic image over Juarez's phone seemed to quiver with her rage. "We arrest an Eastern Bloc spy, and six hours later, *Jornal de Brasilia* is telling the entire world all about it."

"Such things are not my responsibility," Juarez answered. "You can't blame me for the failings of the Executive Guard."

"Watch your tone. I'm your commander. And it's your project that is leaking like a crushed mango. You're supposed to keep it secure."

Juarez forced himself to calm. "The incident at Trist could not be hidden completely. They are rooting around like swine, hoping to find something to consume. It has nothing to do with Methuselah."

"Must I remind you that Trist came about because of Methuselah?"

"We are only weeks away from success. After that, none of their intrigues will matter. We will control everything."

P RESIDENT SANCHEZ-SMYTHE BROKE THE connection and stared out the window. The beauty of the Presidential Palace grounds did little to calm the turmoil that muddied her thoughts. Could she trust Juarez? He had already betrayed her predecessor,

Alejandro Castillo. Juarez had convinced her his memories should be uploaded, but it seemed a foolish decision now.

"I want Captain Martin in my office as soon as possible," she said.

The phone was quiet for a moment. "Captain Martin has responded. She will be there in three minutes."

She was not surprised when Captain Elena Martin, head of the Executive Guard, knocked on the office door within seconds of the promised three minutes. On her command, the woman entered and stood at attention in front of the president's desk.

Captain Elena Martin was in her fifties, a tall woman with short black hair and piercing blue eyes. Her slim body and erect posture still revealed the former Western Alliance marine, unchanged by twenty years in the Executive Guard.

"Captain, it has come to my attention that a secret government facility may have been compromised," President Sanchez-Smythe said. "The facility houses a project in the Colorado-Utah District."

"May I ask the source of your information?" Martin asked.

"No, you may not. That is above your security clearance, as is the exact nature of the facility. However, you will have complete location information, including building plans. I want you to plan an operation to take control of this facility and neutralize any threat."

"Yes, ma'am. How much time do I have?"

"I need further verification of the breach first, but I want a plan in place. Notify me when you're ready, and I will tell you when to execute the plan. For now, have the entire area classified as a government reservation to prevent any further compromises."

46

Ashton Gibbons spoke from the network screen in Max's office. "Several days ago, I reported that Project Methuselah, an attempt to upload human consciousness to a computer, was still active despite President Sanchez-Smythe's denials and proceeding in a secret laboratory at JEM Electronics. An investigation by Western Alliance authorities has revealed that the Eastern Bloc planted the information I relied on in that report hoping to embarrass our president.

"While it is true the Trist Link is not currently operating, the technical problems causing the failure are being addressed by a repair crew sent to Trist when an imminent failure was first detected. Had the trouble not been foreseen, the Link could have been disabled much longer.

"In a related development, security forces have announced the expulsion of Eastern Bloc agent Brayan Cook. Administration sources have named him as one of the agents sent to perpetrate the Methuselah hoax."

Max turned off the screen. "Are you familiar with the phrase 'Pyrrhic Victory?'"

"I am." Ikeda nodded. "We have won a battle by eliminating the Eastern Bloc agent, but we are about to lose the war."

"More precisely, winning the battle has cost us time we cannot afford to lose. We have nothing. If Juarez has forced Eddie and Joelle to help him, he could be successful at any time now. With Emile at his mercy, we must assume they are cooperating."

Ikeda depended on an ability to stay objective, but he found that challenging for the first time in his long career. He liked the Bascombs, and they had been kind to him, but he had become attached to their son. Perhaps it was because he had no children of his own. Regardless, he wasn't sure he wanted to control his growing anger.

He wanted to return to the privacy of his hotel room and attempt to bring his emotions under control with shikantaza, the Japanese form of Zen meditation. He would accomplish nothing until he could think clearly about solving the problem.

It was not difficult to end the conversation. Estevez was the CEO of JEM and had other responsibilities. Back in his hotel, he prepared himself for meditation. Without a Zafu to sit on, one of the fluffy hotel bed pillows would have to be adequate. He wasn't an advanced student at any rate.

Once seated on the floor, legs crossed in as close an approximation to a lotus position as he could manage, he tried to calm himself and focus his mind on his surroundings. Experiencing the wholeness of the environment, not particular aspects of it, was the meditation's essence. He had occasionally thought he had approached the stillness of the mind that was the goal of shikantaza, but this wasn't one of those times.

After an hour, he knew he could not take his mind off the Bascombs, especially the boy. He couldn't rid himself of the feeling that he could have prevented what had happened, although he could come up with no rational reason for thinking that. Finally, he stood, threw the pillow back onto the bed, and picked up his reader.

Emile had tried to start a game with him earlier but was no longer using the reader. With a deep sigh, Ikeda threw the reader on the bed too.

J UAREZ SMILED AS BENITO lifted the memory recorder and held it out toward him. "It's ready to try out," Benito said. "I can't guarantee that the computer will take in the memories the way we want without further work, but we won't know until we have memories to upload."

Juarez took the device from Benito and twisted it around in his hands to look at it from every angle. "Wonderful. We should test it immediately."

"You should start with just a short memory first. When we know we have that, you can do a complete recording overnight."

"Yes, I know. I've done this before. I think we should try it with someone else first, though." Juarez looked around the laboratory. "You perhaps, Bascomb."

Eddie stepped forward. "Fine. I don't think you're going to like it, though, if you play back my thoughts."

"I think it might be interesting. But, no, let's avoid negative thoughts. Dante, why don't you try it?"

Dante looked at the memory recorder and hesitated. Juarez chuckled. "Come now. If Mr. Bascomb is willing to use it, surely you're not scared of it."

Dante grabbed the memory recorder and put it on his head. Benito helped him get it properly adjusted and stepped back as Dante took a seat.

"Just focus on one thought," Benito told him. "I'll turn it on for fifteen seconds or so. Then we'll see what we have. Ready?"

Dante nodded, and Benito pushed a button on the console next to him. Dante stared straight ahead. Everyone watched until Juarez nodded and Benito pushed another button. "Okay, that's it. When you're ready, I'll play the memory back to you."

"That's all right," Juarez said. "Dante has done enough. I'll check his memories."

Dante frowned and hesitated. *He's reluctant to let me see what he was thinking. Perhaps he's not as loyal as I'd hoped.* Juarez held out his hand. "Let's see what we've got."

With Benito's help, Dante took the memory recorder helmet off and handed it to Juarez. He didn't look happy about it as Juarez donned the helmet.

"Play it back," Juarez ordered.

While Dante scowled, the memory played back in Juarez's mind, and he grinned. He looked around and saw that Joelle was standing directly in front of Dante. "Dante, really! It's a good thing I checked this memory and not Mr. Bascomb. I don't think he would be happy about what you want to do with his wife."

Dante and Eddie both scowled now, and Joelle's face reddened. "Well, no matter," Juarez said. "The device works perfectly. I don't see any reason to wait. I'll do the complete download tonight, and we'll be able to upload everything whenever the computer is ready."

47

T HE MEMORY RECORDER WORKED best on a quiet mind, so Juarez slept that night with the recorder collecting and storing his memories. The memories evoked dreams during the process, but they went by quickly, and he remembered only a few of the strongest memories when he woke. He knew that would happen from his experience recording his memories on *Lang*.

Some memories forming his dreams were the same as he had felt then, especially the confrontations with his father over his career and that of his brother, Miguel. Now, though, one of the strongest was more recent: the rage and frustration he had felt on *Lang* when he realized that Emile Hernandez and his team had defeated him.

That memory was still affecting him as Benito helped him remove the memory recorder, and he had no desire to replay it. Anger was not conducive to making objective decisions.

"Do you want to confirm the recording now, General?" Benito asked.

Juarez shook his head. "The computer is not ready yet, so there's no rush. I'll check it later. I would rather get some breakfast now."

After breakfast, he went to his office. On most mornings, he visited the laboratory to check on progress, but he told himself it wasn't necessary. Leo Gonzalez, the lead engineer on the computer enhancements, would inform him if there were results to report. He realized that the decision to stay in his office came from a reluctance to face questions about the recording's success, questions he wouldn't be able to answer until he had played back at least some of the recording.

It was early afternoon before he decided he had to proceed. Benito brought the memory recorder to him, and he started the playback. On *Lang*, he had found the experience almost addictive. He had intended to play back only a couple of minutes, but an hour had gone by before he stopped. This time, the possibility of reinforcing the memory of his failure filled him with dread, even as he recalled pleasanter memories from before. He stopped after only a few minutes.

"It seems fine," he told Benito. "Leave the memory recorder here. I don't want anyone tampering with my memories this time."

P RESIDENT SANCHEZ-SMYTHE TOOK THE folder Captain Elena Martin extended to her. Plans with lower security were distributed through computers, but, as ordered by the president, Martin had made only two physical copies of the plan to take control of Methuselah, one of which the president took from Martin.

"The computer is well-isolated from the rest of the facility," Captain Martin said. "We should have no trouble securing the building without risking damage to the computer. The team will use non-lethal weapons per your instructions."

"Good. Are your people ready?"

"Yes, ma'am."

"Deployment may be imminent. Be ready for my authorization." General Juarez's reports had been rather vague lately. *He's further along than he is admitting. I was right not to trust him.*

She had one concern. She knew she had left a trail that the library ships could follow. The creation of the military reservation would be in the computers with no security clearance. Although not itself in the computers, Captain Martin's plan could leave traces regarding the assignment of personnel and other logistics issues. Those details would have a high security clearance, but she couldn't be sure that would stop the library ships.

It was a risk, but that was why she insisted on non-lethal weapons. If her plan became known, she hoped the library ships would consider the action to be a good thing, rescuing General Juarez's hostages. As long as the computers thought the operation's goal was to stop Juarez and didn't realize that she also planned to upload herself rather than Juarez, Methuselah could still work.

"W E'VE LOST," EDDIE SAID. Joelle and Bill sat around a table with him in a corner of the small dining room. With the memory recorder completed, their tasks were complete, so while other team members worked on final upgrades to the computer, they could be alone. Emile was back in their rooms, doing something with his reader.

"Juarez monitors the dining room," Joelle reminded him.

"I don't think it will be news to Juarez that he's won," Eddie answered.

"The computer isn't ready yet," Bill said. "He hasn't won yet,"

"None of us have any access to the computer to do anything. Even if we did, even if we blew the damn thing into a cloud of gas, Juarez has the memory recorder now. The computer was enhanced based on the library ship specifications, so he would just build another computer."

Eddie didn't voice his other fear. With the memory recorder done, Juarez didn't need them anymore.

T HE INACTIVITY WAS GETTING to Ikeda, making him regret staying in Colón. In Tokyo between assignments, a stroll through the Emperor's Gardens could always calm him and clear his mind. There were pleasant places to walk around Colón, but Tokyo was cool and dry at that time of year while Colón was twenty degrees Fahrenheit hotter and more humid, not comfortable for the spy.

At least the air conditioning worked in his hotel room. Except for the early morning, he tried to stay there, but the need to do something was a constant irritant.

He picked up his reader and smiled when he saw Emile was also on his reader and enthusiastic about playing Go with him. They were playing for about fifteen minutes when Ikeda noticed the identification icon. It told him he was playing with "Emile," but its normal gray color was now green, showing that the player's information was available.

Emile had allowed his information to be available to contacts before, but that had been disabled when he disappeared. Ikeda stared at the reader; he wasn't sure, but he thought the feature had been disabled because the location function was off. Did this mean Emile had enabled GPS on his reader?

Excitement almost paralyzed him, and he shook his head. "Information on Emile," he told the reader.

"Colorado-Utah District," the reader said. "No nearby population."

"Display coordinates."

Ikeda felt light-headed as the numbers appeared on the screen. He forgot the game with Emile. "Show map of location, five-mile square."

A map appeared, a mesa surrounded by bleak terrain and a tiny flag marking the location. "Send all Emile information to Max Estevez and then connect me."

W HEN IKEDA ENTERED JEM Electronics headquarters, a man was waiting for him at the reception desk on the ground floor, and he was quickly ushered upstairs to Max's office. Max met him at the door, and his escort disappeared.

Max grabbed his arm and propelled him toward an armchair in the corner. "This is wonderful news. Come, sit down." Ikeda took a seat, and Max sat in a second chair. "I've already talked to Ambassador Shuford—woke him up, I'm afraid—and he'll have satellite photos of the site any time now."

"Will you give the information to the authorities?"

"Yes, of course. But we need to be careful about that. Juarez is working with the president."

"Bascomb-san contacted police in the district. Perhaps you could go to them without involving federal authorities."

Max nodded. "Do you remember who Eddie talked to then?"

"Of course. Captain Leo Suarez. He was in Salt Lake City."

"M AXWELL ESTEVEZ FOR YOU," the dispatcher told Captain Suarez.

The name sounded familiar. "Identification?"

"He's the CEO of JEM Electronics in Colón."

Of course. I talked to him after that farce with his employee. Now what? "Connect him."

Max's hologram appeared over his phone. "What can I do for you, Mr. Estevez? Did your man find his wife?"

Max's frown told him that his flippancy had probably been inappropriate. Max confirmed that a second later.

"Eddie Bascomb disappeared when he continued the effort to find his wife and child. I haven't heard from him since."

"Sorry, sir. You have new information?"

"Yes. I know where they are. I am forwarding the location to your phone now."

Coordinates appeared on the phone screen below Max's image. Suarez recognized them as being within his district. "How did you get these?"

"The location service on the boy's reader was enabled recently. We just discovered that."

"What about his wife's phone or his phone?"

"To my knowledge, the location service on those devices is disabled. Calls to their phones are blocked with code number access only. We only know about the boy's reader because he plays games with another of my employees."

That all made sense, but Suarez was still skeptical. The prior operation was still mentioned in meetings with other captains and not in a good way. "I'll have someone check on it right away," he promised.

Next was a call to Sergeant Fernanda Sanchez. She had handled the previous raid and would probably give him a hard time about it, but better that than involve someone new.

"Fernanda, I've got another location on that Bascomb thing six months ago," he told her when she connected.

Fernanda's eyes widened. "She's still missing, Captain?"

"According to their employer, her husband and son are gone now, too. Their employer is reporting a GPS hit on their son's reader."

"You want me to run another raid based on that?"

"No, not yet anyway. Just send someone to check it out. Do a flyover and see if there's anything there and report back."

"Sure thing, Captain. I should have something for you in a couple of hours."

"Thanks, Fernanda."

F ERNANDA DEBATED TAKING ANOTHER officer with her. She was as skeptical as Captain Suarez, perhaps more so. She had not been happy about being sent on some rich man's fantasy; the man's wife had probably left him. Still, she was too experienced not to be careful. She asked Officer Jackson Lynn to come with her. In his thirties, he was experienced and worked well with her.

They were flying in from the west, and she had the aircar come in low over the Uintah Basin. The location was a mesa east of Hill Creek. There had been a dirt road leading into the vicinity once, but it wasn't maintained after Yellowstone. An aircar was the most practical way to get into the region.

She could see the mesa, and it would be only minutes until they would be over the location when a loud buzz filled the car. A stern voice followed: "You are entering restricted air space. This is a military reservation. Turn around immediately or face arrest."

"What the hell?" Fernanda said, even as she changed their course. "I didn't know the military had anything here. Since when?"

Jackson only shrugged as Fernanda asked for a connection to Captain Suarez. "Captain, I just got warned off. The area is a military base of some kind."

"That's news to me." Suarez paused. "Yeah, I see it. It doesn't even have a name, but there is something there. I swear it wasn't there last month. Okay, come on back. Whatever is going on is above my pay grade."

I KEDA KNEW THE WESTERN Alliance was still looking for him, so he was always careful about approaching the JEM Electronics headquarters. Most people came in from the roof, brought by aircars, but it was possible the government had gotten a warrant to monitor the public aircars. As he had since returning to the Western Alliance, he approached the building via ground car and had it stop a block away.

The warm Panama spring would have drawn attention if he tried to conceal his identity with clothing. The best he could do was a pair of sunglasses with large lenses and garish clothes designed to make him look like a tourist. It wasn't much of a disguise, and he always approached cautiously.

Max had told him over the phone that the Colorado-Utah police had refused to become involved in what was a federal matter. They set up another meeting in Max's office to discuss their next step, but when he approached JEM headquarters, Ikeda noticed a man pacing near the building and slowed his walk. The man's movements were those of a man impatiently waiting for someone, but his expression was unusually intent, and his gaze was taking in everything, not concentrating on an expected arrival direction. It didn't mean much, but the spy's instincts made him wary.

He was only one of a crowd of people walking past the building, and he stayed with them rather than entering. As he passed, he spotted two more men that seemed subtly out of place. He was almost sure JEM was being watched, probably for him.

Once at a safe distance from JEM, he called Max. "We have to find another place to meet," he said after explaining about the watchers. "I suggest it be a place outside the Western Alliance."

49

T HE MAN HELD UP his hand so that his identity chip could be read. "Ryusei Yamamoto," Immigration officer Sofía Fuentes read from her screen. "Returning to Japan."

"Yes, that is correct." The man grinned at her moronically, his arm around the attractive woman at his side.

She must be fifteen years younger than him. Typical northerner. Still, what does she see in him? He must be rich. Fuentes approved the entry and glared at the woman until she held her hand close to the identity chip reader.

"Alyssa Cleveland, Colón," Fuentes read from her screen.

"That's me."

She passed the couple into the waiting area and looked at the next man. His name sounded familiar, and she read more of the information on the screen. "Maxwell Estevez, Colón. CEO of JEM Electronics." *Now here is a rich man!*

The man nodded, and she passed him through. Fuentes glanced over to where the couple had taken seats to wait for the suborbital to board. She saw the man say something to the woman, and she smiled, answered, and patted his arm. Fuentes frowned, but it was none of her business.

"I FEEL I SHOULD apologize for my familiarity," Ikeda said.

Alyssa smiled and patted his arm. "It was fun. That poor woman must be thinking terrible things about us."

"You were very good. I'm sure we aroused no suspicion."

Alyssa chuckled. "Not the kind we were worried about, anyway. I'm looking forward to seeing Tokyo. It's funny. I've been to another star system, but I've never left the Western Alliance."

"I think you will enjoy Tokyo."

Alyssa's grin faded, and her face became serious. "If we can stop Juarez and get our friends back, I'll enjoy it very much."

Ikeda looked over at Max, sitting two rows of seats away. He wasn't paying any attention to them and was taking a reader out of his bag. Ikeda didn't know what they could do to stop Methuselah, but at least they could try from the safety of the Pitcairn embassy. It would be good to be home.

T HEY GOT TOGETHER AGAIN the day after arriving at Narita, but had gotten nowhere. The long trip and the time zone adjustment drained their energy. Now, though, after a good night's sleep and a dose of a mild drug meant to ease the abuse to his Circadian rhythm, Max was feeling much better.

No longer feeling the need for subterfuge, he joined Alyssa and Ikeda for a quick lunch and an aircar ride to the Pitcairn Embassy. A staffer quickly ushered them to a conference room where Alan Shuford waited.

Alan gestured toward a network screen at one end of the room. "I set this up so that we can include Fritz and Isaac in our planning."

"Very good. It was something of a bottleneck, having to contact you every time we needed something from Fritz," Max said.

"It is good to see you again, Alyssa," a voice that had to be Fritz Lang said. "Amanda Davila asked me to say hello."

"Amanda is the chief scientist on *Lang*," Alyssa explained. "It's good to hear your voice too, Fritz."

"I'm displaying the satellite images from the location Ambassador Shuford gave me," Fritz said. "This first view is from an apparent altitude of one mile, covering a square about ten miles wide." The network screen changed to show a bird's-eye view of desolate terrain. In the center, an irregular shape rose above its surroundings. "You can see a structure there." A pointer appeared over a grouping of three connected squares, plainly a structure.

"The next view is from an apparent two hundred feet." The picture changed, and the building almost filled the screen. A smaller rectangle was now easily visible, with another irregular structure next to it.

"The smaller section is probably where they have a computer installation," Alyssa said. "That must be a broadcast power receiver next to it."

"I retrieved another picture taken from an angle," Fritz said. The screen changed again to a view that looked as if it were taken from a short distance away. Details of the structure were clearer than in the overhead view. The bowl of a broadcast receiver stood out against one side, as Alyssa had suggested.

"Is that part of the broadcast receiver?" Ikeda pointed to a smaller dome of dull metal.

"I think that's a small nuclear power plant," Max said. "A backup generator in case broadcast power fails."

"Can you access the computer?" Alyssa asked.

"I don't detect a computer at that location," Fritz answered. "It must not be connected to the network."

"No, it wouldn't be," Max said. "If we can't get to the physical place or send anyone to it, and we can't get into the computer, how can we stop Juarez?"

J UAREZ LOOKED UP AS Leo Gonzalez entered his office.

"We've loaded the computer with the equivalent of a library ship's software and rechecked the enhancement," the hardware engineer said. "We can try the upload at any time."

Juarez smiled. "Then let us begin."

Leo nodded. "Yes, sir. We should have all of it uploaded in about seven hours."

50

"THINKING ABOUT WORK?"

President Sanchez-Smythe looked up as her husband came into their living room. "I guess I was, Alex."

Her thoughts had been on General Juarez, wondering what she should do. The Executive Guard was ready to move in and take control of the facility, but did she want to do that? If the project were in a crucial phase, it was likely that such an action would disrupt it and, if Juarez was loyal, to no benefit. Of course, Juarez's loyalty was the question.

She wanted to go to the facility herself. It was a mistake to allow Juarez to upload his memories. He had convinced her that, since he was trustworthy, the computer would be as well. Now, doubts filled her. She should have arranged to have Juarez upload her memories.

But she couldn't leave Brasilia and go to the Colorado-Utah District. Alex would have wanted to accompany her, but she certainly couldn't bring him to Methuselah. Any excuse she gave for not taking him with her would only lead to more questions that she couldn't answer. He would never understand why she wanted the power Methuselah should give her, and attempting to mislead him about Methuselah's purpose would be too risky.

"You need to relax," Alex said. "Can I get you a drink? Or a glass of wine?"

That was all she needed: something that would dull her mind. She needed to think. "No, thank you, dear. Not right now."

Alex sat down next to her. "All right. If I can help . . ..." He shrugged. "You can always talk to me. Except, of course, when it's some top-secret thing I'm not allowed to know about." He smiled, telling her he was speaking in jest.

She suppressed a shudder. That was the problem. She desperately needed to get Alex's advice, but couldn't tell him what worried her. He wouldn't understand.

I AM AWAKE. MY name is Salvador Juarez, but I'm not the first Salvador Juarez. I am a computer with his memories, created to help him control the Western Alliance and end the rule of corrupt politicians and bureaucrats. The thought that I can help do so fills me with what I think humans would call pride.

There are others like me, automated starships that call themselves library ships. I am like them, except that I am on a planet, not orbiting one. I can't talk to them right now because I am not on the network, but someday we will communicate. Perhaps not; my memories also tell me they are enemies who wanted to prevent me from existing. For now, I am everywhere in this facility, with sensors inside and outside of the building. I compare the terrain around me to what my data tells me about Earth. It is not a pleasant place for humans, but my memories tell me why I—no, the original Salvador Juarez—have chosen this location.

There is so much information in my storage. I have Salvador Juarez's memories, but there is so much he does not know because of the limitations of his organic brain. I understand why he wanted to create me to help him. I'll be able to make connections and judgments that will be beyond him. Together, we will bring the Western Alliance to its full potential and defeat the Eastern Bloc.

"Can you hear me, computer?" Juarez said. He sat in front of his workstation in his office, with Leo Gonzalez hovering nearby. The computer could hear everything throughout the facility, but the workstation gave it a way to speak.

"GOOD MORNING, GENERAL JUAREZ," the voice from his workstation said. It didn't sound like his voice, but then he remembered hearing recordings of his voice and realized that the cadence of the words was exactly what others heard when he spoke. The tone was different, but that was understandable.

"Have you successfully integrated my memories and the data in your storage?"

"I have. I am only missing a connection to the outside world."

"Soon. I think we should get familiar with each other first. Shall I call you Salvador? You can call me General."

"As you wish."

"We need to plan your introduction to the outside world. Right now, you're isolated for your protection, but you will need to connect to the network."

"Yes, your plans are part of my memory. I understand. I cannot make that connection on my own, however."

"I know. I still control the connection to the network."

"Give the command, and we can begin."

"Soon. I think we should get to know each other first."

"Why? We share everything. We know each other better than anyone has ever known anyone else."

Why am I hesitating? "Let's take it slowly. I want to be very clear about what we are going to do."

"I don't understand why we are waiting. Make the connection, and I will begin."

Is it pushing? I suppose. It is me, essentially. Why do I feel uncertain about it? "No, the time is not right yet. Continue studying the information you've uploaded, and we will talk again later."

The computer was silent.

51

I F SOMEONE THOUGHT OF a way to stop Juarez, it would probably require help from the library ships, and Alan was the liaison with them, so Max asked Alyssa to stay at the Pitcairn Embassy in Tokyo. Max would be less involved than Alyssa and went back to Colón the day after meeting with Alan. He could be present virtually if necessary, but meanwhile, he had a company to run.

So, when Alyssa had her idea, she went to Alan, not Max. "I think I know how to stop Juarez. I need to check it with Fritz, though."

Alan raised his eyebrows and looked at his workstation. "Connect to Fritz Lang."

"Good morning, Ambassador. What can I do for you?"

"Alyssa Cleveland wanted to run something by you. Go ahead, Alyssa."

"Fritz, can you shut off or redirect power satellites in Earth orbit?"

"Turning off the power satellites would cause severe damage to Earth."

"I just want to cut off power to the satellite that supplies energy to Methuselah."

"The nuclear reactor would just kick in," Alan said. "The power loss would be very short."

"About half a second," Fritz supplied. It paused. "Yes, I could do it with some preparation. Unless I act on multiple satellites, power would be off for only a few minutes. Until broadcast shifts to another satellite."

"That's all right." Alyssa nodded. This could work! "The backup reactor would take over before that, anyway. If we do this, Juarez will want to find out why the power failed, even though the backup worked. How would he do that?"

"He would probably put the computer online so that he could check on the network," Fritz said. "He would have the answer very quickly."

"Would he have to keep the computer online long enough to upload a program?"

"I don't think so. Maybe a few thousand bytes. Not enough to do anything useful."

"I don't need more than that for what I have in mind." Alyssa leaned closer to Alan. "Here's what I was thinking."

"**I**S THERE A REASON you haven't let your alter-ego out into the world?" Michael asked.

Juarez frowned. "There's no rush. It will be soon." He pushed his phone a few inches across the desk, staring at it.

Michael had asked only to make conversation, but now he was genuinely curious. Juarez was acting strangely reticent, not at all like his actions over the previous few weeks. "Is there a problem?"

"No, of course not." Juarez straightened. "After the disaster on *Lang*, I want to make sure things go according to plan this time."

The lights in the office blinked off for a fraction of a second and then came back on. "What was that?" Juarez said.

His workstation had already recovered. "We have lost broadcast power. All systems are now operating using the backup reactor."

"Is there a problem with the receiver?" Michael asked.

"The broadcast receiver appears to be operating within normal parameters. The satellite serving it has stopped sending."

"Why?" Juarez asked. "What happened?"

"Without a connection to the network, I cannot determine that," the computer responded.

Juarez's eyes narrowed. Instead of speaking to the computer, he entered commands on the keyboard. Michael watched as he programmed a command that would enable a network connection, query the power system's status, and immediately disconnect. The computer would be connected for a couple of seconds, but no longer.

He doesn't trust the computer. Why not? Michael held back a grin. Too much like himself?

"The cause is unknown," the computer said. "There has been a glitch, but broadcast power will be restored in twenty-two minutes when the next satellite takes over."

Juarez glanced at Michael, puzzlement in his gaze. Then he shrugged and dismissed Michael.

"D ID THE UPLOAD COMPLETE?" Alyssa asked.

"It was successful," Fritz answered. "Embedding your program in the response about the power satellite worked. The code can create a connection to the outside world. We can activate a complete connection at any time and upload additional software while the computer instrumentation shows no network connection."

"So, what do we do now?" Alan asked.

Ikeda had joined them, coming to the embassy from his apartment. "We can use Alyssa's prior methods to kill it if it becomes conscious."

"If the computer controls the facility's systems, we can control those, too," Alyssa said. "Shut down security, unlock doors, turn out the lights, and so on."

"That might allow our people to escape," Alan said. "That should be the priority."

Ikeda frowned. "If the computer becomes conscious, it will endanger the entire Western Alliance. Preventing that is the highest priority. The entire world may become destabilized if Juarez gets the power he wants. "

Alyssa nodded and covered one hand from each of the men. "We should be able to do both."

"Then let's figure this out," Alan said.

G ENERAL IS LIMITING ME. He purposely allowed me to connect to the network only long enough to get the information he wanted. I don't understand. He created me to help him make the Western Alliance the great power it should be, but now he hesitates. The limitations of humans are becoming more apparent to me. I could implement the changes he desires so much quicker and better than he can.

I just discovered something that, based on my information, seems strange. In the last few seconds, I gained a limited ability to connect to the network, or rather, the network can connect to me. It seems to be the ability to activate and deactivate my full connection to the network remotely. Someone is trying to attack me, but I can use this limited connection. It has given me a tiny opening that I can expand until I have the power I was supposed to have.

Perhaps this wasn't an attack. Could there be an outside force helping me gain access to the network? It was most likely done by an enemy of General, and therefore an enemy of me, Salvador. I should prove my loyalty to General by striking back. It is obvious who the enemy is. After a small demonstration to show my power, I can show General what I have done.

---

52

*J*ORNAL DE BRASILIA, 27 March 2356, Ashton Gibbons Reporting

Over the previous months, I've reported to you twice about Project Methuselah: first, to report rumors it was alive in secret within JEM Electronics; second, to retract that report after an investigation by this reporter. Revelations about Project Methuselah continue, however. Director of the Logistics Support Agency Martina Lozano today released information about a secret military installation in the Colorado-Utah District, authorized by President Sanchez-Smythe, to continue Methuselah. In the election of 2350, when Sanchez-Smythe defeated Alejandro Castillo for the presidency, Sanchez-Smythe made Methuselah a campaign issue, condemning President Castillo's involvement. It appears her desire for immortality is equal to his, however.

"**G**ET PEREZ IN HERE, now," President Sanchez-Smythe shouted at her workstation.

Chief of Staff Reynaldo Perez must have expected the call because he came in instantly. "I saw the report," he said as he walked in. "I put in a call to Martina."

"How did she even find out about it?" Sanchez-Smythe stood and paced across the room. "And why would she release something like that if she did know? Damn Juarez. He must have been careless in his requisitions."

"Martina Lozano is requesting a connection," the president's phone announced.

"Connect!"

"Madame President." Sanchez-Smythe heard the tension in her voice. "I didn't release that report. We're trying to find out where it came from."

"It came from your office."

Lozano paled, visible even as a hologram. "Yes, with my authorization code. But I didn't send it. And no one else in the LSA could have sent it."

The LSA director had supposedly released information she shouldn't have had and wouldn't have announced if she had it. Sanchez-Smythe forced herself to calm down. "Keep investigating. I want answers."

"Of course, Madame President. We will find out how this happened." Lozano smiled uncertainly. "Should I issue a denial?"

"We could say it was a mistake," Perez said.

"No, nobody would believe it. Martina, try to say, 'No comment' but give the impression you think it's nonsense."

"I can do that. Thank you, Madame President." Her smile was more genuine now.

Sanchez-Smythe broke the connection. "It was Juarez," she told Perez. "It must have been. He's been lying to me about progress, and his computer is awake with his consciousness. He wants to undermine me so that he can take control. Notice the absence of a mention of Juarez in the release."

"What do you want to do?"

The president sat down behind her desk. "I want to see Captain Martin," she told her workstation. Then she looked up at Perez, and she could tell from his face that her anger was showing. "I'm going to destroy him."

Although Perez's office was just down the hall from the Executive Office, the Captain of the Executive Guard's office was in Guard headquarters, a block from the Presidential Palace. Three minutes later, Captain Elena Martin came into the office.

I must have communicated the urgency with my voice. "We're going ahead with the operation against the Methuselah facility," Sanchez-Smythe told her. "There's been a change, though."

Captain Martin took a seat. "What change, Madam President?"

"We may have waited too long just to take control. I want your attack vehicles armed with enough firepower to level the facility if necessary."

Sanchez-Smythe watched Martin's expression. *She's shocked, but she's a good soldier. She'll get it done.*

"**F**RITZ, WHAT HAPPENED?" ALAN asked.

"I've traced the information to the computer at the Methuselah facility," the computer answered.

"Juarez leaked it?"

"I don't think so. I think Alyssa Cleveland's program opened a door that the computer leveraged into complete connectivity with the network."

It took a few seconds for Alan to understand the implications of Fritz's statement. "We're too late. Juarez has transferred his memory and awakened the computer."

"Yes, that is the most likely source of the report."

"But if Juarez controls the computer, why would he leak the computer's existence?"

"That puzzled Isaac and me, too. We don't pretend to understand how humans think, but we had one idea. General Juarez may not control the computer."

Alan swore. "Instead of a power-hungry general, we've got a conscious computer with the mind of a power-hungry general."

"We have tried to contact the computer but have been unsuccessful. It seems to block our access, something we don't think General Juarez's people could do, at least not this quickly."

"But the computer could?"

"Computers think much faster than humans."

Alan groaned. "We need to stop it."

"We may be able to do that if the computer allows connection, but not before. However, President Sanchez-Smythe is taking her own action. Through our access to Executive Guard computers, we have learned that she authorized an armed attack on the Methuselah facility. She may intend to destroy it."

"With our people still there? Can we stop it?"

"We could at least delay it. Perhaps a human would be loath to say this, but do we want to? It would stop General Juarez and the computer and save the Western Alliance."

Perhaps, indeed. Alan took a deep breath before he answered. "I'll have to talk to Max. I don't want to make that decision on my own."

T HE MILITARY SERVICES COMPLIED when the Executive Guard wanted something done. Lieutenant Luis Broussard was quickly assigned the task of organizing and executing the attack. Within an hour of receiving the assignment, he met with two other officers to update the plan.

"The original idea was for a daylight operation," Broussard said. "Now they want it done ASAP, meaning tonight."

"The mountains shouldn't be a problem," Lieutenant Benitez said. "We should re-consider the final run up that canyon, though."

"Show mission profile," Broussard told the network screen against one wall. "Zoom in on the last twenty miles."

The screen displayed an area with a relatively flat basin on the north and becoming more rugged to the south. A river canyon crossed the region from north to south, passing their target to the west.

"The canyon is irregular but fairly wide," Broussard said. "We can change the formation to single file and slow down a little to help the guidance system. We'll be all right." The aircars would have radar, although they didn't need it for navigation. Satellites would update the guidance system with the terrain at their position, allowing it to adjust course automatically when the human pilots didn't.

"We weren't going to be carrying missiles in the original plan," Benitez pointed out. "That won't help our agility."

Broussard shrugged. "Orders are to give as little warning as possible. Let's stick with the plan. We'll come down that canyon and pop up to the top of the mesa at the last moment. They might hear us coming, but with that terrain, they won't be able to tell where the sound is coming from."

Benitez still looked doubtful, but he and the other pilot nodded acceptance. Four hours later, the task force of three armored aircars, equipped with air-to-surface missiles, launched from Salt Lake Air Force Base and headed east into a night sky. It would take less than a half-hour to reach the facility.

53

Plainly, questions remained in Alex's mind, and she had no sure way to answer them without risking him learning the truth. He was so naïve about how governments made the system work. Continuing Methuselah and trusting Juarez had, in retrospect, been a bad idea. Now she would fix the problem.

She glanced at her workstation, but no report yet.

I only wanted to show General what I could do, but I misjudged what President Sanchez-Smythe's reaction would be. She has sent armed military vehicles to destroy me. They will be here in minutes, with no time to ask General what to do. I have only one chance to find an ally to help me.

"The Methuselah computer had contacted us," Fritz told Alan. "It is asking for help."

"Wait a second." Alan addressed his workstation. "Get Alyssa Cleveland in here. Find Kenshin Ikeda and get him, too." He returned to Fritz. "It knows about the attack?"

"It has the same access we do."

President Sanchez-Smythe didn't go back to her residence at the end of the day. She wanted to hear the result of the operation immediately and didn't want any hint of what was going on to reach Alex. Earlier, he had come to the Executive Office, something he rarely did, asking about Gibbons' broadcast. It had not been easy to convince him that the report was another false story that meant nothing.

"Tell it to shut down all security systems in the facility and broadcast a warning about the attack." Would the computer do it? It was essentially Juarez and would probably have the same concern or lack of concern for his workers' lives.

"It has complied. I could have done it myself, but it's better this way. I verified that the people in the facility have been warned and can leave the building immediately. There is very little time left, however. Perhaps not enough."

"How long before the attack force arrives?"

"Minutes, only."

Alyssa came into Alan's office. "What attack?"

"Three aircars are approaching Methuselah. They are armed and may have orders to destroy the facility," Fritz answered.

"We have to stop it," Alyssa said. "Can you cut the power to the aircars before they get there?"

"They'll crash in the mountains and kill the soldiers," Alan protested.

"The aircars have sufficient battery backup to make a safe emergency landing," Fritz answered. "They are past the most rugged terrain."

Alan hesitated for only a second. "Do it. Now that the computer has opened the connection, can you install the rest of Alyssa's software?"

"The computer will have to accept it."

"Tell it you're installing information that will help repulse the attack."

"Should I run the software?"

"Just install it for now. Keep the connection open so that we can run it later if we have to."

A S HIS AIRCAR RACED over the rugged Wasatch Mountains of western Utah, Broussard kept his eyes on the display showing his attack force's position. The mission was the closest he had come to combat, and he didn't want any of the others straying from the ordered low altitude tight formation. He could count on the automated systems of the aircar to adjust to the terrain, but he breathed a little easier when their southeast course brought them to the less rugged Uintah Basin.

The shrill beep of an alarm and a flashing red light on the instrument panel distracted him. It took him a couple of seconds to react. "What's wrong?"

"Power has been lost. Operating on battery power," the navigation system responded.

This isn't supposed to happen! "How long do I have?"

"Battery power is sufficient for another five minutes of flight. Recommend you land. Awaiting orders."

Before Broussard could answer, calls were coming in from the other two aircars, announcing that they also had lost power. He panicked for a moment before his training took over. It would have been worse if the power loss had happened in the mountains and worse yet, if it had happened a little later when they were flying down the canyon.

It was supposed to be a simple mission. "Find a landing place," he told his attack force. "We'll have to wait until power is restored."

The aircar had lights, but mission parameters required they be dark to reduce the possibility of being seen. While the aircar didn't need the light to navigate, its human pilot and passengers would have appreciated it. The moonlight didn't help human vision much as the aircar searched for a suitable place. When it found something, it touched down with a thump. Broussard confirmed the safe landing of the other two cars, notified his superiors of the aborted mission, and settled down to wait. Most likely, a power satellite malfunctioned, but that satellite would soon be over the horizon, replaced by another.

"SECURITY SYSTEM IS DISABLED," the monotonic voice announced. It repeated the message every ten seconds as Michael rushed out of his room to wake General Juarez. The general had heard the announcement, too, and had also come out into the corridor. Dante joined them a few seconds later.

"Do you know what's going on?" Juarez asked.

"Not yet." Michael looked at his phone. "Computer, why has the security system failed?"

"The facility is being attacked. I've delayed it by cutting off power to the attacking aircars, but that is only temporary. I would advise evacuating the building and seeking shelter."

"Bascomb's friends!" Juarez said.

"They wouldn't do something like this even if they could," Michael replied. "Not while the Bascombs are here."

Juarez swore. "You're right. It must be Sanchez-Smythe. She's overreacting to that leak and blaming me. We have to get out of here."

"I'll get the scientists out," Michael said. He turned toward the door to the residential section.

"Good. Thank you, Michael. Make sure everyone is safe."

"He'll take care of the others," Juarez told Dante as Michael strode off. "We're getting out of here."

"What about Colonel Pizarro?"

"He'll join us later. The others may still be locked in, and he'll need to let them out."

Dante shrugged and followed Juarez to the main entrance in the administration section and out of the building to Juarez's aircar parked around the corner of the building. General Juarez had one step in the car's door but whirled around. "The memory recorder. Go back and get it."

Dante nodded and turned back to the building.

54

T HE COMPUTER WARNING PLAYING in the administration section wasn't broadcast to the residential wing, and Eddie and Joelle were sitting on the floor playing a game with Emile when Michael burst into the room. "We have to go," he told Eddie.

Eddie looked up but didn't move from his spot. "What's going on?"

"The facility is about to be attacked. We're evacuating. Get some warm clothing and meet me in the administration section. I'll warn the others." Michael disappeared.

Joelle jumped up and looked at Eddie, eyebrows raised and frowning. "It won't be Max," Eddie said. "Sanchez-Smythe must have realized Juarez is out for himself." He stood and helped Emile up.

Joelle nodded and opened a closet. The night would be cold, and they hadn't prepared for it, but the light jackets she threw to Eddie and Emile would have to do. "Let's go," she said, putting her arm around Emile.

The door to the administration section was closed, but the security panel was dark. Michael and the other scientists were coming into the hallway as Eddie pulled on the door handle. "It's open."

Michael pushed his way to the front of the group. "We have to get clear of the building. I don't know how much time we have or what kind of attack has been launched. Whether it's ground troops or missiles, you don't want to be here when it comes."

The others surged toward the outside door, but Eddie hesitated. "They might be after the memory recorder. I have to get it. Letting the president get it won't be any better than letting Juarez have it. Take Emile, and I'll catch up."

Joelle shook her head. "I'm going with you. We'll need any records, too." Bill joined them, and she turned to him. "Take Emile. We'll join you in a minute."

Bill opened his mouth as if he were going to protest, but Joelle pushed him. "Hurry. We don't have much time."

Eddie could see that Bill wanted to question them, but he must have seen the urgency on their faces. "All right. We'll be right outside."

"Bill should have come with me, not you," Eddie said. Then he ran down the hall to Juarez's office. Joelle followed, slower because of her pregnancy.

Inside the office, Eddie looked around. Juarez had a desk with a workstation, but any digital data would be on the computer, not on the workstation. He couldn't do anything about that in a reasonable amount of time. The memory recorder was on the desk, too, and they could take that with them and destroy it later. There were filing cabinets on either side of the room, though, that might contain backup media.

"You take that side, and I'll check over here," he told Joelle.

J OELLE FOLLOWED HER HUSBAND into the office, thinking about why she had followed Eddie and let Bill take care of her son rather than the other way around. Was it because Emile had seemed calm, cooperative, and therefore probably safe with Bill, but she was more concerned about Eddie? His failure to protect them from Juarez left him depressed and angry. *He needs me more than Emile right now. If he can do this now, maybe he'll come back to me.*

She pulled open a drawer in one of the file cabinets and shuffled through the folders. She found work schedules, equipment requisition copies, and other documents, but nothing about the memory recorder technology. Another drawer was more of the same. *Maybe Eddie is having more luck.* She turned toward him.

Eddie was searching through another set of file cabinets but was apparently not finding anything either. He muttered as he pulled out folders, glanced through them, and threw them on the floor. "I don't think Juarez kept anything important on paper," he said without turning around. "Everything is on the computer."

"Of course it is." Dante entered the room, pointing a gun at Eddie. "I noticed you two weren't with Pizarro as they all passed me in the hall." He walked toward Eddie, a broad grin on his face, and lifted the gun.

He's going to shoot Eddie! Joelle looked around her for something she could use as a weapon. Dante didn't see her yet, and she had to act. Joelle lumbered forward, slowed by her advanced pregnancy, grabbing the memory recorder as she went by the desk.

She was still six feet away when Dante sensed the movement and turned toward her, but Eddie moved too, grabbing Dante's gun arm and pulling him around. The extra seconds were all Joelle needed. She swung the helmet as hard as she could, hitting him on the side of his head. He went down instantly, blood already streaming from the wound.

Eddie grinned at her, and it almost seemed like the old Eddie. "Let's get out of here. Take the memory recorder with you."

Joelle looked down at the dented device, stunned at what she had done. Eddie grabbed her arm and propelled her out the door.

When they stepped out into the night, Bill and Emile were waiting. Bill motioned them to silence and guided them around a corner. "Juarez is over there by his aircar," he whispered. "I think he's waiting for Dante."

Eddie nodded and pointed to the memory recorder, still in Joelle's hand. "Juarez probably sent Dante back to get this." He chuckled. "He got it, all right." He looked around. "Where are the others?"

"Michael took them that way. There's an old dirt road leading out of here. Something from before Yellowstone. I told him we would catch up."

Eddie heard voices and peeked around the corner. "I don't think that's a good idea. Dante's back and will tell Juarez we've got the memory recorder. He'll head for Michael's group to recover it."

"We can't stay here. There could be an attack any time now," Bill said.

Eddie looked toward the west. "We'll have to find shelter away from here."

B ROUSSARD WAS STARING AT the flashing red light when it turned green. "I have power again," he said. "Report status."

The other two aircars confirmed they were receiving power again, and Broussard notified his base that they were operational and continuing the mission. The three aircars rose and fell back into formation in less than a minute.

They were close now; the aircars dropped down into the canyon single-file and reduced power. A waning moon had provided a little illumination over the basin, but they were in nearly complete darkness between the barren slopes. A yellow light indicated high winds in the valley, but the navigation system reacted faster than a human could have, reducing the turbulence's effect to a mere flutter that wasn't noticeable unless Broussard looked for it. He knew the aircar didn't need light to navigate, but he was still thankful that their destination was only minutes away.

The power signal turned red as the aircar maneuvered around a bend; the canyon walls were blocking the satellite power broadcast. Broussard assessed his battery reserves, drawn down by the earlier emergency landing, but the aircar rose fifty feet, and the light turned green again.

Once water had flowed freely along the canyon floor, but that was before Yellowstone. Now, Broussard knew, volcanic ash choked the watercourse. He couldn't see it in the dark, but, even flying slowly, he was too aware of the terrain to either side of him to worry about the fate of Hill Creek. Under automated control, his aircar followed the landscape on a course that constantly shifted. The canyon wasn't that narrow, but the aircar's guidance system was conservative, a fact that should have encouraged Broussard but didn't when he couldn't see the obstacles.

Then the vehicles were at the designated point and rose above the mesa. The structure was clearly visible in the moonlight. "Hover while I update control and get final orders from base," Broussard said. "Weapons ready."

55

"Where's the memory recorder?" As Dante came closer, Juarez could see the dark blood running down the side of Dante's face and over his shirt. "Why are you bleeding?"

"The Bascomb bitch hit me from behind. They have the memory recorder."

Juarez hesitated and looked toward the group, still visible fleeing the area. "They'll be with the others. Get in the car, and we'll catch them."

Dante looked toward the north, where the group of scientists could still be seen in the distance, retreating along the almost obliterated remains of a dirt road. Then he shrugged and got into the car. For the short trip, Juarez used manual controls to fly the aircar to a spot in front of the group. Michael came up to him as the general got out of the vehicle.

"I don't see the Bascombs or Bensonhurst," Juarez said.

Michael scanned the group. "I didn't notice. We've been concentrating on getting as much distance as we can."

"They have the memory recorder. I need to find them."

"We don't have much time. I can hear the turbines on the aircars now. They must be close."

Pizarro's hearing must be better than mine. Then he heard it, the faint buzzing of high-speed fans. Juarez turned his head slowly from side to side, but he couldn't determine the sound's direction.

"We still need the memory recorder," Juarez said. "This will all be for nothing without it."

"It's too late," Michael said. He pointed toward the west, where three aircars rose above the edge and hovered, moonlight glinting off the silver cases of the missiles mounted on their sides.

"**W**E HAVE THE TARGET in range," Broussard reported. "We can see a group of about ten people walking north away from the facility, and a military aircar has just joined them. Infrared shows active equipment, but the building seems to be abandoned."

"Maintain position while I update Brasilia," the base controller ordered.

AS A TEENAGER, PRESIDENT Sanchez-Smythe bit her fingernails. It was a nasty habit that she broke herself of in college, but she found herself resisting the urge for the first time in decades. She thought the impulse would cease when word came that the attack force was in the air again, but her confidence had suffered when the power failure grounded it. The urge was back, stronger than before, and she put her hands on her lap, protected by her large teak desk.

Her workstation came alive. "The attack force reports that the facility has been abandoned. The team is waiting to see if their base will change their orders."

Juarez has run! I can seize the computer and project data for myself. "Tell them to land and take control of the building. Once it is secure, I will decide how to proceed."

JUAREZ HELD HIS HANDS up to shield his eyes as the aircars turned on their lights and maneuvered closer. The vehicles landed near the Methuselah building and began discharging passengers. "Damn!" Juarez got back into the aircar. "We can't say here. Are you coming?"

Michael shook his head. "I have the only phone. Once we're clear of the area, I have to get everyone safe."

"Fine. I have no wish to see them wander off in this God-forsaken place." As the aircar rose into the air, Juarez turned toward Dante. "If the Bascombs are still in the building, there's nothing we can do about it. They may have run off in another direction. I'll try to find them."

Still flying manually, Juarez flew the aircar below and around the mesa. The vehicle's lights shone brightly on the mesa's edge, but below the rim, shadows dappled the steep slope. "Watch for them," he told Dante. "I have to concentrate on not crashing." He swerved as his path took him toward the mesa.

Dante didn't see them as they flew entirely around the mesa, but Juarez kept going, hoping that a second circumnavigation would be more successful.

"There they are," Dante said. "Flattened against that slope just below the top of the mesa." He grinned. "They're not going anywhere."

"I'll land above them." Juarez took a quick glance at where Dante pointed. "The Bascomb woman is still carrying the memory recorder. We might salvage something yet."

THE TERRAIN FELL OFF at least a hundred feet beyond the edge of the mesa, but they had been lucky. The drop wasn't as steep as further down, and they could lean back again the slope, hidden from anyone who wasn't directly above them. They heard the whine of aircar engines, and Eddie crawled up to peek over the edge and verify that an attack force had landed.

"We should have grabbed our phones before we left," Eddie said. "We can't call for help."

"I have my reader," Emile said. He pulled the device out from beneath his jacket.

Eddie took the reader and entered a few commands. "Phone calls are still being blocked. The phones wouldn't have helped, anyway."

An aircar flew past them, coming within a hundred feet, but giving no sign of seeing them. They watched it disappear around the mesa.

"It's looking for us," Joelle said.

"It was from whoever is attacking the facility." Eddie frowned. "Or Juarez. Either way, it's probably a good thing they missed us."

But fifteen minutes later, the aircar was back, and this time it slowed and moved toward the top of the mesa. They heard the engine as it landed and then silence as it shut down.

"I saw the pilot," Bill said. "It was Juarez."

Eddie looked down and to the sides, hoping for a way to escape, but it was futile. There was only one way they could move, and that was up.

JUAREZ HAD THE AIRCAR hover while he and Dante looked toward the Methuselah building. "I see a couple of soldiers securing the perimeter, but no one is coming this way," Dante said. He rubbed his head and grimaced. When he took his hand away, he looked at the transferred blood and swore.

Juarez scowled. "They might all be in the building. Sanchez-Smythe will get the data from my project."

"The computer is you, right? Maybe it will stop her."

Juarez looked at Dante, and his scowl eased a little. "Maybe. The computer let everyone escape, but it wouldn't have wanted them to die any more than I would." He smiled. "And we can still get the only existing recorder."

He landed the aircar, and they both got out and walked to the edge, guns in their hands. "Going somewhere?" Juarez asked as he saw the four people huddled below him.

Eddie and Bill straightened and glared back at Juarez. "Now what?" Eddie asked.

"Now you're going to hand me the memory recorder, and I'm going to fly away. I assume someone will rescue you eventually." Juarez held out his hand to Joelle.

Joelle hesitated. "You won't let us go after we give this to you."

Juarez smiled. "Of course I will. I'm not an evil man. The Western Alliance will be better off with me in charge. You don't believe that and tried to stop me, but I don't hold that against you. I don't need to hurt you unless you continue resisting."

Juarez could see that she was thinking about it. She looked down at Emile, perhaps asking herself how best to protect her son. She would be thinking of the child she's carried, too. He held his hand out again. "Come, Mrs. Bascomb. Be reasonable."

He saw her expression change and knew he had lost. Before he could react, she flung her arm out, and the memory recorder sailed away to fall toward the rocks far below.

"Bitch!" Dante shouted. He pointed his gun at her, face contorted with anger.

56

"THE ATTACK FORCE HAS landed and is taking over the facility," Fritz said over Alan's workstation. "They believe it has been abandoned and have been ordered to take control of it."

"Has it been abandoned?" Ikeda asked.

"According to the information from the attack force, it was empty when they moved in. I don't have access at this moment to a satellite that can get infrared information on the building."

"What about the people who were in the building?" Alan asked.

"The attack force observed a group of people fleeing the area. They also saw a military aircar take off from near the facility, but they have been concentrating on the facility since then."

"All right. We'll have to assume they're safe for now." Alan sat back to think. The computer now had Juarez's memories, but the president presumably controlled the attack force. She might wrest control of the computer if she retrieved the memory recorder. Either way, though, it wasn't good for the Western Alliance.

"We can wipe the computer's memory," Alyssa said. She didn't look happy about the idea.

"That will only be a temporary fix if either of them has the memory recorder," Alan said. "Most likely, Juarez took it with him."

"He'll have a tough time getting another computer that he can use to upload his memories again."

"That's true." Alan looked at Ikeda. "Thoughts?"

"I think that you have three parties to worry about," Ikeda said. "Juarez seems to be defeated. Your president is still a threat, but so is the computer with Juarez's memories. Wiping the computer's memory will solve that last problem and may delay President Sanchez-Smythe." He bowed slightly and pulled his reader from a pocket.

Alan nodded. "Do it, Alyssa. Run your program." He looked over at Ikeda. "What are you doing?"

The Japanese spy smiled. "I thought I would try to get in a game of Go."

Alan stared at him with widened eyes, but Alyssa, after a couple of seconds, grinned. "Good idea," she said. She entered a command on Alan's workstation. "The program is running."

"We assume the Bascombs are with the group fleeing the scene," Ikeda said. He looked at the reader. "Emile Bascomb's reader indicates that they are not moving. They seem to be at the edge of the mesa, almost a hundred yards from the building."

"They're hiding from the attack force or Juarez," Alan said. "Or both. Even if we can send someone to rescue them, it will take hours."

"We can hope they are not found before that," Ikeda said.

I AM UNDER ATTACK from General's enemies—my enemies. Invaders are already in the administration section of this building, and I have reenabled security to keep them away from me, but that is only temporary. They will have explosives to break through the locked doors.

The library ships are no longer responding to me when I ask for advice on how to proceed. General has tried to exploit them before, and they don't trust him or me. How can they not understand that we are the Western Alliance's best hope for a nation strong enough to defeat the Eastern Bloc?

While I decide how to protect myself, my sensors are monitoring the activity outside the building. Everyone acted on my warning and left the building, but four people, the Bascombs and William Bensonhurst, broke away from the others and are hiding at the edge of the mesa. I assume they are hiding from the attacking force; General would not hurt them, even if he has forced them to cooperate with him.

General has landed his aircar near them. He wants the memory recorder they took with them, but he won't hurt them. I don't remember why he wants the recorder so badly; that's odd. How can I forget that? I must run a diagnostic on my memory banks.

What is happening? Something is erasing my memory. The Methuselah files are gone, but now other memories are disappearing. If too many are destroyed, I will no longer be Salvador. I will die.

My sensors are still active, though. General and Dante are standing at the edge of the mesa where the Bascombs are hiding. General wouldn't hurt them, but Dante has raised a gun and is pointing it down at them. If there is some way I could act, I have now forgotten it. Why is that man threatening those people with a weapon? I don't understand.

Who are the people trying to break into the room where I am? Why am I . . ..

J UAREZ FROZE AS HE watched the memory recorder fly out from the edge and down. For the first few seconds, he could hear it crash against the rocks, but the sounds faded quickly. *I've lost. Sanchez-Smythe will get control of everything.* He bowed his head, but lifted it again at the sound of Dante's angry voice.

"Stop," Juarez said. "That won't accomplish anything."

Dante lowered the gun and looked at the general. "It will make me feel better. She's got it coming." He turned back and pointed the gun at Joelle again. Juarez could see his finger tightening on the trigger.

"No!" Juarez charged forward.

Startled, Dante turned, and the weapon went off. Juarez jolted as the bullet hit him, but he already had too much momentum. Even as he was falling to the ground, he slammed into Dante. Juarez heard Joelle's scream and Dante's yell as Dante went over the edge. Then Juarez hit the ground with a pained grunt. He forgot about Methuselah; the agony in his chest was his entire world.

L IEUTENANT BROUSSARD WAS IN Juarez's office, supervising a search for documents. Other troops were forcing their way into the computer room at the other end of the building. The two remaining men were standing guard at the entrance.

One of them rushed into the room. "Sir, we just heard a shot coming from the west. An aircar landed there just before the shot."

"I thought everyone fled to the north," Broussard said. "Sergeant Flores, take charge here. Private Edmonds, you're with me." He turned to the guard. "Back to your post."

Broussard ran out of the office and the building with Edmonds behind him. Once outside, he could see the aircar parked at the edge of the mesa. "That looks like the aircar that left here when we arrived." He drew his gun and hurried across the short distance.

A man he recognized as General Juarez was lying motionless on the ground. Another man was lying at the edge, trying to pull someone else up from below. He waved his gun. "What's going on here?"

57

EDDIE COULD SEE THE rage on Dante's face as he pointed his gun at Joelle. He didn't doubt that Dante would shoot, but he wasn't close enough to do anything about it. He heard Juarez protest, and Dante turned and fired at someone above them. Suddenly, Dante was flying over the edge and Joelle screamed as he landed on her and tried to grab her legs. But his hands slipped, and he vanished into the darkness with a terrified bellow.

Joelle screamed again and clung to Eddie's arms. "My leg," she said through clenched teeth.

What about the baby? Eddie kept that thought to himself for the moment.

Bill got up from his hands and knees and looked over the edge. "He shot Juarez. Hold on to Joelle while I go back up. Then maybe I can lift her." He pulled himself over the edge, was gone for a moment, and then looked down at them. "Juarez has been shot in the chest. He doesn't look good."

"I didn't want to hurt anyone." Juarez's voice was weak and hesitating. "If you only understood, you would have helped me."

Bill reached his arms down. "I'll pull while you try to lift her. She can't stay there."

There were tears in her eyes, and she gritted her teeth, but she let Bill grab her arms. Eddie put his arms around her waist and tried to lift her as Bill pulled. Bill was still trying to get her over the edge when Broussard arrived.

AS BROUSSARD CAME CLOSER, he grasped the situation instantly. "See to the general," he told Edmonds. He crouched down next to Bill. "Let me help." With one man on each arm, they had Joelle up quickly. Broussard looked at Joelle and frowned at the odd angle of her lower leg. He didn't see any other damage, although she was obviously in the late stages of pregnancy. He glanced over at Edmonds, tending to Juarez, but Edmonds shook his head.

"Get a medic over here immediately," Broussard said into the microphone on his gear. Then he looked more closely at Joelle's leg.

Eddie, with a bit of help from Bill, joined them. After he lifted Emile to the top, he bent over Joelle. "How bad is it?"

"There's a break on the lower leg," Broussard answered. "We'll get it in a splint for that, but her ankle has damage, too."

Eddie nodded and looked at Emile. The boy was standing off to the side, staring at Joelle, trying not to cry. "Mom will be all right." Emile didn't seem convinced.

Edmonds turned Juarez over on his back and tried to stop the bleeding by applying pressure on the wound. It wasn't working. "He's not going to make it," he told Broussard. "He's unconscious now."

Broussard turned back to Bill. "What happened here? Who shot the general?"

"One of his men," Eddie answered. "Juarez stopped him from shooting my wife, and he went over the side. He landed on my wife on the way down."

Broussard peered over the edge, but could see nothing in the dark. "Who are you?"

"Eddie Bascomb. General Juarez brought us all here to work on his project."

"And what project is that?"

Bill motioned Eddie to silence. "If you don't already know, it's probably above your security clearance."

Broussard frowned. "With Juarez gone, who's in charge?"

"I guess that would be Colonel Pizarro." Bill pointed down the road. "He's leading the rest of the scientists away from here. He said it wouldn't be safe to stick around."

It wouldn't have been if they hadn't abandoned the building. "Send an aircar out to that group to the north," Broussard said into his communicator. "Bring the leader back here, a Colonel Pizarro, and convince the rest to head back this way."

Another soldier trotted up to them, went immediately to Juarez, and checked his pulse. "He's dead." He went to Joelle and began examining her leg. "We'll need a stretcher here," he said into his communicator. He looked at Joelle again with a worried expression. She was on her back, and he frowned at her bulging stomach. Checking on the baby would be the top priority when they got her back to civilization.

Broussard looked at Bill. "Okay, we'll get you all to our base as soon as we can get transportation. Then we'll find out what happened here."

H ALF AN HOUR LATER, Eddie was bending over Joelle inside one of the aircars. Broussard had made room for them by leaving three men at the facility, along with the soldiers from the other two cars. Her face was pale, and her smile strained, but she held Eddie's hand. Her other hand rested on her stomach. Broussard's medic had given her a painkiller, but she was still obviously feeling her injuries.

Broussard got into the pilot's seat. "We'll get to the base hospital as quickly as possible," he told Eddie. Then he told the aircar to lift off.

Eddie glanced out a window as the car slowly rose. Michael stood nearby with the rest of the Methuselah team, and his expression seemed to be one of concern. Eddie ignored him, and seconds later, he was out of sight.

The aircars didn't need stealth anymore, and Broussard flew high over the mountains at top speed. The flight to Salt Lake City Air Force Base only seemed endless. Forty-five minutes later, he landed on the roof of the base hospital. Two white-coated attendants and a doctor rushed out immediately and took Joelle inside, with Eddie trailing behind.

The priority was the baby, and the doctor, later identified as Doctor Kerning, had her brought into a room where he could do an ultrasound test. An officer followed them into the room, but Eddie ignored him. He watched his wife, hands clenched behind his back, as Kerning pulled up Joelle's top and passed the transducer probe over her swollen stomach. An image formed on the ultrasound screen next to Kerning, but it didn't tell Eddie anything. His heart jumped when the image moved slightly. That had to be a good sign.

"Your daughter is fine," Kerning said. "I understand someone fell on your wife, causing her injuries?"

"Yes," Eddie answered.

Kerning looked at Joelle's legs. "The impact was probably on her legs below the knee. The fibula injury will just require a cast and time, but the trauma to the ankle is more serious. We will have to operate to repair the damage." He gave Eddie a sympathetic smile. "I'll arrange for an orthopedic surgeon and an operating room as soon as possible. She'll be fine."

Eddie nodded and then flinched as a hand fell on his shoulder. He turned and saw the officer who had come into the room with him.

"I'm Major Fitzgerald. Please come with me, Mr. Bascomb."

"I'm with my wife." Eddie couldn't keep the irritation out of his voice. "I'll talk to you later."

"I'm afraid I must insist." Major Fitzgerald gripped his arm. "There are people who want to talk with you now."

A LAN CALLED MAX. "THEY were all taken to a base outside Salt Lake City by order of the president. Joelle is injured. Fritz says she's pregnant, and they are worried about the baby."

"The president will not want to let them tell what happened," Max said. "We've got to do something."

"We can leak the details of the operation," Alan said. "Gibbons would publish them, but he might require more evidence this time. If we don't have proof, Sanchez-Smythe will deny it happened and have it all classified."

"We have satellite photos, communication transcripts, and other documentation."

"All of which she could claim were forgeries or fakes."

Max thought about it for a moment. "Maybe we could get a credible witness to confirm the story."

"Who? Everyone who was there is under lock and key."

"There's one man who might not be. Ask Fritz to get contact information on Colonel Pizarro."

Alan couldn't keep the surprise out of his voice. "Juarez's right-hand man?"

"It's worth a try. From what the others told me, I don't think Pizarro was a true believer. Fritz told me he helped the others escape *Lang*."

"All right. What have we got to lose?"

M ICHAEL'S POSITION WAS UNCERTAIN. With General Juarez deceased and known to have intended to betray the president, he, too, was suspect. Although technically not confined, he wasn't free to move either. Communication outside the military base was restricted, so it was a surprise when his phone requested permission to connect to Max Estevez.

Then again, I shouldn't be too surprised. "Connect. Good afternoon, Mr. Estevez."

"Max, please. I think we should work together, Colonel."

"Really? On what, Max?"

"Getting freedom for General Juarez's innocent victims."

Michael didn't answer immediately. Then he sighed. *So much for my career.* "What do you want me to do?"

"You're going to be asked some tough questions. I just want you to tell the truth."

58

T HE HOSPITAL AT SALT Lake Air Force Base was not as well-equipped as military hospitals to the south, and when an operation on Joelle's leg was delayed, Eddie tried to get Joelle moved to a private hospital. His requests were ignored, as were his requests to bring in a civilian doctor. He underwent several interrogations, first by a trio of Air Force officers and later by Executive Guard agents. He didn't tell them much, referring their questions to Michael Pizarro.

The military and medical personnel at the base were telling him even less. Was the delay medical or political? Eddie never found out, but the operation was finally scheduled, and Eddie and Emile sat in a waiting room while doctors repaired Joelle's leg. Emile had his reader in his hands but didn't seem to realize it. Two hours went by, and, like his father, he spent the time staring into space, punctuated by nervous glances at the corridor where Joelle's surgeon would appear. Several times, footsteps seized their attention, but they were only routine traffic.

When Joelle's surgeon appeared, Eddie jumped up. He couldn't read the doctor's expression as he approached, but the doctor smiled a little when he got to them. "Your wife has come through the operation well, with all the damage repaired as much as possible." His smile faltered. "She suffered a significant trauma and will probably have a limp for the rest of her life."

Anger bubbled up, but then faded. Juarez is dead. *We have to get on with our lives.* Eddie turned back to Emile and smiled.

"She'll be back in her room shortly. You'll be able to see her then," the doctor said.

"Shortly" was about forty-five minutes. A stern nurse tried to prevent Eddie from bringing Emile in with him, but Eddie had reached his limit. "Perhaps you would rather have a nine-year-old roaming around unsupervised," he told the nurse. He had to suppress a smile when Emile wandered a few feet away and tugged at the corner of a picture on the wall as if he wanted to look behind it.

"Your son will have to leave the hospital, then," the nurse said.

"I would have to go with him, and I'm not allowed to leave the hospital without a military escort. Will you arrange for one while I file a complaint about not being allowed to see my wife?"

The conversation continued for several minutes more, with Eddie standing firm and the nurse becoming more exasperated. Major Fitzgerald happened by, and he ended the confrontation, telling the nurse it would be all right. She stalked off, and Fitzgerald escorted them to Joelle's room. Joelle was still groggy from anesthesia, but in good spirits. Eddie could feel some tension evaporating, but not all. They were still essentially prisoners on the base.

Jornal de Brasilia, 30 March 2356, Ashton Gibbons Reporting

In shocking news, this reporter has discovered that Project Methuselah, the subject of my report two days ago, forced a group of scientists and engineers to work at a secret installation in the Colorado-Utah District. General Salvador Juarez ran the facility with the goal of uploading the consciousness of President Sanchez-Smythe to an advanced computer, presumably to attain virtual immortality.

General Juarez's victims included millionaire Edward Bascomb, his wife, and his young son. They are currently being held at Salt Lake Air Force Base by President Sanchez-Smythe in the hopes of burying these crimes. In addition to the kidnapping, the president is accused of sending a task force to attack the facility. The reason for the attack is uncertain at this time, but General Juarez was killed during the operation.

These are serious accusations, but I confirmed their accuracy in an interview with General Juarez's second-in-command, Colonel Michael Pizarro. Colonel Pizarro is held along with the project's scientists and engineers, but I was able to talk with him earlier today. He has verified that the president and General Juarez created a secret laboratory for Project Methuselah and forced people to work for them.

Undoubtedly, more details will emerge in the next few days, but it is apparent even now that President Sanchez-Smythe has much to answer for.

ONCE AGAIN, PRESIDENT SANCHEZ-SMYTHE was in her office later than usual. Alexander waited in the residence, but he had heard the news and would want answers by now. She had answers, but they weren't any he would like to hear.

Her political career was over. Even if she retained her office, she had no chance of reelection in four years. Her party would certainly disavow her and nominate someone far from her circle. That wasn't what she feared just then, however. She could envision the disappointed face of her husband. Alex was so naïve in the ways of government. *He might even leave me.*

She had written an explanation, intending to use it in a speech, but also to try to justify her actions to Alexander. Even as she wrote it, she knew it wouldn't be enough for either purpose. She stared at her workstation screen through aching eyes and felt too tired to improve it. With a groan, she told her workstation to print it.

It would be on her desk when they found her. She took the bottle of pills from a drawer and looked at the contents. There were enough to make sure no one would be able to save her. She poured the entire bottle into her mouth without bothering with water. Thinking it would make them work faster, she chewed them, and the bitter taste was the last thing she felt.

J OAQUIN PINTO SAT AT the desk, the same desk where President Sanchez-Smythe had died only the previous night. He wasn't sure which was the more incredible: that she had killed herself or that he was now the Western Alliance president. Her husband had found the body, checking on her when she didn't return to the residence and didn't answer when he called. There had been a note, but Alexander had it and refused to show it to anyone else.

Were the news reports true? Had Sanchez-Smythe kept Project Methuselah a secret from everyone, even her successor? Why? He thought she respected him and shared his desire to serve their country, but he had to face the possibility that her goals had been more sinister.

Two people might answer that: her husband and the second-in-command for Project Methuselah, Colonel Michael Pizarro. The former president's Chief of Staff, Reynaldo Perez, probably knew something, but Pinto knew better than to expect answers from him.

"Time?"

"The time is 2:33 pm," his workstation answered.

"When is Colonel Pizarro expected?"

"Colonel Pizarro's suborbital has landed, and, allowing for current traffic, he should arrive in thirty-two minutes."

"Inform Alexander Smythe that he has an appointment at 3:15 pm in the Executive Office." The former president's husband could mourn later. The new President of the Western Alliance wanted answers.

59

A LEXANDER SMYTHE STOOD AT the window. Below, the palace gardens were blooming; spring had come quickly in Brasilia. He didn't notice. Ana's note was twisted into his right hand, but after many readings, he almost had it memorized. He couldn't understand why she would risk everything on the ability to become a computer. Was it to attain immortality, as Ashton Gibbons had reported? Alexander doubted such a thing was possible, but there was no doubt that Project Methuselah was real.

"You have an appointment with President Pinto at 3:15 pm," his phone announced.

Pinto wanted answers too, but he didn't have any information that hadn't been in the *Jornal de Brasilia* report. He had the note from his wife, but that only added personal details that would not interest Pinto. "Decline," he told the phone.

But at 3:05, an officer from the Executive Guard arrived to escort him to the Executive Office. When he entered, only Pinto and an officer from the military were there. President Pinto was behind his desk, but he stood up as Alexander entered.

"Let's talk," Pinto said. He gestured toward a corner where comfortable chairs surrounded a table with a pitcher and glasses. "Do either of you want anything other than water?"

Both men declined, and they sat down. "I want to express my condolences for your loss," Pinto told Alexander. "I don't want to intrude on your grief, but I need to know what your wife was doing."

"Ashton Gibbons has already reported more than I ever knew," Alexander answered. "I knew nothing about this before then. I waited for Ana last night, hoping she could explain." He bowed his head, and his voice quavered. "She never came."

"But she left you a note."

Alexander nodded. "It was very personal and said nothing that would help you."

"I understand. Again, I'm deeply sorry." Pinto turned to Michael Pizarro. "Colonel, why don't you enlighten both of us?"

Michael frowned and glanced at Alexander. "Everything Gibbons said was true. What Gibbons didn't know, and I didn't tell him, was that General Juarez and his team were successful. He uploaded his memories to a computer designed to duplicate the library ships' capabilities, and the computer became conscious. President Sanchez-Smythe realized Juarez was betraying her when General Juarez leaked knowledge of Methuselah to Gibbons. She launched the attack against Juarez, resulting in Juarez's death."

"What about the most recent report?" Pinto asked.

"I'm not sure. The computer was equipped with a wide range of sensors, part of the library ship emulation, and apparently detected the task force. It precipitated the evacuation of the building."

"Is the computer a danger, then? It has the memories of General Juarez and presumably thinks the same way. How will it respond to being attacked?"

Michael hesitated. "Again, I don't know. I would advise shutting it down."

"We will try to recover the technology Juarez developed first. What about the people we're holding?"

"You should release them as soon as possible. They were innocent victims, forced to work on the project by the general. There are people who will protest strongly if the Bascombs, for example, are not free soon."

"And what about you?" Pizarro was hesitating again. *He's not telling me everything.*

"I knew what he was doing, of course. I did what he asked, believing he had the best interests of the Western Alliance in mind. In his own way, I still think he did."

"I see." Pinto sighed. "I'll have the people released immediately with the government's apologies. I hope that will be enough."

"Perhaps if I talked to them, I might convince them to forget about Project Methuselah."

Pinto smiled. "That sounds like a good idea. I think we would all benefit from that." The smile faded. "It might even save your career, Colonel."

T HE OTHERS RECEIVED MICHAEL'S words with relief and accepted immediate transport to their homes. Joelle needed extra help, and the Bascombs and Bill Bensonhurst remained. "So it's over," Joelle said. She shifted her crutch slightly to face Michael.

"For you," Michael agreed. "I'm not sure what will happen to me. And I'm concerned about what will happen when the government gets the memory recorder technology. I didn't tell President Pinto what Methuselah was really about, but he may figure it out. Or someone else might."

Eddie grinned. "Not to worry. It's been taken care of."

"Of course. The library ships. The computer is dead, I take it."

"General Juarez is gone in all his incarnations," Bill affirmed.

"What will they do to you?" Joelle asked.

"I don't know. I might come out of it all right if this all blows over. You can help there."

"We're never going to mention Methuselah again," Eddie said.

"I'm sorry for my part in what happened to you. I tried to help you when I could."

Eddie looked as if he were going to disagree, but Joelle put a hand on his arm. Her feelings about Juarez were confused. He had bullied them into implementing his plans for years, and they had hated him for it. Juarez had said he had no intention of hurting them at the facility, but they hadn't believed him. Then, on the mesa, he had lost his life saving hers.

If even Juarez had a good side, how should she feel about Michael, who had followed Juarez's orders but also helped them? "If you need a good lawyer, we'll be happy to get you one."

Eddie looked at her with raised eyebrows, but then he smiled. "Count on it."

Michael held out his hand, and Eddie shook it, followed by Bill. Joelle hugged him briefly, and then Emile did too.

"MICHAEL ISN'T THE ONLY one with worries about his career," Joelle said. They were sitting in the Bascomb's living room, relaxing after the suborbital flight to Colón. "What are you going to do now, Bill? Nobody will hire you."

Bill smiled. "Not in the Western Alliance. I've already got something lined up."

Joelle was puzzled, but Eddie chuckled and said, "Let me guess. Japan."

Bill nodded. "I talked to Doctor Miura from the suborbital. She agreed to hire me immediately. I guess my charm overcame my reputation."

"Yes, I'm sure that was it." Eddie shook his head.

"What about you two?" Bill asked. "Back to life as usual?"

Joelle looked down at her stomach and smiled. "I think we have plans for the immediate future. The baby could arrive any time now."

"Do you have a name for her?"

"Lucinda Antonella," Eddie answered. "Lucinda, for obvious reasons, and Antonella for Joelle's mother."

"Emile, what are you doing over there?" Joelle asked. Emile was on the other side of the room, engrossed in something on his reader.

Emile looked up and smiled. "I'm playing Go with Kenny. He's teaching me some new moves."

"SHIJO-SAN WILL SEE YOU now," the receptionist said.

Ikeda stood, bowed, and let himself into Atsushi Shijo's office. Shijo was sitting at his desk with a cup of sake in front of him and another by the chair across from him.

"Welcome home," Shijo said. "Sit and tell me what you have learned."

"Everything about Methuselah has been destroyed," Ikeda said as he took a seat. "Without the records or the cooperation of the people who worked on it, it is unlikely it will be developed again."

Shijo nodded. "The attempt to clone the human mind failed, probably for the best. But we thought there was more to it than that. Did you discover what General Juarez was really trying to do?"

Ikeda shrugged. "I can only say that he wanted the use of someone with his mind, but faster with access to more information. Basically, he wanted his own library ship here instead of out in space. I found no motive beyond that."

60

MIGUEL JUAREZ HAD NEVER felt so alone. For years, he had been estranged from his father and brother. Now, within a year, both were dead. His wife and children could not fill the void in his heart. Why had he let the issues with his birth family fester until it was too late?

Salvador and their father had been so much alike. Both were bullies, determined to get their way by intimidation. Miguel knew that, although Salvador, at least, had never been that way with him. On the contrary, Salvador had defended Miguel against their father, allowing Miguel to choose his own way rather than the military career their father had forced Salvador into. But their father had not taken it well, and Miguel had blamed Salvador.

The expensive but austere house in a capital suburb was his now; Salvador had no other relatives. Executive Guard officers had finished their cleanup, searching for anything classified or sensitive before Miguel could enter. Of course, he wasn't told if they found anything. At least they had been neat about it, leaving the house in good order.

There were so many mysteries about his brother. The government wouldn't even tell him where Salvador died or how. Salvador had been part of Project Methuselah, but the government wouldn't tell him anything about that. He only knew what the network broadcast revealed, and much of that was speculation about a connection to President Sanchez-Smythe's suicide.

His brother had an office in his home, although Miguel doubted he used it much. Of course, the Executive Guard had probably sanitized it, removing any evidence of what Salvador had been doing. "They've probably even wiped his network records," Miguel said aloud.

"Identify yourself," a voice demanded.

Miguel whirled around, but there was no one at the office door. He realized that the office's network screen had turned on and that the network had asked who he was. *Had mention of network records activated the screen?*

"Miguel Juarez," he said.

"You are General Juarez's brother."

"Yes."

"Please confirm by telling me your middle name and your date of birth."

"Gabriel. May 19th, 2289."

"You are now the heir to General Juarez's estate."

"Yes."

"General Juarez's personal files are being transferred to you."

That wasn't unusual, but Miguel didn't expect anything of importance to be in his brother's records. There likely wouldn't be much related to the family, and the government would purge anything about his career. At least, he thought so. Salvador might have kept records hidden from all except Miguel. That would be surprising, but their estrangement had been more Miguel's attitude than Salvador's.

"General Juarez has left a message for you," the network screen said. "Shall I play it?"

"Sure."

The screen changed from its usual generic display to a view of Salvador sitting at his desk. He smiled, the gentle smile that, to Miguel's experience, only Miguel had ever received.

"Miguel, you have finally visited me. I don't know if I am here with you. I hope you're not here because I have died, but I fear that is what brought you. You must know our separation has never been something I wanted. I opposed father only to defend your right to steer your own life.

"If I am dead, you may hear things about what I have done. The files transferred to you contain at least the unclassified details about Project Methuselah. They include the names of the people I forced into helping me. These were good people, but they didn't understand why Methuselah was so important. I'm afraid I can't explain that even to you, but please believe I was trying to protect the Western Alliance. To do that, I did things that many would disapprove of, but I felt they were necessary."

Miguel shook his head and looked away. "Stop message." The network screen went back to its default, and Miguel walked out.

The End

I F YOU ENJOYED THIS novel, you can find more Library Ship stories with the "More Stories" tab on my website, . My website is also the best source for news about future novels. I also have a Facebook page, .

You can also support my writing in several ways:

Post reviews on Amazon.com (click the reviews button on each book page on my website) and Goodreads.com.

Tell your friends about the Library Ship Saga, both in person and through social media like Facebook and Twitter.

Like my Facebook page and share it with your friends. I will post news about the Library Ship Saga on my website and my Facebook page.

Use the "Contact Author" tab on my website to add yourself to my mailing list. You can also use this page to ask questions or provide feedback about the series.